RAVE REVIEWS FOR ANNE AVERY, *ROMANTIC TIMES* REVIEWERS' CHOICE AWARD-WINNER!

A DISTANT STAR

"The impressive debut of a splendid new talent."

—*Romantic Times*

"*A Distant Star* is a must read. . . . Anne Avery has a bright future!"

—*Affaire de Coeur*

"*A Distant Star* sweeps the reader into strange and wonderful worlds filled with high adventure and love!"

—Kathleen Morgan, author of *Crystal Fire*

FAR STAR

"Ms. Avery delves deeply into the hearts and minds of her intriguing characters. Impressively textured and filled with haunting pignancy, this [is an] emotionally powerful love story."

—*Romantic Times*

"*Far Star* grabs your heart and gets it pumping. You'll care about the wonderful characters Anne Avery has created. . . . *Far Star* is a must read."

—*The Talisman*

THE HIGHWAYMAN'S DAUGHTER

"Anne Avery provides a spirited romance with her delightful sense of humor, three-dimensional characters and lively plot."

—*Romantic Times*

VOLUNTARY AMNESIA

"Cold, Kate? I know how to warm you. Remember?"

He cupped the curve of her shoulder with his palm, then slowly, lightly, ran his hand down her arm. She could feel the heat of him even through her robe. When she tried to slide away from him, he seized her other arm and dragged her hard against him.

"You didn't shrink from me once, Kate."

The words were soft and dangerous, and they set her nerves humming. His grip was hard and outright threatening.

He leaned closer still, then bent his head to hers. His tongue traced the line of her mouth.

"Remember?" It was scarcely a whisper.

"No!"

He jerked back. "Liar."

She wrenched free, tears spilling. "I don't *want* to remember. Don't you understand? I don't want to remember *any* of it!"

"Then you shouldn't have come back."

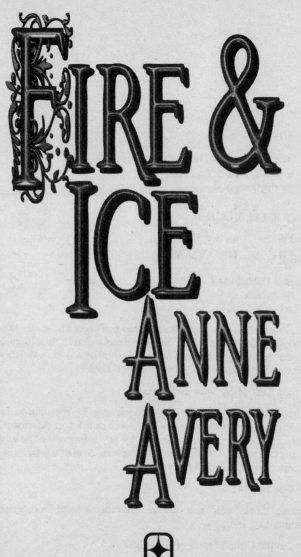

FIRE & ICE

ANNE AVERY

LOVE SPELL   NEW YORK CITY

A LOVE SPELL BOOK®

July 2001

Published by

Dorchester Publishing Co., Inc.
276 Fifth Avenue
New York, NY 10001

ISBN 0-505-52442-2

The name "Love Spell" and its logo are trademarks of Dorchester Publishing Co., Inc.

Printed in the United States of America.

Visit us on the web at www.dorchesterpub.com.

To my editor, Alicia Condon,
who showed me the way out of the dark.

Chapter One

Late January 1933

Maybe she'd made a mistake after all.

Nausea rose in her at this first sight of Grand House. Kate Mannheim stared out the pitted windshield at the stark North Dakota landscape and the looming mass of stone and mortar that stood on the horizon, limned against the forbidding gray clouds. From this distance, the house looked unchanged from the last time she'd seen it, ten years before.

Ten years. It was crazy to come back to this grim mausoleum after so long. It was even crazier to come back because of a few shadowy memories and the dreams that had begun when her grandmother died two and a half months ago. But if the diamonds really *did* exist . . .

Kate squeezed her eyes shut, forcing out the image of Grand House.

If her mother's diamonds existed, then coming back would be worth it. And if they didn't . . .

If they didn't, her employers would have to sell the small New York bookstore to someone else, and her years of working and saving to buy it would go for naught. Now that his wife was dying, Jonathan had no choice—and neither did she.

Kate forced her eyes open.

Though still more than half a mile away, the house filled her vision, dominating the vast sweep of winter-killed prairie just as it dominated her dreams.

No, not dreams. Grand House always came to her in nightmares. Dark, twisted images that jerked her awake, panting and sweating, with her heart pounding in her chest.

Perhaps by coming back, by confronting the past, she could lay those dreams to rest at last. With any luck, she'd find the diamonds, too.

With luck. Kate's mouth twisted. Since when had anything tied to Grand House ever brought her luck?

The thought made her straighten in her seat. She made her own luck now. Wasn't that why she was here?

At the lane leading to Grand House, Hod Simpson pulled his rattletrap pickup off the road. His hands, callused and scarred from years of unremitting work, squeezed the cracked steering wheel for an instant, his shoulders hunched as if he wanted to hit something. Reluctantly, he dragged his gaze off the road ahead and turned to face her.

"You'll forgive me for not takin' you all the way up to the house. But it's only a quarter mile or so and, well, Ruth Skinner, she hates me just like she hates pretty near everybody around 'cept old Gar. Now she's lord of the manor . . ." His big hands opened helplessly. "You'll understand."

Kate nodded. She did understand, all too well.

"You sure you want to do this, missy? You don't want to, you just tell me. Times are hard, but the missus and me, we'd be glad to put you up for a day or two. I'll be goin' back into town end of the week, and I can take you to the station then. There's trains passin' through every day. One of 'em'll take you to New York, you want to go. All you gotta do is say."

Worried furrows in his work-worn face mirrored the concern in his voice. He must have seen an answering fear in her eyes because he added, more harshly: "Your Aunt Ruth, she's not goin' to welcome you back. You know that same as me."

Kate swallowed, nodded. "I know that, Mr. Simpson, but . . . I *have* to. My—my mother's things are in that house. They're mine now—they belong to *me*, not to . . . *her*."

He blinked at her sudden vehemence, then slowly nodded in understanding and, she thought, regret.

"All right, then. You go on, but remember, you got trouble, you come to us. We're only a couple miles along the road. Far enough this time of year, but not so far you can't walk it if you have to. Lord knows Ruth Skinner won't put herself out to bring you to us, let alone haul you all the way into town, but if you gotta leave . . ."

The words trailed away, laden with warning.

With a muttered thanks, Kate climbed out of the old truck, then dragged her cheap canvas suitcase out of the back. She hauled it to the side of the road, waving as Hod drove off. He didn't look back.

We're only a couple miles along the road, he'd said. And they were the closest neighbors around.

Hunching her shoulders against the wind, Kate drew her coat closer about her, then bent and picked up her suitcase and set off up the lane. As she walked, she deliberately kept her gaze fixed on the rutted dirt road in front of her. She didn't want to see Grand House growing bigger and bigger with every step.

The lane wasn't as wide as she remembered it, perhaps because of the winter-dead vegetation

14

encroaching on either side. It cut through fields that hadn't been worked since her mother died, fields that had long since gone to weeds and sand—once disturbed, the tall prairie grass never came back, as though the touch of humans had poisoned the land itself.

The quarter-mile walk seemed endless. Though she walked almost everywhere she went in New York, this was harder. The ground was hard-packed and worn by weather and the wheels of farm wagons into ruts and ridges that seemed designed to twist the ankles of the unwary. Her shoes, so comfortable on paved city sidewalks, weren't suited to this rougher surface at all—she could feel every stone and bit of gravel through the leather soles. The wind was cruel.

By the time she reached the tall stone gateposts that marked the edges of the main yard, Kate was ready to swear her small suitcase weighed twice what it had when she'd climbed off the train in Mannville that morning. She set it down on the dead grass beside the drive and slowly flexed her hand, trying to work out the cramp and chill, shivering in the cold. She'd worn her best coat, a sturdy brown wool one she'd found in a secondhand shop in New York, but the bitter wind easily cut through the heavy cloth. Her exposed cheeks and throat and her stocking-clad legs stung from the wind's constant assault.

15

For an instant, she wished she'd worn the single, scandalous pair of wool trousers folded in her suitcase, but at Grand House, comfort always came a distant last when judged against propriety. Gertrude Mannheim had been proud—so proud she'd insisted her husband take *her* last name when they'd married—and rigidly proper. Perhaps to make up for her status as poor relation, Ruth Skinner had taken those qualities even more seriously. And now she was mistress of Grand House.

Not that Grand House was looking so very grand these days, Kate noted with a sense of shock. Her grandmother had taken enormous pride in her gardens and her carefully tended grass, driving the hired help mercilessly, though there weren't many visitors to appreciate the effort, even then. Yet the yard, like the neglected fields, clearly had been surrendered to weeds long since.

Bare patches of packed earth showed through the winter-dead grass, and the once vibrant flower beds didn't look as if they'd been tended for years. Spirea bushes that had once been a mass of white in the spring were broken and straggly, with here and there a gap in their ranks where one of their number had died off. Climbing roses that had once bloomed against the gray stone walls were fallen, their branches a tangled mass of bare canes and sharp thorns. The fences that had kept out the livestock were sagging or, in spots, fallen altogether.

Only the huge stone gateposts and the stone house itself seemed unchanged, as if the gray granite blocks that had been transported so far and at such a cost refused to yield to the unforgiving land into which they'd been dropped. Her great-grandfather, Charles Gordon Mannheim, had wanted to build it so the house would last for generations. What would he say if he knew it had come to this so soon?

There was no car in the rutted gravel drive that led around the side of the house, no lights in the windows on any of the three floors. Picking up her suitcase again, Kate started to walk around to the kitchen door, as her grandmother had always required. She took five steps in that direction, then stopped.

Her grandmother be damned.

With a decisive grating of her heel against the stones, Kate spun about and walked toward the front of the house, following the narrow graveled path from the drive. She barely glanced at the dead grass and barren shrubs. Her attention was fixed on the impressive sweep of stone steps leading to the massive double doors of the front entrance.

The first time she'd come to Grand House, a terrified three-year-old desperately clutching her mother's hand for reassurance, Kate had entered by those doors. The memory of their slow climb up each of the seven steps still had the power to wake her, trembling, in the night.

Her mother, Kate knew now, had been too frightened herself to pay much heed to her daughter's fears. Kate could still remember how her mother's hand had trembled, how she'd mounted those steps with a desperate determination even a child could sense. For each of Sara Mannheim's steps, Kate had taken two, hurrying to keep up, tripping on the uneven stones, pulled off balance because her mother wasn't leaning down toward her tiny daughter as she usually did, wasn't allowing for her smaller strides.

Kate halted at the base of the steps. For an instant she hesitated, then, before she could retreat, put one foot firmly on the first step and started to climb. *This* time her tread was sure, deliberate.

All those years ago, each stumbling step had brought Kate and Sara closer to the grim-visaged woman who'd stood in the yawning black entrance, her arms crossed on her bosom, silently staring at them as though she'd been a statue carved from the same granite as the house behind her.

Kate's feet faltered at the top. For a moment, she almost expected the massive doors to open and her grandmother to appear, still stern and disapproving.

The doors remained shut, their leaded glass panes staring at her accusingly, as though shocked by her temerity in approaching the house from this side.

Kate couldn't remember how old she'd been when she'd realized those doors rarely opened except for distinguished guests, weddings, and funerals.

There'd been no weddings and seldom any guests. The last time Kate had seen the doors open was for her mother's departure.

Sara Mannheim's coffin had been plain, unvarnished pine, the cheapest available. The mortician's men had carried her out of the house to the waiting hearse and from the hearse to the grave because there was no one else to perform that last office. There'd been no mourners, no memorial service, and only the briefest of prayers spoken over the gaping hole dug with such effort in the frozen prairie soil.

Under the circumstances, her grandmother had told the nine-year-old Kate, it was a great deal more than Sara Mannheim deserved.

Kate wondered whether anyone besides the mortician's men and Aunt Ruth and Uncle Garfield had been here two and a half months ago to watch her grandmother's departure. According to the letter Ruth sent her at the time, the coffin had been of solid oak with the finest brass fittings and a padded satin lining, ". . . as befits a woman like Gertrude Mannheim."

Ruth hadn't said whether El had been present. Kate's jaw muscles tightened uncomfortably. Where was he after all these years? Where had he gone?

It was useless to wonder.

She crossed the stone porch in three long strides. The heavy brass door knocker was tarnished but only slightly pitted from the sixty-plus North Dakota winters that had assaulted it. After an instant's hesitation, she lifted the knocker and pounded it once, twice against the striker plate.

Kate waited, expecting to hear the reverberating echoes. There were none. The house had eaten the sound, swallowing it whole.

She pressed her face against the leaded glass and tried to peer in. All she could discern in the gloom were the vague, bulky shadows of furniture. Even the ancient mirror that hung on the wall across from the entrance reflected none of the gray winter light, as if it no longer responded to anything other than what lay within the granite walls that surrounded it.

Irritated, Kate stepped back from the door to scan the windows of the upper floors. Still no light, no hint of motion behind their dark, flat surfaces. She had no choice, then, but to go around back to the kitchen.

Kate's foot was on the bottom step when a

sharp *thwack!* from the far side of the house, away from the drive, caught her attention. For a moment, she couldn't identify the sound; then it came again. *Thwack!* Someone was chopping wood, and doing it very efficiently, too.

Grateful for any excuse to delay knocking on the kitchen door, Kate followed the worn path that led toward the sounds. Her first impression as she rounded the edge of the house was that something was wrong, out of place. Then she stopped abruptly as she realized what that something was.

The ancient elm her great-grandfather had planted so long ago no longer spread its massive branches in a sheltering arc along the west side of the house. What was left of it was stretched on the ground in a pathetic heap of broken limbs and wood chips, exposed to the weather it had defied for so many years. The bulk of it had already been cut into thick logs, then split into firewood and neatly stacked in a waist-high pile.

A man dressed in faded work pants and a plaid flannel shirt stood in front of the knee-high stump, his back to Kate. With an easy, graceful swing that spoke of long practice, he raised an ax over his head, then brought it down with vicious force. *Thwack!* A chunk of wood somersaulted off the stump onto a pile of similar chunks.

He raised the ax again and brought it crashing

down, then again. With each swing, Kate marveled at the strength, the raw power in the man that enabled him to wield the heavy, double-bitted ax with seemingly effortless efficiency.

Three strokes more and he'd reduced the log to a heap of neatly sliced pieces ready for a fire. The man straightened, then turned to select another log.

As he turned, Kate could see his face for the first time. The sight of those dark features struck her like a blow from the ax. The suitcase slid from suddenly lifeless fingers.

"Elliott." The name was barely a whisper, yet it burned across her tongue and lips.

He'd recognized her in the same instant. Even at this distance, Kate could see her shock and surprise mirrored in his face.

With a careless fling, El tossed the ax aside and took two quick, eager steps in her direction. Then he stopped, as if brought short by an invisible barrier in front of him. In an instant, the eagerness drained away, leaving his expression stiff and hostile.

He hasn't forgiven me, Kate thought. The wind whipped a lock of hair into her eyes, drawing tears. Ten years and he still hasn't forgiven me.

Uncertain whether to walk forward or turn and flee, she stood immobile as El shook free of his momentary paralysis and strode across the yard to her. He stopped a good two feet away, but Kate reeled as though he'd run into her.

He's changed, she thought, then wondered why that fact should surprise her. Ten years was a long time. A long, long time.

He wasn't any taller than the six feet she remembered, but he was heavier, more muscular. Kate studied him, searching for signs of the young man she'd once known.

His hair was still long and thick and unruly, tangled by the wind, but now there were premature strands of silver mixed with the inky black. The broad, flat planes of his cheeks and the square jaw were the same, but the once sharp beak of his nose had been slightly flattened and skewed to the side. Lines etched the corners of his eyes now, and deep grooves carved the sides of his mouth. His skin was coarser, darker, as though it had been baked by a harsher sun than North Dakota's, but the dark shadow of beard was the same. From the day he'd turned sixteen, Kate remembered, he'd shaved twice a day. Probably still did.

Her eyes slid down his neck to the open collar of his shirt. He still had to shave all the way to the base of his throat. Distracted, she studied the curling chest hair exposed by the open collar, remembering.

"You shouldn't have come, Kate."

His voice was deeper, rougher. Once, it had

been gentle, but now it rasped Kate's nerve endings and made the heat rise in her wind-chilled cheeks.

Irritated by her involuntary reaction, she defiantly lifted her chin, then immediately wished she hadn't. His eyes smoldered with all the heat that should have belonged to the hidden sun.

"Why did *you?*" she retorted.

For an instant something cold and bitter flickered in those dark depths. But only for an instant. A moment later his eyes, like the windows of the house, turned a flat, reflective gray, hiding what lay behind them.

The left side of his upper lip quivered in the beginnings of a sneer. "Surely you heard. Thanks to your grandmother's death, Aunt Ruth is wealthy now. Why shouldn't I play the dutiful great-nephew and come home, take advantage of the situation?"

"You wouldn't!"

"You don't believe I'd try to get some of that money Ruth inherited from your grandmother?" One dark eyebrow lifted in a mocking query. "That's not what everyone else around this damned county thinks. And you believe *them*, don't you?"

"Should I?" Instead of the scorn she'd intended to put in her voice, Kate heard uncertainty, even a note of fear.

This man wasn't the protector and friend she'd

known. Not any longer. He was a dark force, an angry power whose influence swept away her resistance, leaving her vulnerable.

El moved a step closer, then another, until he loomed over her.

Kate tried to speak, but her mouth was too dry. She stared, mesmerized, at her own image reflected in the gray glass of his eyes.

El leaned even closer. His lips parted slightly, and his jaw worked, as though he was struggling against the words that wanted to come out. Abruptly, he brought his hand up to within an inch of her face, then slowly, very gently, ran the tip of one finger along the side of her face.

Kate flinched but refused to draw away. *Couldn't* draw away. It had been so long since they'd been this close, since she'd felt his touch. Even in the bitter wind his nearness and the brush of his hand against her skin were like heady drugs that stirred her senses and stifled her will.

"They said I killed her—that I killed Louisa." El said the name slowly, consideringly, as though savoring it on his tongue. His finger moved across Kate's lips and down her throat in a delicate, feather-light caress. "They're still saying that. Even now, people still whisper behind my back when I walk down the street."

His lips pulled back from his teeth in a frightening mockery of a smile. His eyes had changed again. Now, instead of her own reflection Kate saw the hot, black flames of the hell he'd lived in these past years, the hell he'd carried with him ever since that moment when he'd been arrested and charged with the murder of one of his former high school classmates.

"*You* believed I was guilty," El said suddenly, his voice harsh. "Didn't you, my beautiful Kate?"

Kate tried to deny his accusation but found she couldn't—his fingers were suddenly locked around her throat. She stiffened, then strained upward on her toes, fighting to keep her balance. She grabbed his wrist, but her meager strength was useless against the raw power that vibrated within him.

"I strangled her. Remember, Kate? That's what the sheriff's men said, anyway. According to them, it was easy. All I had to do was squeeze. Like this." Elliott's eyes glittered, and his fingers tightened even more. "The killer had large hands. Powerful hands, like mine. The coroner said so. He could tell by the locations of the bruises on her throat. Remember that?"

"El! Elliott!" The croaking sounds that came from Kate's throat were scarcely intelligible, but El heard her.

For an instant, he froze. Then his eyes grew wide, and the air whistled between his lips as he drew in a deep, shuddering breath. Abruptly, he released his hold on her, almost shoving her away.

Kate swayed, suddenly unsteady. Without thinking, she put out her hands and braced herself against his chest. It was like touching the wall of a house where an angry fire raged inside. For the first time she could feel the animal heat of him, a heat that defied the wind plucking at them so insistently. With an exclamation of dismay, Kate jerked her hands back, then crammed them into the pockets of her coat.

El shut his eyes, squeezing the lids closed tight as though he could make her go away by merely blocking the sight of her. His shoulders tensed, and his head dropped. His hands balled into fists. Kate could see his fingers digging into his palms.

After a moment, he took one deep, ragged breath, then opened his eyes to stare at the distant horizon. "Why did you leave before I was even released?"

"I . . ." The words stopped in Kate's throat, choking her. In spite of herself, she shivered.

El caught the slight movement. "You've forgotten how cold North Dakota can be in January," he said gruffly. Again his hand came up toward her throat. Kate jerked back, but this time he simply adjusted the collar of her coat more closely around her.

The gesture robbed Kate of all capacity for speech. She studied his face, searching for some clue to his thoughts. Before she could respond, another voice interrupted.

"El?" The single word was a plaintive query.

Kate turned to see a frail, wizened old man she didn't recognize shambling toward them from the back of the house. He was dressed in a neatly starched and pressed white shirt and black pants held up by black suspenders, but his shirttail stuck out in two places, and his pants sagged on his bony frame. He had bedroom slippers on his feet but wore no coat or hat despite the biting chill of the wind. Kate was about to ask who the man was when Elliott abruptly left her to go to him.

"Uncle Gar," Elliott called, swiftly moving toward the old man. "You shouldn't be out here. It's too cold."

Uncle Garfield? Kate stared in shock. It couldn't be! The tall, powerful old farmer whose laughter rattled windows couldn't possibly have changed into this trembling, uncertain stranger in the space of ten years.

Shaken, Kate hurried after Elliott.

"Why aren't you in school, El?" Garfield Skinner quavered, looking up at his great-nephew with eyes that were the washed-out blue of old age. "Aren't in trouble, are you, boy? I can talk to the teacher—"

"There's no school today, Uncle Gar," Elliott said, suddenly gentle. He tried to turn his uncle

28

around and lead him back to the house. "Why don't we go back to the kitchen and get some tea from Aunt Ruth?"

"This your teacher?" Gar demanded, peering at Kate. He patted his head in confusion, trying to remove a hat that wasn't there. "El's a good boy, ma'am. There's no cause to—"

"This is Kate, Uncle Gar," Elliott interrupted. "Kate Mannheim. Sara's daughter. You remember her, don't you?"

"Can't believe it's Kate that's in trouble." Gar shook his head, frowning. "Can't be Kate, ma'am. She won't say boo to a horsefly."

Kate felt rather than saw Elliott flinch at his uncle's bewilderment. Tears stung her eyes. How cruel life could be, to play this kind of joke on a man as strong and vital as Garfield Skinner had once been.

"Kate's not in trouble and neither is Elliott, Mr. Skinner," Kate said soothingly, struggling to force out all thoughts of El and focus instead on the immediate problem of getting Gar back in the house and out of the cold.

She took the old man's other arm and helped Elliott lead him toward the back door. "They're both very good children. I just came to get a cup of tea. Do you think Mrs. Skinner would make us some tea if we asked her to?"

Kate kept up the calming chatter all the way around the house and up the sagging wooden steps that led to the back porch. Once she glanced up and caught Elliott watching his uncle. Kate didn't look at him again. Even after what had passed between them in the yard, she couldn't bear to see that kind of helpless, angry pain.

Once inside, Elliott guided his uncle to a battered easy chair placed near the massive, wood-burning stove that was keeping the kitchen almost tropically warm. "Here's a comfortable chair right by the stove, Uncle Gar. Why don't we put this shawl around your shoulders, get you warmed up."

While Elliott tended to his uncle, Kate hovered near the door, uncertain what she ought to do and disoriented by the move from outside to the once familiar, enclosed little world of the kitchen. She shifted uncomfortably on her feet, then hunched her shoulders and wrapped her hands around each other, still chilled from the cold but unwilling to move closer to the stove, or to El.

What madness had possessed him, to attack her like that? What insanity had caused her to respond to him in spite of it? Had they both changed that much?

The answer was there in the man and in herself, in the nervous doubt that still fluttered through her veins.

Yet some things never changed. Around her,

the house sighed and creaked, and the wind whined at the old sash windows, seeking entry. They were the same sounds she'd heard for years, the sounds that had either soothed or terrified her, depending on the moment, but that had always been there, an inescapable backdrop to her every thought.

It was as if the house itself were drawing her back, reminding her that she could run, but never far enough to leave the past behind.

Her mother had tried to leave once. Had tried, and failed, and come dragging back with a small child only to die in the house she'd fled nine years before.

A sharp gust of wind hit the house suddenly, shaking the window panes, shrieking in protest at being denied entrance. Kate jumped. Her heart sped up, sending the blood pounding through her veins. She clasped her hands together tightly until her muscles hurt from the tension.

Was it going to be like that for her now? Kate wondered. Was she deluding herself by thinking she'd escaped ten years ago? By thinking she could escape now?

As the doubts and fears grew, the room around her seemed to grow, too. Larger and larger, then larger still until it was as she remembered it from her childhood, a vast, echoing cavern in a stone mountain from which Kate would never find her way out.

"Are you going to do anything useful, or just stand there gaping?"

Kate gasped, startled by El's sharp words. With a sigh that must have been the wind, the kitchen shrank abruptly until it was merely a substantial farm kitchen, and she was once more a grown woman who hadn't moved five feet from the back door.

Elliott frowned at her, eyes narrowed with an emotion she couldn't identify. Contempt? Distaste? A combination of both—and more?

She forced her shoulders back, willed her hands to stop trembling, her heartbeat to calm, then took off her coat, hung it from a hook by the back door, and moved purposefully toward the sink.

"I'll make some tea," she said, trying to ignore the unsettling effect El's gaze was having on her.

Since the old, cast-iron kettle was already on the stove, filled with the hot water that was always kept ready at Grand House, it was a simple matter to set the tea to steep in the old china pot, then collect the cups, spoons, and sugar bowl on a tray.

She carried the tray across to set it down on the table near the stove. Though she avoided looking at Elliott, she could feel his nearness, his tension. "How's Uncle Gar?"

"That's a stupid question."

Kate jerked and her head came up, a protest already forming on her lips. She glanced at Elliott, then at the old man sitting in the chair, staring at his hands in his lap and mumbling vaguely to himself.

The protest died unspoken. "You're right," she said, her shoulders slumping. "I'm sorry."

The words were so inadequate, so useless, but what else could she say? Had anyone ever found words to ease the pain of watching the physical and mental disintegration of someone they'd loved, someone who'd been as important to them as Gar had been to Elliott?

"No, *I'm* sorry. I didn't mean to snap at you, it's just . . ." El's voice trailed off.

Kate glanced up, surprised at his hesitation. The big man stood staring helplessly at the sad wreck of a human being who had once stood as father and friend to him. With an awkward gesture of frustration, El dragged a hand through his hair and looked away from Gar. His gaze met Kate's.

It was absurd, but Kate would have sworn she caught the gleam of a tear in the corner of his eye.

He blinked. Suddenly, the hostility that had flared between them in the yard was gone, as if it had never existed.

In an instant, Kate had crossed the few feet

dividing her from Elliott. Without stopping to think of the consequences, she wrapped her arms about him and laid her head against his chest, drawing him close.

"I'm sorry," she whispered. "Oh, Elliott, I'm so very sorry."

Before he could react, a voice with edges like shards of ice spoke from across the room.

"Like mother, like daughter. Isn't that so, Katherine Mary? Not an hour in this house and already you're rutting in the kitchen like a cat in heat."

Chapter Two

The harsh words bit deeper than the bitter wind outside. With a gasp, Kate pushed herself away from El.

"Aunt Ruth!"

The tall, big-boned woman in the doorway drew herself up to her most imposing height. Her already thin-lipped mouth narrowed in disapproval, and the edges of her eyes squeezed up with repressed anger.

"You shouldn't be so surprised to see me, missy," Ruth snapped. She tugged sharply at the waist of her long-sleeved gray dress, adjusting it as if she were preparing for battle. Stiff with indignation, she marched into the kitchen.

"After all, *I* own this house now. Or did you think you could get away with indecent behavior in *my* kitchen and not have me know about it?

Your grandmother would never have permitted it, and neither will I."

"I was just . . . We weren't . . ." Kate fumbled for an explanation, still too startled and embarrassed to think clearly.

"The wind spooked her, Ruth, that's all." El shifted his position, moving so he stood between Kate and his aunt. Ruth was big—intimidatingly so—but El was bigger and even more intimidating.

He gestured to Gar, who was still muttering to himself, oblivious to what was going on around him. "Kate helped me bring Uncle Gar in the house. He wandered out without a coat."

Whatever sharp words hovered on the tip of Ruth Skinner's tongue died unspoken. With an exclamation of concern she bustled across the room to lean over her husband, both Kate and El forgotten.

"Gar? You all right? You shouldn't have gone out like that, you know. I've told you a hundred times it's getting cold. You hear me, Gar?"

Ruth kept up a soothing, scolding monologue as she brushed her husband's few remaining strands of hair back from his face, tucked in his shirttails, straightened the starched white collar that was too big for his scrawny neck. She even helped him hold the cup of hot, sweet tea that Kate had prepared, praising him for each sip he took as if he were a child just learning to feed himself.

Kate watched without speaking, bemused by the older woman's solicitous concern for her husband. Ruth's love for Garfield Skinner was the only softness Kate had ever seen her show.

Ruth and Gar had once been well-matched—physically, at least. They'd both been tall and big-boned, with strong-featured faces worn by exposure to the elements and hands that were heavily callused, toughened by years of hard, manual labor. But there the similarities had ended.

Ruth had been raised with her cousin, Kate's grandmother. Even though she'd been the poor relation, Ruth had adopted all the arrogance and unpleasant airs that had made Gertrude Mannheim so thoroughly disliked in the community. But where Gertrude was tolerated and kowtowed to because of her wealth, Ruth was disliked and generally shunned.

Ruth might have lived out her life in the shadow of her wealthy cousin, uncomplainingly performing the menial tasks that were beneath Gertrude's dignity, if it hadn't been for Garfield Skinner.

Gar had been a transient field hand, a kind, unambitious man with a ready laugh who'd never met a man, woman, or child he didn't like. He'd married Ruth while he was working for

Kate's great-grandfather—swept her off her feet, he liked to say—then settled as tenant farmer on a Mannheim farm.

It was Gar who had insisted on taking in his great-nephew, eight-year-old Elliott Carstairs, when his father abandoned him, and Gar who had comforted a sobbing Kate when her mother died.

Kate and El had grown up in fear of Ruth's sharp tongue and quick temper. Gar possessed their unquestioning adoration. For them, and for Ruth as well, he was like the sun on a cloudy day, the one source of light and warmth in an otherwise cold, gray world.

Kate watched now as Ruth arranged a throw over Gar's lap and solicitously tucked in the edges. What would become of her if Gar died? Kate wondered. What would Ruth do when the man who had been the center of her world for so long was gone?

Ruth straightened, then turned to face Kate. She frowned and her lips almost disappeared in the hard line of her mouth.

"Why did you come back?" she demanded. "There's nothing for you here. Gertrude left everything to me."

Even through she'd expected it, Kate flinched at the antagonism in Ruth's voice. "I don't want anything that was Gertrude's," she said firmly. "I only want what is rightfully mine."

"Yours! There's nothing here that belongs to you! And if you think you can just waltz back here and—"

El, who had been tending to the tea that Kate had abandoned, cut short the increasingly shrill tirade by crossing the room and thrusting a steaming mug at Ruth.

"Here's a cup of tea," he said. His voice was flat, uninflected, conveying no hint of the emotions behind it.

"And one for you," he added, extending a second mug. "You take lemon, no sugar. Right?"

"Right." Kate hesitated, then accepted the proffered mug, careful to take it by the handle without touching him. "Thanks." She could feel El's eyes on her as she took a tentative sip of the hot brew.

"Why *did* you come back?" he asked in the same flat tone he'd used with his aunt. He took a sip of tea, but his eyes never moved from her face. "I asked you that out in the yard, but you never answered. Remember?"

"I don't owe you an explanation," Kate snapped, uncomfortable under his unwavering gaze and irritated by the way he stood, feet firmly planted a foot apart, totally still.

"You owe *me* the explanation, missy. It's my house now, and don't ever forget it." Ruth slapped her mug on the table, causing tea to slop over the rim, then aggressively propped her hands on her hips, ready to defy any attempt against her newly acquired property.

Kate's stomach twisted. She'd never dared to confront Ruth before, never, in all the years she'd lived in Grand House, fought for anything she wanted, anything she believed in.

Her hands trembled and her fingers, even though wrapped around the hot mug of tea, felt like ice. For an instant, Kate considered running, just as her mother had. Just as she had run ten years earlier.

But only for an instant. Then anger rose within her, pushing down the fear. She had a right to be here, a right to claim what was rightfully hers. No one—not Ruth, not El, not *anyone*—was going to stop her.

Kate brought her chin up a fraction and forced her eyes to meet El's cold gaze, then Ruth's hostile stare. "I don't want your money. I want the books and photos and other things that belonged to my mother. The things that should have come to me when she died."

The carefully rehearsed explanation came out far more smoothly than Kate had expected. It was the truth, but only part of the truth. She had no intention of letting anyone learn the real reason behind her return.

"When she died! That's a nice way to put it, I must say!" There was unmistakable scorn in Ruth's laughter.

"Aunt Ruth!" El's sharp words cut his aunt's laughter short.

"Kate's request seems reasonable," he continued smoothly. He stared at Kate for a moment, as if he expected her to say more, then straightened and strolled over to the sink and dumped his tea. With his back to them, he added: "Let her get the things she wants. That way, she won't have any excuse for coming back."

El placed his empty mug on the drain board with exaggerated care, then swung around to face Kate. He leaned back against the edge of the sink and crossed his arms over his chest. His expression was hard, unreadable, but Kate could see a muscle jump at the side of his mouth.

"That would suit you, wouldn't it, Kate?" he said. His words sounded like an insolent challenge. His right eyebrow arched.

"That would suit me just fine." Kate fought against the sudden tightening at the back of her throat. How could it hurt so much to hear him put her own thoughts into words?

El pushed away from the sink. He seemed relaxed, at ease, yet something about the way he held his shoulders, about the angle of his head, tilted to one side, spoke of tension ruthlessly held in check.

"I'll get your bag," he said, moving toward the door. "You dropped it in the yard, remember?"

Kate nodded. "I remember."

El didn't bother to acknowledge the admission, just swung open the door and stepped out onto the enclosed porch. As he pulled the door shut, a sharp gust of wind slipped past him into the kitchen. Kate shivered, but the physical reaction was only partly due to the icy draft.

The sound of the screen door banging shut made Ruth jump. She dropped her hands from her hips, but Kate knew she hadn't changed her opinion. Hostility radiated from the woman like heat from the old stove.

"I suppose you'll have to stay," Ruth said grudgingly. "But don't think you're staying long. I've enough to do without taking care of you, as well."

"I always did my fair share of work around here," Kate retorted, stung.

"And that won't change! You can start by making your own bed. Your grandmother didn't touch your room except to have it cleaned, and neither have I. The linens are where they have always been." Ruth stared at her, as though daring her to object, then abruptly turned to tend to her husband.

Ruth's curt words were all the welcome she'd get, Kate knew, but she couldn't prevent the twinge of resentment that tugged at her. Without speaking, she crossed the kitchen to the back hallway and the servants' stairs that led to the upper floors of the house.

The stairs, hidden behind a paneled, white-painted door, were as narrow and difficult to navigate as she remembered.

Kate stopped on the landing at the top. In front of her, firmly shut, was the door leading to the second-floor hallway. To her left, the stairs continued onto the third floor where the servants' quarters and Kate's old room were.

She hesitated for a moment, then, with an odd sense of defiance, of taking a liberty she wasn't permitted, opened the door to the second floor and stepped out into the wide, central hall beyond. With her hand still on the knob, she studied the scene before her.

Everything was as she remembered it, unchanged and silent. Even the smell—a heavy, musty scent compounded of floor wax, furniture polish, and closed rooms—was the same.

The hallway ran the length of the house. Dark mahogany bedroom doors, four to each side and firmly shut, stood like sentinels, wordlessly staring out on the hall.

A large window at the far end of the hall, heavily draped in velvet and lace, allowed a dim, gray light to filter in. The light reflected off the polished wood floor, making the dark shapes of the furniture nearest the window seem to float in midair, as if suspended in the vague luminescence. Little of the light reached as far as the servants' stairs, leaving the rest of the massive

Victorian furniture scattered along the length of the hall shrouded in shadows, like specters, silently waiting, watching.

Involuntarily, Kate shivered.

It was the cold, she told herself firmly. The heat from the kitchen stove hadn't penetrated this far. If Ruth ran things as her grandmother had, most of the heat registers in this part of the house were turned off.

Kate turned back, ready to start up the second flight of stairs, when an icy draft of air from the hall behind her blew past her ear.

Startled, Kate spun about. No one was there. The heavy drapes on the window hung perfectly still. Not even the lace curtains stirred. The doors along the hall remained shut, the rooms behind them silent.

It was the wind, Kate chided herself, willing her heart to slow its sudden, rapid pace. In this old house the wind could always find a chink to slip through.

Kate waited, without knowing why she did so, wondering if the draft would come again. Nothing moved.

The hall seemed colder than it had a moment ago, but that had to be her imagination.

With an uncomfortable, dismissive shrug, she pulled the stair door closed and flicked the light switch for the upper stairs. Nothing happened.

Feeling her way, she crept up the remaining

stairs in the dark. At the top, she fumbled for the door handle. It turned in her hand but the door refused to open.

Again that draft of wintry air blew past, and a voice, very faint, whispered in her ear. "Not true."

Kate's skin prickled. She whirled to see who stood behind her on the stairs. Her foot missed the narrow tread. Panicked, she lunged for the wobbly door handle. Her hand slipped on the cold porcelain knob, but her grip was just enough to keep her from tumbling down the stairs.

"What? Who . . . ?" The anger in her voice was a poor disguise for the sudden fear behind it.

Still clinging to the door handle, she shifted to look back down the stairs toward the landing on the second floor. Pale light filtered up from the first floor, but it was too weak to reach the doorway to the third floor.

Weak though it was, however, the light was enough to show her whether anyone was on the stairs.

No one was there.

Someone on the third floor then, at the other side of the door. But that was impossible. There was no one in the house except her, El, Aunt Ruth, and Uncle Gar—was there? Surely she was the only one on this floor.

"Is anyone here?" Her voice quavered slightly.

"Who's there?" she called out, this time more loudly.

No answer came, not even the sound of the wind.

"This is ridiculous." Putting her shoulder against the door, she shoved. It gave way with a screech of protest, opening outward to the third-floor hallway.

Even as she silently scolded herself for being foolish, Kate couldn't resist a quick glance behind the door. There was no one there, just as there was no one in the barren hallway, and nowhere that anyone could hide.

It was the wind I heard, Kate tried to convince herself. The wind and nothing more.

This upper passage was devoid of furniture, its only adornment a worn runner tacked down on the plain plank flooring. Even the window at the far end was uncurtained, though the dust that had accumulated on the panes was almost as effective in softening the light.

For as long as Kate had lived in Grand House, most of the cramped, narrow rooms on this floor had been closed up or converted to storerooms for castoff furniture and old clothes that had gone out of style but were still too fine to be given away. Despite an all-consuming pride in her family and her position, Gertrude hadn't kept the large staff that Kate's great-grandfather had deemed essential for his comfort. A housekeeper who also served as cook, and a maid or two had sufficed for running Grand House, even to Gertrude's exacting standards. The gardener and his occasional boys had slept in the bunkhouse and taken their meals in the cookhouse with the rest of the hired men.

Rather than pay good money for more help, Gertrude had driven her hirelings like a mule driver his mules, never trusting them, never stooping to anything that might make them think they were her equals, paying them only what she had to and giving them nothing they didn't need to do their work.

The housekeeper, an old, pinched woman who had worked in Grand House since it was built, had died here, alone in her bed, a few weeks before El had been arrested. One of the maids had found her when Gertrude had angrily sent to know why her morning toast and tea weren't ready when they were supposed to be. Only Gertrude had mourned the woman's passing, for she'd been as sour and unloving as her mistress. Kate had often wondered whether her grandmother's grief had more to do with the loss of cheap, familiar help than any real regret at the woman's death.

The maids had come and gone. They'd been farm girls, for the most part, accepting Gertrude's poor wages because they hadn't had much else to choose from, and because they hoped what they'd learned here would qualify them for better paying service somewhere else. A couple had been kind to Kate when she was little, but most had merely tolerated her, a few even smugly pleased that their mistress's daughter and granddaughter were forced to suffer the same discomforts and indignities they were. Not even the kindest dared presume to offer real friendship. Gertrude would never have tolerated such presumption, and they knew it.

Pushing down the urge to open every door along the hall and let out the ghosts behind them, Kate crossed to the third door on the right from the stairs. Behind it was the small, bare, three room suite that had once been reserved for the housekeeper, then been turned over for her and her mother's use—Gertrude hadn't considered either her erring daughter or her unwanted granddaughter worthy of one of the more stately rooms on the second floor. After Sara's death, the suite had been Kate's alone, the only place where her grandmother hadn't bothered to erase every trace that her mother had ever lived.

For a moment, she hesitated outside the suite, her hand on the cheap, white porcelain door-knob. Ten years ago she'd shut this door behind her, vowing never to return. It wasn't too late to turn back. Hod Simpson had offered her shelter and a ride back to Mannville at the end of the week. It wouldn't be easy carrying her suitcase those two plus miles in this wintry wind, but it might be easier than staying. And safer.

The thought made her sweat, despite the cold. She pressed her forehead against the painted wood, her fingers squeezing the knob as if it might disappear while she worked up the courage to move.

Think of the bookstore, she told herself. *Think of the diamonds. Your diamonds!*

It didn't work. The future lay ahead, insubstantial and out of reach, while the past crouched on the other side of the door, waiting to drag her back.

Back to El, she thought, and trembled. Her hand tightened convulsively around the knob.

Her eyes were open and staring blindly at the painted wood of the door, but what she saw was his face. Not the thin, angry face of the boy she'd first met, nor the eager face alight with dreams she'd known so briefly just before their world had shattered around them, nor even the cruel, cold visage from the yard that had pierced her soul. This face was some tormenting amalgam of them all, with lines and edges that blurred and shifted with each breath she took and each thudding beat of her heart so that she wasn't sure what she saw, or what thoughts lay behind those cold, accusing gray eyes that seemed to stare out of the wood and straight into her heart. A terrible, dangerously changeable face, and so very, very desirable.

The muscles of her neck tightened with the remembered feel of his hands about her throat, his fingers digging into her flesh. Her breasts peaked with the remembered feel of his hands on them so long ago, of his body pressing hard and hot against hers.

With a deliberate effort, she forced herself to straighten, then turned the knob and pushed. The door swung open with a creaking protest as though reluctant to yield even that much to her. Nothing roared out to devour her, but the hallway seemed colder than ever.

Kate took a deep breath, then stepped into the room. It was like walking through a mirror straight into the past.

The middle room of the three had served as their sitting room. It was simply furnished with a pine table and two chairs in one corner, an uncomfortable-looking sofa pushed against the far wall, and a small bookcase stuffed to overflowing with books. Everything was old and well-worn, castoffs Gertrude had grudgingly allowed them to take, but not before she'd battered them with endless reminders that they were virtual beggars and dependent on her charity. Sara had sewn the curtains herself out of fabric she'd found in an old trunk in the attic—there had been no money to buy new even if Gertrude

Mannheim was the richest woman in the county.

Narrow doors at either end led to the two small bedrooms on either side. Both were shut, as if trying to hide the shabbily furnished rooms behind them.

Kate stood in the empty doorway, her gaze sliding from one familiar object to another, then another, then back again. When she'd left, she'd sworn she'd never come back, yet she remembered carefully straightening the worn cloth on the table and dusting the bookshelves and tugging the pillows into place one last time as if there were anyone left to care about what remained.

She'd swear she could feel her mother's presence, as if Sara had just stepped out to fetch something and would be back at any moment. The room seemed to engulf her, sucking her back in.

The thought made her shiver. Or maybe it was just the room. She'd forgotten how very, very cold Grand House could be in the winter.

Kate knelt to touch the brass heating grate set in the floor. It was ice cold. Not a whisper of warmth had worked its way this far up in the house. Not that she had expected anything else. Despite her wealth, Gertrude Mannheim had always begrudged the coal needed to keep the big furnace in the basement working hard enough to heat the upper floor. With no servants occupying this floor, Ruth, who'd spent her life pinching pennies, had probably shut off all the registers up here and in the unoccupied rooms below.

No servants. Kate rose, frowning. Why were there no servants? She couldn't imagine her grandmother living in Grand House without servants. Gertrude Mannheim had never dusted a table or swept a floor in her life; she would have died rather than try.

Had Ruth let them go when she'd inherited the property? But why? If anything, Kate would have expected her aunt to add even more hired help so she could wallow in leisure and have the satisfaction of ordering people about, knowing they would jump when she told them to.

Had the servants simply left? Walked off the job rather than put up with Ruth's famously sharp tongue and bad temper? It was difficult to believe anyone would give up a paying job in these hard times, but Ruth might well have been so determined to establish herself as mistress at Grand House that she'd ended up driving them away.

Or had she perhaps sent them away because of Gar? Ruth's pride was huge, and it had claws. She'd hate having anyone see Gar as he was now, knowing people would pity her for what her husband had become. But surely even Ruth's pride had to give way before the overwhelming demands of caring for her husband and maintaining a house that was ten times the size of her old one?

At the thought of Gar, tears stung Kate's eyes. At least she knew now why El had come back. He'd come for Gar.

Wherever he'd been, whatever he'd done, he wouldn't have forgotten Garfield Skinner, the only person in the world besides herself who had ever loved him. And Gar was the only one who had never abandoned him. Even when the people of Mannville had started muttering of lynching, Gar had been there, fighting for the great-nephew who was as close to a son as Gar would ever have.

Gar had been there three months later when El had been released from the county jail at last, the murder charges dropped for lack of evidence though not, Kate knew, for lack of suspicion. By then, she'd been two weeks gone, driven away by El's anger and her own fears. Only months later, when she'd finally worked up the courage to write her grandmother and tell her where she was in New York did Kate learn that El, too, had disappeared, fleeing Mannville and the suspicions still hanging over his head—all without a word to anyone except Gar.

The boy's loyalty clearly lingered in the heart of the man. El's presence here was proof of that.

But then, he had cause to be loyal. El's mother had died shortly after he was born. His father, a foul-tempered, feckless soul much given to drink, had dragged him around the country for seven or eight years, depositing him with resentful relatives when he became inconvenient, snatching him up and dragging him off again when drink and loneliness combined to make Daniel Carstairs maudlin and convinced of his love for the boy.

When Carstairs died—killed in a drunken brawl in Chicago, or so Gertrude had said—the social workers had tried to place him with his relatives, but without success. They'd had the boy before, one family after another had protested. None of them had liked Daniel Carstairs much. No one had been willing to take his son.

No one, that is, except Garfield Skinner, who had been Carstairs's uncle by marriage. It was a distant relationship, but enough to convince the welfare people to send the boy to North Dakota.

Ruth, who never spoke of her own childless state, hadn't hesitated to voice her resentment at having yet another mouth to feed, another batch of clothes to wash. She'd put El to work quickly enough, but no matter how he'd labored, it had never been enough to satisfy her. Her dislike of the boy had been matched only by Gar's genial devotion.

The stair door creaked open and footsteps crossed the bare hall to her door. Kate squared her shoulders and turned to face the door, then flinched it was thrown open without a preliminary knock.

El stood there holding her shabby cardboard suitcase in one hand as easily as if it weighed no more than a sheet of paper. His other hand was still wrapped around the doorknob. His powerful body filled the doorway.

For a moment, neither of them spoke. All that needed to be said was in the single, angry glance he threw her, and the silence was her only reply.

He was the first to look away. Roughly, he shoved the hall door back and crossed to the closed bedroom door on his left, flung it open, tossed the suitcase on the narrow bed, then slammed the door shut behind him.

"Anything else?" It was a challenge, not a question.

Their gazes met, locked.

"Thank you. For bringing my things up." She forced the words past a sudden constriction in her throat.

His eyes held her.

"I won't say you're welcome." He almost spat the words. "You're not wanted here, Kate."

Coming from him, that slashed deep.

"I know."

His gaze swept the shabby room, arrogant and cruelly dismissive, then swung back to her.

"Your mother was little more than a beggar here. What could she possibly have had that was worth coming back for?" Acid, now, to burn in the wound he'd opened.

Despite the cold, bare stretch of floor that separated them, he seemed to fill the room, pressing against her until she could scarcely move or think or breathe.

It took all Kate's strength just to meet that hostile, angry gaze. "The value of things isn't just in the price you paid for them."

"No?" He sneered. "I would have thought the price would have mattered a great deal. It always did to your grandmother."

"I'm not my grandmother," she shot back, stung.

He studied her, eyes narrowed and sharp with suspicion. "If you'd really wanted a bunch of old photos and letters, you could have dug them out years ago. Gertrude never paid any more attention to you than she had to. It wouldn't have been that hard to search for them . . . if you'd wanted."

He took a step toward her, compressing the air around her even further. "Why didn't you look for them then, Kate?"

Kate knew the answer to that. It was fear. She'd been afraid to touch anything that had been her mother's, afraid she'd shatter into so many pieces that she'd never be able to put herself back together again. Sometimes the only way she'd been able to endure her mother's absence was to pretend she'd never existed at all.

All she said was, "What does it matter? It's not important."

"No?" He took another step forward, driving her back. *"I'd* say it was important, Kate. Very important. Very, very important."

With each "very," his voice grew softer, silkier, more dangerous.

"I know damn well you didn't come back because of Gertrude. You sure as hell didn't come back because of me."

"You're right about that," she said, defiantly standing her ground. "I didn't come back because of you."

He smiled. It wasn't the smile she remembered, the warm, gentle smile he'd always had for her, and for her alone. This smile was hard, feral, and it struck fear into her heart.

Kate backed up farther, until her calves hit the edge of the old sofa. He followed her, relentless.

"Was it Ruth?" he asked. His eyes mocked her.

She shook her head, mute.

"Or Gar? Did you come back because of Gar, Kate?"

Kate shivered and closed her eyes, unable to look into that threatening face she'd once loved. Tears squeezed out from beneath her lids, burning salty trails down her cheeks.

"I didn't know about Gar." It was barely a whisper.

He didn't say anything, didn't move, yet she

would swear she could hear him breathing. She could feel the animal heat of him, like a fire in the icy stillness of this long-abandoned room. Awareness shimmered through her, igniting every nerve end.

She forced her eyes open. "I didn't know about Gar. I would have come if I had."

Nothing moved in his face, yet she would swear it became harder, more unforgiving. Like granite, and just as inhuman.

He reached out his hand—she had to steel herself not to flinch—and delicately brushed away a tear with the tip of one finger.

For a moment, he held her there, pinned with the force of his gaze. Then his lashes lowered, cutting her off as though she no longer existed. With the cool, detached air of a scientist examining a drop of water beneath a microscope, he studied the crystalline drop of liquid that had beaded on the tip of his finger.

And then he lowered his head and licked off the tear. Carefully, as though he thought it might scald his tongue.

Held in thrall by mingled fear and fascination, she watched as he tasted the tear, then slowly licked his lips as if he wanted to be sure to gather every molecule of it. Her chest hurt from the effort it took to breathe.

His lashes raised, allowing her to look straight into the cold gray depths of his eyes. Once, she'd seen desire burn there, and, she'd almost believed, love. Now she could read no emotion whatsoever. Nothing but cold gray winter like the winter that whined outside the window.

"It's bitter," he said, "and it tastes of salt."

"Tears do." She looked away. The hostility she'd seen in his eyes in the yard had been easier to endure than this coldness and strange, dark intimacy.

If she could, she would have shoved past him and put more distance between them, but El showed no sign of moving away, and she couldn't bring herself to touch him. Not so much because she was afraid of what he might do, but because she was afraid of what *she* might do if she were ever rash enough to try.

Her hands clenched, fighting the urge to press them against that broad chest so close to hers. Her lips burned to feel his hard upon them. Her body remembered every detail of what they'd once shared, and ached for it.

Again his lashes lowered. His gaze lingered on her lips, slid over her chin to the row of tiny pearl buttons that closed the neck of her dress, then lower, to her breasts. She could see his nostrils flare and the rise and fall of his chest, deeper now, as if he was forcing himself to breathe.

Nothing else changed. Not a muscle in his face twitched.

She thought of the way he'd grabbed her

throat, and tensed, wondering what this cold anger might drive him to next.

Instead of touching her, he abruptly turned away. He was in the middle of the room before he stopped and turned back again.

He's afraid, too!

The thought struck with such force that her knees suddenly gave way. She plopped down on the sofa. She couldn't take her eyes off him.

His dark brows knit, shadowing the gray depths beneath. His hands hung at his sides, clenching into fists, then opening, then clenching again.

No, he's not afraid of me, she thought, and felt her heart constrict. *He's afraid of himself, of what he might do.*

His anger burned in the silence between them.

"You really didn't know about Gar?"

She shook her head. "No."

"Or about me?"

A pause. "No."

He stared at her, as if willing her to tell the truth. "Would you have come if you had?"

A longer pause. She shook her head again. "No."

She had to fight the urge to push herself deeper into the sofa, to curl into herself until she was nothing more than a tight, impenetrable ball. Only five feet of bare floor separated them.

Five feet and ten years.

"You shouldn't have come back," El snarled, echoing her doubts. "Whatever your reasons, I promise you'll be sorry you did."

A heartbeat later, he pulled the hall door shut behind him. Kate listened as his footsteps faded into silence. When the keening of the wind outside was the only thing left to keep her company, she drew up her feet and wrapped her arms around her legs, and shivered.

Chapter Three

"There's meat, boiled potatoes, and corn. If you want any more than that, you can go into town for it yourself." Ruth slapped down a plate stacked with slices of white bread, then took her seat beside Gar.

For an instant, she glared across the table at El and Kate as though daring them to challenge her offering. Neither made any comment. They kept their attention strictly on the plates in front of them, but that didn't seem to mollify Ruth. She snorted in disgust. "Not good enough for you, *Miss* Mannheim? Should I have served it on the best china and silver in the dining room, just like your grandmother did?"

Kate eyed the unappetizing portions before her. Even in the dim light of the oil lamps, the food looked gray, bland, and unappealing.

Ruth had never been noted for her cooking, but then, with only her and Gar to work the farm for so many years, she hadn't had much chance to learn. Gertrude, on the other hand, had always kept a cook as well as a housekeeper and had made a point of having her meals served formally. If there was anything that more clearly indicated the vast gulf between the circumstances of the two cousins, Kate couldn't imagine what it might be.

"It's fine, Aunt Ruth," she said, trying to force a note of enthusiasm. "And the kitchen is much more practical. Really." Involuntarily, she glanced at Gar.

His chair was at the far end of the table, in front of the stove where it was warmest. In an effort to get a spoonful of corn, the old man had chased the mound of yellow kernels around his plate, shoving corn, potatoes, and the bite-size bits of meat that Ruth had cut for him off the plate onto the table. As Kate watched, he tried to bring the spoon to his mouth. His hand wavered. Instead of his mouth, he hit his lip, spilling the few kernels he'd collected down his front and onto the floor.

Embarrassed for him, Kate flushed and averted her gaze. But not quickly enough. Ruth had caught her pitying glance.

"This is our house, now," she snapped. "Gar's and mine, and we'll do as best suits us."

For the rest of the meal, Kate kept her gaze firmly fixed on her plate, but her effort at avoiding unpleasantness was wasted. Ruth's resentment hung in the air like coal smoke in New York, thick and oppressive.

Across from her, Ruth alternately fed Gar and ate her own meal, shoveling up her food with uninterested efficiency and ignoring both Kate and El.

At the end of the table, El sat stiff and silent. Like her, he appeared to be keeping his attention focused on the meal before him, but Kate suspected he was as uncomfortably conscious of her as she was of him. When she reached for the pepper, his hand was there a moment before hers, pushing the ceramic shaker toward her. When she dropped her fork, he picked it off the floor first, then, without speaking, rose and fetched her another.

His silent awareness was more unnerving than any overt challenge, for there was no way she could respond, no possibility of confrontation.

"Have you gotten such high-flown airs that you waste good food, now, missy?"

The sharp question brought Kate's attention back to Ruth with a snap. A quick, guilty glance at her plate revealed she'd done little in the past twenty minutes except shove her food around, just as Gar had earlier. At least she hadn't slopped it onto the table.

"I'm sorry, Aunt Ruth. I guess I'm just tired."
Even as she muttered the apology, Kate had to
repress a stab of irritation at being called to task
as if she were still a child.

"Humph!" Ruth eyed the uneaten food, then
glared at Kate as though inviting a protest.
Abruptly, she pushed back her plate and laid her
hands flat on the table.

"Just where were you planning to look for your
mother's things?" she demanded. "Assuming
they even exist."

For a moment, Kate met Ruth's gaze. There
was a belligerent challenge in the older woman's
eyes and something else Kate couldn't identify.
In anyone else she would have called it uncertainty, even fear. But not with Ruth. It was lu-
dicrous to think of those two emotions in
relation to this angry, embittered woman.

Kate's eyes dropped to Ruth's hands. They
were big hands, broad and long-fingered, and
they were pressed hard against the table as
though Ruth didn't trust herself to keep them still
by any other means. The skin that covered them
was rough and wrinkled, discolored by age and
too much sun, but they were striking hands
nonetheless and still strong.

"Well? I asked you a question, miss."

Kate jumped. "I don't know," she admitted.
Tension tightened the muscles of her shoulders.
"I thought perhaps I'd start with some of those

old trunks in the attic. Unless you know of somewhere better."

She glanced over at El. His head was bent, and he was meticulously adjusting the position of his plate by pushing it first with the index finger of his left hand, then with his right until the edge of the plate was perfectly aligned with the edge of the table. Kate could see a muscle in his jaw jump as he ground his teeth together.

Ruth ignored him. "The attic's as good a place as any. But I don't want you meddling with anything that's not yours," she added sharply. "You can have your mother's things—I don't want them anymore than Gertrude did—but that's all. Do you understand? That's *all*."

"I—"

"And I'll have no fooling around between you and El, you hear me?"

"What? What do you mean?" Kate couldn't stop the heat that rose to her cheeks. There was too much truth behind the unexpected accusation, and far too much guilt.

Ruth glanced at El, then turned back to her. "You think I don't know what you did? What was between you two back then?"

Kate sucked in air, but her lungs didn't seem to be working. The thought of anyone knowing about what she and El had shared made her feel dirty, suddenly tainted. She couldn't bear to think of the one bright, good thing in her life being soiled by ugly, spiteful gossip and others' prying.

She set her fork down, fighting for calm. "What do you mean?"

"Ruth." El didn't say anything else, but something in his look made Ruth hesitate.

She glared at Kate. "Everyone knew. Like mother, like daughter, isn't that right, Katherine Mary? Like mother, like daughter."

Kate stared at her, glanced at El, silently pleading for help.

Oblivious to her plea, El abruptly pushed back his chair. "Uncle Gar! The stove doesn't need any more wood. It's just fine as it is."

Kate glanced at Gar, who was trying to lift the handle on the stove door with a chunk of firewood. He staggered slightly, trying to catch his balance, and his hands trembled so, he could scarcely hold the piece of firewood he'd taken from the box. She hadn't even noticed him leave his chair.

In an instant, El was around the table and taking the wood from Gar's hands.

Ruth was a heartbeat behind El. "I've told you, Gar, you can't work the stove. Don't you remember? If you want more wood on the fire, you ask me or El. We'll do it for you. Don't you try." The exasperated scolding went on as Ruth shifted her husband's chair farther from the fire, then helped him back to it.

Quietly, Kate slid out of her chair and crossed to the servants' stairs. She'd make her escape now, before either Ruth or El could notice her departure. But just before she slipped through the door, Kate hesitated, then glanced back over her shoulder.

That was a mistake.

El was standing in front of the stove, watching her. He'd pulled up one of the stove's cast-iron lids, ready to stuff Gar's piece of firewood into the flames. The fire's glow cast strong, red-orange highlights along his arm, across his chest, and over the hard lines of his face, etching it in fire and shadow. Even from across the room, Kate would swear she saw the flames' reflection in his eyes as he watched her, unmoving.

For an instant, she stood frozen, caught between the cold darkness of the stairwell behind her and the hot, red glow of firelight that molded him. But only for an instant. Then she turned and pulled the stairway door shut behind her.

Eleven o'clock. The luminous dial on her cheap alarm clock glowed eerily green beneath the muffling towel. Kate groaned and let the towel fall back into place.

The darkness pressed on her like a weight, making it hard to breathe. She twisted under the heavy wool blankets, trying to find a more comfortable spot on the hard bed, but there wasn't any to be found. There never had been, not even when she was little and such things mattered less.

She'd hoped to get a few hours' sleep before she started the first part of her search, the part she didn't want Ruth to know about, but despite her weariness, true sleep eluded her. Every time she drifted off, a vision of Elliott rose before her, as sharply etched as if they both still stood amidst the shattered wreckage of that old tree. She could see the shadow of beard along his jaw, the thin, hard line of his mouth, and the stray strands of silver as the wind ran its fingers through his night-black hair. Despite the remembered cold, she could feel the raw animal heat of him. His opaque gaze devoured her.

Yet each time she stepped forward, hand outstretched to touch him, a vicious fire roared up between them. Through the flames, she could see his image changing, his features twisting and blurring in a crackling heat that forced her back, hands raised to shield her from the blaze. A cry of protest burned her throat, but he didn't hear her, and didn't care because he *was* the fire, and as pitilessly cruel.

And then she'd wake again and find herself alone in her solitary room at the top of Grand House with the silence roaring in her ears. After ten years in New York, solitude and silence were as threatening as the past they came from.

El was there in the silence, too. Once, he had been her sun, the bright, hot fire at which she warmed her soul. Now he was . . . what? Not an enemy, not yet, but no longer a friend. Not a lover. He hadn't been that for a long, long time.

With sudden decision, Kate flung back the blankets and swung her feet out of bed. Eleven o'clock was good enough. She couldn't bear to wait any longer, not when thoughts of Elliott consumed the waiting.

She planned to begin with Gertrude's bedroom. Kate had decided that weeks ago. There wasn't much chance her grandmother would have kept anything that had belonged to Sara so close to her, not even the diamonds. But somewhere in that huge, over-furnished room there might be a clue, some hint Kate could use to her advantage. It was a slim chance, but it was a beginning.

The minute her bare feet touched the floor, Kate gasped. The floor was *cold*. She hastily scrabbled for her worn, wool-lined slippers, then reached for the heavy robe she'd laid across the foot of the bed.

She'd have to be quiet and move cautiously, but there wasn't much risk of being found. Ruth wasn't going to hear her. She and Gar were sleeping in a converted parlor on the first floor since Gar couldn't manage the stairs.

The only one Kate might disturb was El. He

had a room on the second floor. She'd have to pass it on her way to Gertrude's, but he ought to be asleep by now, too. There wasn't much chance he'd hear any sounds of her search.

Cautiously, every nerve alert to catch the faintest sound, Kate felt her way down the stairs and pushed open the door to the second floor. Candles and matches were in her pocket, but the risk of someone seeing the light seemed greater than the risk of stumbling in the dark.

Kate could discern almost nothing in the broad passage. There was no moon to provide even a hint of gray at the hall window and only faint shadows, black against deeper black, to tell her where the furniture might be. She stopped a dozen times in her slow progress, straining to catch any sound, however faint. There was nothing. Even the wind had ceased its mournful wailing several hours before.

By the time she reached her destination, Kate's pulse was hammering in her throat, and she was sweating, despite the cold. She fumbled for the crystal doorknob of her grandmother's bedroom, slowly pushed the door open just enough so she could slip through, then shut it behind her just as carefully.

Kate hesitated. Somehow the darkness here seemed deeper, more encompassing than it had in the hall.

Nothing stirred. The very air was still, heavy

with the mingled smells of candles and dark, musky perfumes, old furniture polish and even older draperies.

Despite the silence, Kate could have sworn the room was breathing—deep, slow breaths that matched the nonexistent heartbeat of the house around her.

Did a house eventually gain its own life, a sentience compounded of all the lives that had been lives within its walls? Could people leave the mark of their passing, not just in the furniture and adornments of each room, but on the very air itself?

The thought that any part of her grandmother's spirit might be lingering in the dark made Kate flinch, then fumble for the matches in her pocket.

The single candle did little to dispel the darkness.

She swallowed, trying to ease the constriction in her throat, then rubbed her damp palms on the skirts of her robe. Concentrate on your search, she admonished herself silently. You're not stealing, only looking for what was your mother's and is now rightfully yours. That's all.

But where to begin? Where, in this huge room filled to overflowing with bric-a-brac and ornate Victorian furniture, would she find a clue to where her grandmother had hidden her mother's diamonds?

If it's here at all, Kate reminded herself.

Pushing down her doubts, she arbitrarily turned to the small table that stood nearest the door. She had to begin somewhere, and the table was as good a place as any.

Stooping, Kate began to run her fingers along the table's edges and underneath its top, searching for any secrets that might be there, waiting for her to find them.

Almost two hours later, Kate sank with a sigh into a low chair in front of the marble fireplace.

Nothing. Not even a hint that the diamonds had ever existed.

She'd been prepared for a long, exhausting search, but Kate couldn't repress her discouragement. How much easier it would have been if Gertrude had kept the necklace in her dresser drawer along with all the other antique brooches and earrings and necklace Kate had found.

Kate let her eyes fall shut, then wearily rubbed her neck and shoulders, trying to ease the tension in her muscles.

She was a fool.

She was also tired, frustrated, and—if she was honest—scared.

What if her dream had no substance in reality? What if it was just something her subconscious had conjured to torment her with one last, faint hope?

But it always seemed so real. And her mother *had* spoken of their "chance," the money they'd have once she regained what her grandfather had given her.

Kate opened her eyes to study the room around her, searching for some visual connection to her dream.

In her dream, the room had been as it was now, each piece of furniture in the spot it had occupied since being brought to the house years before. Her mother had stood . . .

Kate tensed, then twisted in her chair, straining to see the phantoms from her dream.

Her mother stood . . . there, in front of the hearth not five feet from Kate.

Her grandmother sat . . . there, in the chair with the ebony carving. Her spine was rigidly straight, her expression coldly forbidding.

"You had no right to pry," Sara Mannheim said. Her words were defiant, but her voice trembled. "No right to take what is mine."

"I've every right. It's my responsibility to protect what my father worked so hard to build." Gertrude's voice sliced through the cold night air. She raised her fist to the light, shaking it at her daughter. Kate could see the glittering strands of a diamond necklace looped around her grandmother's fingers.

"You'd sell them?" Gertrude hissed. "Your grandmother's diamonds? The jewels your grandfather entrusted to you? I can't believe you'd sacrifice such a treasure for mere money!"

Sara Mannheim straightened, drawing her frayed dressing gown about her as if it were a magic cloak capable of fending off all attackers.

"Not mere money, Mother. Freedom! My freedom and my daughter's!" Her voice shook, but this time it was with passion.

"Freedom!" Gertrude sneered. "Freedom to do what? Starve on the streets? Freeze to death? Believe me, without my help that's exactly what will happen. No matter how much this jewelry brought you, you'd manage to squander the money eventually. And then what would you do? Work for a living?" Gertrude's laughter was razor sharp with scorn.

"I could! I could earn a living for Kate and me!" Sara protested. Her words sounded suddenly uncertain, too hesitant to resist Gertrude Mannheim's contempt.

"Just as you did after that no-account bum you ran off with died, right?"

"You can't say that! Not about Richard!"

Gertrude rose to stand before her daughter, an unyielding wall against Sara's frail, trembling figure.

"He didn't marry you, did he? He didn't do anything except get you with child, then die before the bastard was even born."

"Kate's no bastard!" Sara cried. The tears that

had trembled at the edges of her lashes were now streaming down her face. "She's my daughter! You can't say that about her!"

"I can and I will. Just because she's my granddaughter doesn't mean I'm proud of having a bastard in the family."

"Don't say that!"

Goaded, Sara lunged to strike at her mother. Gertrude was faster. Her hand whistled through the air a fraction of a second before it struck her daughter's cheek, sending Sara spinning back against the chair behind her.

Off balance and stunned by the blow, Sara collapsed in a heap at her mother's feet. Her body shook with her sobbing. "Don't say that! You can't say that about my Kate! You can't say it. You can't!"

"You can't say that!" Kate cried, leaping to her feet.

She sprang at her grandmother, but her hands closed on empty air. Her legs tangled in her heavy robe. She stumbled, then fell against the edge of the carved ebony chair. The chair shifted with a sharp grating sound of wood against wood.

For a moment, Kate lay sprawled on the floor, too dazed to move.

The floor was hard and cold beneath her. This far from the candle she'd left burning on the table, the shadows owned the corners and came creeping out from around the looming furniture. She could feel her breath whistling in and out of her lungs and her heart racing in her chest. Her knee throbbed where she'd struck it against the chair.

Kate shook her head, trying to clear it. She must have dozed off. That was the only rational explanation. It was her surroundings, and the memories they'd roused in her, that had caused her to wake this time and try to attack a phantom. But what insanity had prompted her to such twisted imaginings that she had jumped at something that wasn't even there? What if someone had heard her scream?

That thought brought Kate off the floor with a jerk.

For what seemed like eternity Kate stood there, waiting for the sound of footsteps in the hallway. But there was no sound from outside, no sound within the room but the thudding of her own heart.

A chill shook Kate. She hunched her shoulders and wrapped her arms around herself for warmth. The hard, cold bed in her own room suddenly seemed enormously appealing.

Kate glanced about her, checking to be sure she'd disturbed nothing.

Was it only her imagination, or were there shadows in the corners of the room that hadn't been there when she'd entered?

Kate swallowed, forcing down the fear that rose in her throat. She was tired and her eyes were playing tricks on her.

She'd just put her grandmother's chair back in its place. . . .

Her hand froze only inches away from the chair. She couldn't do it, couldn't bear to touch the cold, black wood. Kate drew back, shaking.

Slowly, she backed toward the bedroom door. Tomorrow. She'd get up early tomorrow and put the chair back. Ruth would never know.

Kate bumped into the door. Her gaze still fixed on the room before her, she groped for the candle, then blew it out, sighing as the room was plunged back into the dark. A darkness that now seemed oddly safe and comforting.

Kate fumbled for the doorknob, then tugged the door open and slid out of the room as quietly as she could.

While she'd searched the room, the moon had risen. Its vague light shone through the hall window, dark gray against black. Kate sighed, grateful for the faint glow.

The sigh became a choked scream an instant later as a huge, amorphous shape reared up out of the darkness, blocking the pale light.

Chapter Four

An instant later, common sense returned.

"It's you." Kate sucked in air and backed away.

"Who did you expect?" El asked, his voice low and laced with threat as he followed her. Slowly, like a cat hunting a mouse.

"Not you." In the shock of her vision or hallucination or whatever it had been, she'd forgotten he even existed. The light hinted at the planes and lines of his face, the edge of his shoulder. The rest was as black as the dark that held them.

"Why not?" Something in his voice made her shiver.

He caught that involuntary trembling and moved closer still. She might be half blind, but he seemed to see in the dark.

"Cold, Kate? I know how to warm you. Remember?"

He cupped the curve of her shoulder with his palm, then slowly, lightly, ran his hand down her arm. She could feel the heat of him even through her robe. When she tried to slide away, he seized her other arm and dragged her hard against him.

"You didn't shrink from me once, Kate."

The words were soft and dangerous, and they set her nerves humming. His grip was hard and outright threatening.

He leaned closer still, then bent his head to hers. His tongue traced the line of her mouth.

"Remember?" It was scarcely a whisper.

"No!"

He jerked back. "Liar."

She wrenched free, tears spilling. "I don't *want* to remember. Don't you understand? I don't want to remember *any* of it!"

"Then you shouldn't have come back." With a snarl of disgust, he shoved her away.

Kate's shoulder hit the door with a dull thud, forcing it open.

"What were you looking for, Kate?" El demanded, staring past her into the dark.

"Nothing."

"You lie." She couldn't see his eyes, but Kate could feel him watching her as if he could will her into a confession just by staring.

She pulled the door shut, testing the knob to be sure the latch was properly closed this time.

"Ruth will know if you've taken anything."

"That matters only if I *do* take something. I haven't. I don't want anything that isn't mine. Not from this place. Not ever."

She shoved past him, forcing him to step aside. The small gesture gave her confidence, enough to keep walking. She wanted to run. That brief, unsettling brush of his tongue against her mouth had stirred more heat and confusion than she knew how to deal with.

Kate was halfway toward the back stairs' door when his hand wrapped around her arm, pulling her to a halt, then spinning her around and back into his arms.

"It's not that easy," he snarled an instant before his head lowered and his mouth claimed hers.

It was a cruel kiss, hard and demanding and filled with ten years of anger and resentment, yet she found herself responding in spite of herself.

Excitement mixed with the fear, setting the blood pounding in her veins and starting a humming in her ears strong enough to drown out the voice of reason that warned her she was risking too much, too soon.

The kiss went on and on. She didn't want it, didn't want to need it, but she was powerless to break away. His fingers dug into the muscles of her upper arms with savage strength, yet it wasn't pain she felt. His anger was so hot it singed her soul, yet it wasn't fear she felt now but a deep and aching hunger that had been roused long ago and never assuaged.

When he pulled away at last, a small whimper of protest escaped her. She swayed toward him, unthinking, face upturned for another kiss.

El shoved her away so roughly her head snapped back on her neck.

"Damn you." His voice grated like a saw scraping across the silence.

"You were the one who claimed the kiss." That came out more sharply than she'd intended.

She could feel him flinch. It felt good to fight back.

In the dark, he was little more than a hostile black bulk against the deeper black of the open hall. The gray moonlight slipping around the edges of the heavy drapes was too frail and far away to show her more. She didn't need it to— her body was so charged with awareness that she could have reached out blindly and found his shoulder, his hand, his hip.

Instead, she shoved her hands into the pockets of her dressing gown. With the heat of the kiss and his touch gone, the night air was seeping back, chilling her.

"I'm going to bed," she said flatly, as if daring him to object.

"This time, stay there."

He didn't move as she walked away, but she could feel his gaze boring into her back. He'd had an uncanny ability to find his way in the dark when they were children. She could have sworn he saw every detail now.

When she was once again in the utter black of the servants' stairwell with the door safely shut behind her, she stopped, sagging against the painted door, grateful for its support. No sound came from the other side.

When she was sure she could walk without her knees caving beneath her, she shoved away from the door, then cautiously made her way up in the dark, blindly feeling with hands and feet, one careful step at a time.

She wasn't sure whether it was fear or longing that made her think she heard him following her.

Dawn came with a thin, keening wind and a dull gray light that was as much the fault of the sun as it was the grime-coated windows.

Kate was already awake. She'd roused over an hour before but hadn't found the strength of will needed to throw back the mound of wool blankets she'd burrowed under during the night. The room around her was cold—not as cold as it would be when snow came whirling in the wake of the wind, but cold enough that she didn't care to face it any sooner than she had to.

With the dawn, she had to. Ruth Skinner had always prided herself on being an early riser, and Kate didn't figure she'd changed that lifelong habit just because she'd inherited Grand House. Arriving too late to help with breakfast or, worse, arriving after the rest had sat down to eat, would be marks against her that no amount of good behavior would expunge.

The frigid air rushed under the blankets the minute she pushed them back, instantly driving out the warmth. Teeth chattering, Kate dragged on her robe and slippers, then pulled a blanket off the top of the bed and threw that over her shoulders, too.

The single bathroom allotted to the servants' use was halfway down the hall. El had turned on the water that supplied it before dinner last night, but Kate didn't have much hope of hot water. In the past, what little managed to make it all the way to the top of the house had already cooled during its long journey through the pipes. Five minutes in the wintry air and it had been as cold as if it had never been heated at all.

She was wrong. Somehow, El had worked magic with the old plumbing. The hot water didn't exactly gush from the faucet, but it did steam in the cold air, clearing her head and warming her body.

Impelled by the unexpected luxury, she drew a shallow bath. She didn't give herself time to think, just threw off the blanket, robe, and too-thin nightgown, then climbed over the edge of the tall, claw-footed tub to sit in the swirling water.

Even though her hair couldn't possibly dry before she got downstairs, Kate lathered shampoo into her curls. It had taken her four days to reach Grand House. That meant three nights sleeping on hard train seats or even harder station benches. She'd done her best to keep clean, managing a couple of quick, almost furtive sponge baths from tiny sinks in jolting railroad cars, but they hadn't helped much. To finally wash off all the grime of travel was a luxury.

It was a short-lived luxury. The chilly air cooled the water as quickly as she'd known it would, but by that time her blood was pumping, and it didn't seem quite so miserable. Shivering slightly, she wrapped her towel around her head, threw on her robe over her still-damp body, pulled the blanket over that, and scuttled back down the hall to her room, heedless of the faint trail of damp she left in her wake.

Her teeth were chattering again by the time she put on the sensible wool dress that was her winter "uniform," as her boss liked to tease her, and fastened the last button of the demure collar. She tugged on a heavy sweater over that before undoing the plush towel she'd brought with her from New York.

Good towels were one of her few indulgences. Once she'd found a job and a place to live in New

York, her first purchase had been a large, expensive Turkish towel. The thick, lush kind that soaked up moisture like a sponge.

Gertrude had always begrudged spending money on her for anything the rest of the world couldn't admire, so while Kate had had the best of everything when it came to clothes and shoes, towels had always been thin, and sheets had always been coarse. That towel had been the first tangible proof she'd had that her new life might actually end up better than the one she'd left behind.

She still didn't spend any more of her hard-earned money on clothes than she had to, but she did occasionally indulge in some of the more intimate luxuries her grandmother had denied her—good towels, soft sheets, perfumed shampoos and soaps and lotions. It wasn't much, and sometimes she couldn't even afford that, but she'd long ago decided that being sensible with her money was one thing, being needlessly penny pinching was quite another. And once she found the diamonds . . .

The thought brought the memory of the night before crashing back. Beneath the heavy sweater and warm wool dress, her nipples, already peaked in the cold, tightened further, pushing against the soft knit cotton of her practical chemise.

Kate squeezed her eyes shut, trying to push

away the troubling memory of the shadow lover who'd haunted her dreams. She'd face him in a few minutes, see the reminder of what had passed between them in his eyes. Somehow, from somewhere, she had to find the courage for it.

As she worked a comb through her tangled hair, she silently cursed the ill-fortune that had thrown them together again.

It hadn't been easy to think of coming back. Even with the windows of her small apartment open so that the jangling noise of New York had filled the rooms, she had heard the hostile silences of Grand House waiting for her.

It had taken all her courage to confront those silences and the past that still echoed in them. Not once had she considered the possibility that she would have to deal with El, too.

Or rather, deal with her feelings for him. She'd thought she'd put him and what they'd shared firmly in the past where it could be forgotten. She'd been wrong. Dangerously wrong.

She had bruises on her arm from where he'd held her last night. And the look on his face when he'd asked her, there in the yard, if she'd believed he was capable of murder . . .

Kate shivered, remembering.

When she walked into the kitchen five minutes later, only Ruth and Gar were there.

"I was beginning to wonder if you were going

to show at all," Ruth said snidely, slamming the heavy cast-iron skillet down on the stove. The clank of metal hitting metal made Gar jump. "You may get breakfast in bed in New York, but here you'll work, same as the rest of us."

Kate bit back the question of why anyone had to work at all now that Ruth had inherited her grandmother's money. "I'll set the table, shall I?"

Ruth scornfully eyed her still damp curls, but said only, "El's already eaten."

"Yes, all right," said Kate meekly, turning away. Relief mixed with an unsettling disappointment at the news.

She retrieved three of the crude pottery plates that had been for the servants' use when she was a girl—Gertrude's collection of fine china and crystal was kept in glass cases in the butler's pantry and the dining room—and set them on the oilcloth-covered table. Behind her, she heard the sharp crack of an egg being broken against the rim of the skillet, then the snap and hiss as it slid into the oil.

"You can fetch more eggs after breakfast," Ruth informed her. Another egg slid into the oil, then another. "The hens are nesting in the barn, now, so it's not too bad. Even a city girl like you ought to be able to manage that."

"Hens," said Gar, and smiled. He was already in his place, forearms resting on the table on either side of his plate as if he meant to dig in with both hands when the food finally came. His washed-out gaze wandered hopefully from Ruth to Kate and back again. "I like eggs."

"Watch Gar doesn't follow you out," Ruth warned. "He'll catch his death of cold this time of year."

Kate bent down and, laying her hand on Gar's, said, "I'll bring you a nice, big, fresh egg. Would you like that, Uncle Gar? A beautiful new egg, just for you?"

"Be careful of that ol' banty hen," he warned. "She's a mean 'un. As soon peck you as breathe."

"I didn't know you raised banties, Uncle Gar."

Ruth snorted and flipped an egg. "We've only had one banty hen, and I wrung her neck years ago. Wasn't long after you ran away." She flipped two more. "And give the eggs to me, not him, you hear?"

"You watch 'er," Gar insisted, wagging a big, gnarled finger in warning. "She's *mean*."

Kate nodded, blinking back tears. She squeezed his hand, then let him go and straightened. "I'll be careful, Uncle Gar. I promise."

All Ruth said was: "Toast's in the warming oven. Bacon's on that plate there. Get moving, girl, or it'll be cold before you get it to the table."

Breakfast was a grimly silent meal. Clearing up afterward was a relief. Ruth, who hadn't looked up or said a word all through the meal, gave her a half dozen sharp instructions, then bent to help Gar to his feet.

"Come on, Gar," she said. "Time to go to the bathroom now."

"Don't have to go," he muttered, suddenly obstinate.

"Yes, you do. Come on, now. Might as well get it over with, and then you can take a nap. Would you like that?"

"Got corn to tend to," he objected.

"It's too cold today. You can tend to it tomorrow."

"Today. Got to do it today. Harvest's coming. Got to do it today." With his wife's help, Gar awkwardly heaved to his feet, then stood there, swaying slightly and looking around as if he wasn't quite sure where he was.

"All right, but let's go to the bathroom first, shall we?"

Kate could hear them arguing all the way down the hall.

For the first time in her life, Kate pitied the older woman. Ruth had never been anything but sharp-tempered and disapproving, but she had loved her husband. It had to be hell to watch the man she adored getting more and more lost behind those vague blue eyes. And Gar . . .

This time Kate didn't fight the tears, just wiped them off on her sleeve and kept washing dishes. Ruth still hadn't returned by the time she finished. Rather than face the woman again, she grabbed her coat and the old egg basket and slipped out of the kitchen.

She paused on the steps a moment, searching for any sign of Elliott. He was nowhere in sight, and there were no sounds to indicate where he might be.

She hurried across the packed earth, shoulders hunched against the cold. The barn was farther from the main house than on most farms—her great-grandfather hadn't wanted to be wakened by the lowing of milk cows or the crowing of roosters, Gertrude had told her once. By the time she reached the small door set beside the massive double wagon doors, she was feeling a little warmer and, to her surprise, eager for the hunt.

While she waited for her eyes to adjust to the dusty darkness, Kate took stock of her surroundings. It was slightly warmer inside, the sweet smell of hay overlying the sharper smell of cows and manure in a nose-tingling, half-forgotten aroma that brought the memories rushing back.

When she was younger, the barn had often been her refuge—Gertrude refused ever to set foot in it—and Kate had come here whenever she could. No one bothered her. A couple of the laborers had been kind to her, but most had kept their distance, too wary of Gertrude to risk friendship with a shy child who never had much to say about anything.

Anne Avery

Today the place was almost empty. A solitary milk cow was tied to a stanchion, contentedly munching on hay from the manger in front of her. From behind the slatted walls of a stall a sudden squawk and a flurry of clawed feet scrabbling across the floor attested to the presence of hens. Nothing else moved in the place except dust motes. With only one cow and a handful of hens and chicks to fill it, the place seemed strangely desolate.

Kate suppressed the urge to call El's name. He'd been here—the tethered cow was proof of that—but he wasn't here now, and she couldn't bear to call for him and receive only silence in reply. There'd been too many years when she'd called for him in the dark, reaching out of her dreams and loneliness and longing to find only emptiness and regret.

The muscles in her shoulders relaxed, yet she couldn't repress a stab of regret at his absence. Juggling the wanting and the fear was exhausting.

The cow raised its head when she stopped to pat it. When it became clear that Kate hadn't brought any grain, it placidly lowered its head and grabbed another mouthful of hay, unimpressed. A few of the chickens came up to her, *pruck-prucking* hopefully and scratching at the floor as if to remind her of what was expected. Since the floor was still littered with the corn El had tossed them earlier, Kate ignored them and began searching for their nests.

She was crouched by a broken slat in one of the stalls, trying to reach a nest that some perverse biddy had built in a dusty, abandoned combine that had been pushed up against the opposite wall, when El walked in. She heard the creak of the small door first, opening and shutting, then the faint crunch of his footsteps coming across the barn toward her.

Suddenly breathless, she pulled her arm back and stood, hastily brushing off the bits of hay and straw that clung to her coat.

El stopped dead a good ten feet away. "You! What are you doing here?"

It wasn't a promising start. She held up the basket. "Aunt Ruth sent me to gather the eggs."

His gaze slid down her dusty, straw-adorned coat. Kate tried, but couldn't read anything in his hard face, not even anger. If he was thinking of what had passed between them last night, he gave no sign of it.

"I'll do it," he said. "You'll get too dirty."

There was a note of scorn in his voice that made her spine stiffen. However much he might haunt her thoughts, she was determined not to give in to his intimidation.

"It's no trouble."

"You don't know where the nests are."

"I'll find them. I've already found some of them."

For a moment they simply stood there glaring, silent antagonists divided by ten years and ten feet of dirty barn floor.

And a murder, Kate reminded herself.

A subtle change came over his face, as though he knew what she was thinking and couldn't decide what to do about it . . . or whether he even cared.

She shook the thought away. He cared. The bruises he'd left on her body last night were proof of that.

The silence was an anchor, dragging them down.

"I'd best get busy," she said, forcing herself to turn away. "Ruth will wonder where I've gotten."

"No she won't."

The harsh denial brought her around with a snap. "What do you mean by that?"

"Ruth won't *wonder* about anything. She'll be quite sure that you're out here in the barn making love with me."

"How dare you? How can you say such a thing?"

His right eyebrow arched dangerously. "How? It's easy because that's what I'm thinking. Of making love to you. Right here. Right now."

Chapter Five

With each word he came closer, inexorably advancing, eyes dark now with an angry threat that brought her heart into her throat.

"You . . . you . . ."

"I . . . what? I wouldn't do that? Or I wouldn't dare?" His mouth curved in an unpleasant smile. "Come now, Kate. You know I would. After what we shared, you can't pretend you don't think about it, too. Why even try?"

"I don't—That is, I wouldn't—"

He stopped dead in front of her. His smile turned grim. "No, you wouldn't, would you? You wouldn't admit you enjoyed making love back then, and you wouldn't admit that you think about it now. But you see, that's the difference between us, Kate. I say what I think. You don't. You never did."

Because I didn't dare!

She clutched the basket with its three small, dirty eggs as if her very life depended on it.

Perhaps it does.

That thought shook her even more. She didn't want to believe it. *Wouldn't* believe it of him. Not of El, the boy who had been her only friend, her only lover. She wouldn't even believe it of this cold, hostile stranger who stared at her as if determined to force a confession from her by sheer strength of will.

Did he want her to plead with him? Go down on her knees and beg for . . . what? Forgiveness? Mercy?

Or did he just want her down on her knees begging?

"So say it, Kate," he said, pressing her. "Say it straight out. Tell me what you're thinking."

Kate's breathing turned shallow. Her feet felt as if they'd turned to stone.

"I want you to leave me alone," she said, swallowing the fear that choked her. "I want you to stop threatening me. No matter what you think about me or what I did ten years ago, I want you to stop treating me as if I were some . . . some . . ."

She fought to find the right word and failed. But it was anger that gripped her now, not fear. Anger and a sudden, hot resentment.

"I want you to leave me alone," she stubbornly

repeated, and didn't know whether she lied or told the truth, or both.

She expected him to blow up in anger or threaten her as he had yesterday. Instead, he startled her by staring for a moment, then throwing back his head and laughing so loudly that the cow stopped eating and shifted around to get a better look at them over the side of the stall.

"Good for you, little Kate. There's some fight in you after all."

Slowly, head cocked, he walked around her like a horse buyer inspecting some beast up for sale. His eyes were unreadable slate.

Kate stared back defiantly, determined to hold onto that spark of anger. This was the first time since she'd returned that El had shown any approval of her and she found, perversely, that his approval mattered. She wanted, *needed*, for him to see her as a stronger, braver woman than she really was, perhaps because if he believed it, she might, too.

"What's the matter, Mr. Carstairs? Are you wondering if I've grown a tail since we last met?"

He casually propped his shoulder against one of the massive uprights that supported the roof, crossed his arms over his chest, and smiled as if inviting her to share the joke. Beneath the relaxed pose lay a leashed panther, waiting to pounce. She had to fight the urge to reach out and stroke the beast despite the danger.

"I don't know about the tail," he said at last. "Something's changed, that's for sure."

His voice seemed deeper, suddenly darker and more intimate. It slid over her like a gloved hand, caressing her. Her skin pricked. Kate drew her coat closer about her throat, but it wasn't a chill that had claimed her.

"A whole lot of somethings, actually," he added, amused. "Even under that ugly coat I can tell you've turned into a woman, Kate. A very beautiful woman."

You didn't seem to think so yesterday, she wanted to say.

"Little girls grow up even at Grand House," she shot back instead, hoping that the shadows here prevented him from detecting her flush of pleasure at his approval.

"Perhaps. But they don't usually grow into strong women fighting for what they want." His gaze hardened, locked with hers. "And you do want something, don't you, Kate?"

She didn't have an answer to that. He didn't seem to expect one.

"I need to finish gathering the eggs. Aunt Ruth—"

"Can wait."

She shook her head, tried to turn away but couldn't. El frightened her, yet she wanted to stare at him, to look and keep on looking to make up for all the years when the only time she could see him clearly was in her dreams.

"Aunt Ruth told me to gather the eggs," she insisted stubbornly.

He sighed and shoved away from the post. "If you're going to look for them no matter what, I suppose I ought to help. You'll never find them all, otherwise."

"I can find them."

"Not without me, you can't."

Was it just her imagination that there was any special meaning behind his words? Her imagination and a small, irrational hope?

Kneeling, he stuck his arm through the broken slat and retrieved the egg she'd been trying to reach when he found her. "Here. There's another one underneath, but you can't get to it from this side."

"I already found that," she said irritably, trying to ignore the dangerous spark of satisfaction at his offer of help.

"And the one in the manger?"

"That, too. There wasn't anything in it."

"What about the one *under* the manger?"

"I didn't look there," she reluctantly admitted.

A moment later he emerged with three good-size eggs. "How about in the back, around the combine, or over where the hay's stacked?"

"I hadn't gotten to those places yet."

This was what her own search was going to be

like, she thought. Groping in dark places, trying to second-guess her grandmother and the outrageous pride and spite that had driven her to take the one thing that might have set her daughter and granddaughter free.

Silently Kate followed El around the barn, no longer bothering to hunt for the eggs herself. While he burrowed and stretched to reach the corners and crannies where the hens had hidden their nests, she picked straw out of her coat and tried to think about her own search and not about the way his shirt strained across his broad back as he stretched to reach a nest, or the curve of his buttocks and the strong line of his thigh that were outlined under the heavy twill of his work pants every time he got down on hands and knees to grope under a piece of dusty, abandoned machinery.

At last, irritated by the silence and his pointed efforts to avoid looking at her, she said, "Why doesn't Aunt Ruth just keep these darned chickens in the chicken coop?"

He shrugged, got down on his knees to dig under a rusting wagon. "There aren't enough hens left to bother, I suppose. And no one to clean a coop," he added, placing another egg in her basket. "Past few years, it's been hard to keep the farms going around here. Seems Gertrude let the last of her hired hands go at least five years ago. These are Ruth's chickens, not Gertrude's."

"And the milk cow?"

"Ruth's. They're about the only things she brought with her when she inherited Grand House, far as I can tell. Them and a couple of pigs in the pens out back."

"I'm surprised she bothered with them. I always figured she'd opt for the same life of luxury that Grandmother always had." *And Mother and I didn't,* she silently added.

Impossible to keep the bitterness out of her voice, little though she liked the sound of it.

El grew still for a moment, as if weighing his answer. In the end, he just shook his head and scrunched farther under the wagon, straining to reach a second nest inconveniently located atop a broken springs on the back axle. The effort yielded two small speckled eggs.

Kate's thoughts were still back on Ruth. "Well?" she said. "Why doesn't Ruth hire someone to take care of the chickens? Or a maid for the house?"

"Gertrude had two maids and a cook working for her when she died. They left when Ruth took over."

"Why?"

"I don't know."

"And don't much care," she guessed, trying to read him.

"No." He climbed to his feet, slapping dust and straw off his clothes.

101

"Is it because of Gar? Is she trying to hide Gar away?"

His hand hovered over his sleeve. He frowned at the faded plaid, then carefully picked off a crushed piece of straw and tossed it away.

"Well, is she?" Kate insisted.

"Could be," El admitted reluctantly. "I never asked. Not my business."

It's not yours, either. He didn't say it. He didn't have to.

And yet it *was* her business, if only because she had lived here too long not to wonder what lay behind the changes. Grand House without servants. The farm without hired help. Chickens in the main barn and only one milk cow. The world she'd grown up in had always been off-kilter, but it seemed to have tipped wildly askew since she'd run away, and she wanted, somehow, to understand why.

Had Ruth already lost the money she'd inherited? Had she inherited any at all? The market crash in '29 had made paupers out of millionaires overnight. Maybe Gertrude had lost money, too. But if that were the case, why had she kept living like she always had? Why not sell some of the furniture or the silver to raise some cash? There were still folks with money to spend and a yen for the kind of things Ruth now owned in abundance.

It couldn't be lack of money.

"It *is* Gar." Kate said it with conviction. "That's why Ruth's shut herself away like this, isn't it? Because of Gar. *Isn't it?*"

His met her questioning gaze warily. "Yes, it's because of Gar."

"Ruth is letting her pride get in the way of her good sense."

"Is that really so surprising? The only thing she's ever had is her pride."

"And Gar?" Kate protested. "What about Gar?"

"I can't do a damn thing about Gar, and neither can you." His words snapped like a whip.

"If Gertrude had left the place to me—"

"Be thankful she didn't." He studied her through narrowed, suspicious eyes. "Did you *want* Grand House?"

"No, of course not."

Just the diamonds, she thought. *My diamonds*.

Suddenly, fiercely, he clamped his hands over her shoulders, dragging her to him. His eyes locked on hers. She wondered whether he saw anything other than panic in her eyes.

All she could see in his was fury.

"Listen to me, Kate. Forget Gar. Forget Ruth and Grand House and all the rest of it. What is, *is*. I don't go borrowing worries, and neither should you. Do you understand?"

She didn't understand any of it, but she wasn't about to admit it.

"Damn fool," he said, and shoved her away as

roughly as he'd grabbed her. The eggs in her basket rattled. "Whatever it is you're after, it's not worth it. Trust me, Kate. It's *not worth it.*"

"It is to me."

When he remained silent, she pointedly shoved past him. She had a house to search.

Before she'd taken a second step, he grabbed her sleeve and pulled her back.

"Watch where you're going," he growled. "You damn near stepped on that chick."

A fat brown hen had wandered out from behind the old wagon, herding a half dozen chicks in front of her. The one she'd almost crushed scratched at the floor in front of her foot, doing its best to look like a grown up hen, then pecked at a bit of grain the other hens had missed.

Kate set her basket down, then picked up the bold little creature at her feet. The chick struggled for a moment, then gave a little cheep, fluffed out its nonexistent feathers, and settled contentedly into the warm cradle of her hands. She gently stroked the chick with the tip of one finger.

El knelt beside her. "I'd forgotten how much you always loved the babies around the farm," he said, picking up another chick.

"I always wanted a pet," she admitted a little sadly. "If you and Uncle Gar hadn't let me drag your old mutt around, or pet the rabbits, or pester the hens, I don't know what I'd have done."

He made a funny little sound at the back of his throat. The chick cheeped as his work-roughened thumb gently stroked it.

Kate pushed away memories of El's fingers stroking her just as gently, once.

"Remember that old apple crate where Uncle Gar used to keep the chicks near the stove, where they'd be warm?" She smiled at the half-forgotten picture of big, booming Gar on his knees, gently cradling a tiny ball of yellow down in his palm and crooning soothing nonsense. "He certainly loved his chickens."

The chick in El's hand suddenly panicked, flapping its useless little wings in a desperate effort to get away. Expressionless, he set it down. It hesitated for a moment as if uncertain whether it was really free, then scampered off, cheeping madly.

Kate reluctantly let her chick go as well and glanced around the big, empty barn. "I'm surprised Ruth doesn't bring him out here more often. I think he'd enjoy watching the chickens."

El's mouth turned hard. "She used to until he tried to start the old tractor in the shed and nearly blew himself up. When he started chopping wood on his own . . ."

He shrugged and looked away, unable to complete the thought. A long, broken bit of straw on the floor caught his attention. He picked it up, studied it, frowning.

She had to fight the urge to touch him, to lay a comforting hand on his shoulder and tell him things would be all right, even if it was a lie.

"You came back because of him, didn't you?"

"I came back"—she noticed he didn't say he'd come home—"two months ago. There was something I wanted to talk to him about, something I had to . . . get clear. I needed answers."

"And you didn't get them," she said softly.

He shrugged and wrapped the straw around his finger. "He can't tell me what I need to know. Not anymore."

There was a world of loss in that matter-of-fact statement, though he didn't seem to hear it. She tried to imagine the lonely wanderings he'd endured, and found she didn't want to.

The pain of it all squeezed her heart.

The last thing she'd wanted was to feel pity for any of them.

He frowned, then angrily tossed the straw away and got to his feet. He didn't offer a hand to help her up.

She retrieved her egg basket and stood. The all too brief understanding that had blossomed between them had withered again, burned up under that forbidding black look.

"I'd better take these eggs in," she said, uncertain now just how to act. "I promised Uncle Gar I'd have an egg just for him. Which do you think he'd like better, that speckled one, or this big brown one?"

"Who in hell cares? I don't want to talk about Gar. I want—"

He squeezed his eyes shut, breathed deep, then opened them and stared some more.

"God, you're beautiful, Kate," he said. It was barely a whisper. "Even more beautiful than I remembered."

And then he leaned forward and kissed her.

It was a gentle kiss, tentative and hungry, with none of the fury of last night's kiss. But the fury was there underneath. She could taste it on his lips. She could see it lurking behind his eyes and feel it in the barely leashed power of his hands and body. Even as the heat and hunger worked their way through her blood, it terrified her to think of it.

Despite the doubts, she couldn't help but respond. The eggs rattled softly in their basket. She ignored them. Last night's kiss had seared her senses and burned its way through her dreams. This kiss was far more dangerous, laden with possibilities she didn't dare believe in.

She wasn't sure who broke it off first. Perhaps they both came to their senses at the same time.

Not that she'd ever had much sense when it came to Elliott Carstairs.

Not that she'd ever thought she'd need it, she reminded herself, compressing her lips against the sudden cold now that he'd stepped back.

El glanced at the basket of eggs, then over toward the cow, who had emptied her manger and was now placidly contemplating the barn wall.

"Guess I'd better get to work," he said, deliberately not looking at her. "There's the milk to store, and Ruth said Gar wanted chicken for supper. I'll have to tend to that, too."

Kate murmured a dazed agreement without really taking in a thing he said. That rough, angry note was back in his voice, lurking just under the words. It grated down her spine like a hard wind, warning of a storm to come.

Somehow she got out of the barn without stumbling. It wasn't until she'd set the basket of eggs on the kitchen table and started to remove her coat that she realized she needed to talk to El. Really talk to him. Clutching her unbuttoned coat closed in front of her, she dashed back out into the cold.

The barn was empty, the cow gone. El was nowhere in sight. Frustration rose in her. She had to tell him that it was going to be all right. It was *all* going to be all right. Somehow she had to say the words out loud if they were ever to have a chance of coming true. She was sure of it.

She found him in the weed-grown yard outside the chicken pens. He had a scrawny gray chicken under one arm and was adjusting a loop of rope over a branch of winter-bare cottonwood. He didn't see her, but from this angle, she could see the grim, cold expression that seemed carved into his face.

Satisfied with the loop, he stepped away from the cottonwood and took the chicken's head in his right hand. Too late, she realized what he was doing.

With one quick, practiced flick of his wrist, he swung the chicken around in a circle, like a rock tied to a string. The weight of that circling body was enough to break the creature's neck, killing it instantly.

Another quick motion and he'd wrenched the head off and tossed it away. The body he tied up by the feet from the ready loop, letting the blood drain out through the crudely severed neck.

Through it all, his expression hadn't changed. It was still grim, forbidding, as if he dwelt on thoughts that suited the brutal, bloody deed. He would, she knew, have managed to get not a drop of blood on his hands or shirt.

Forcing down the bile that had suddenly risen in her throat, Kate turned back to the house. It took every ounce of will she possessed to keep from running.

Chapter Six

The attic to which Kate fled proved an uncomfortable refuge. It was dark and cold, yet the smell of dry, musty summer lingered unpleasantly, trapped among the boxes and trunks stacked on the plank-covered rafters and tangled in the ungainly forest of discarded furniture.

How many lives were hidden away up here? she wondered. Her great-grandfather, Gertrude had often told her proudly, had gone to great lengths to protect his ancestors' heritage. The detritus of all those lives—letters, clothes, carefully preserved treasures that had no value save to someone a hundred years dead—had been stored away here, carefully wrapped in paper or tucked in fancy-work boxes, then forgotten. Even the mothballs had long since vanished, leaving nothing but a faint, nose-wrinkling odor behind.

Kate crept along the narrow path of bare boards laid over the naked rafters that ran from one end of the attic to the other, peering into the confusion on either side and trying to decide where to start. Though she'd brought one of the big, reflecting work lanterns, the light from that single kerosene-fueled flame could only drive the shadows back a few feet and no farther. Beyond that, its battle against the dark was reduced to casting a distorted mural upon the ceiling, a mural made of shadows that shifted with her every step like monsters lurking just out of sight, waiting to pounce.

She had always hated the attic and everything it contained. To her, it had seemed more a monument to the dead than the storehouse of treasures that her grandmother considered it. Sometimes, when she was a child huddled in her bed, caught between sleep and waking, she'd thought she could feel the weight of all those dead people and their possessions pressing down on her, crushing the life out of her.

Though she was an adult now, the place still made her shiver. The ceiling here at the midpoint was a good five feet above her head, yet she found herself stooping to get beneath it, hunching her shoulders and tucking her elbows to her sides as if by making herself smaller she could somehow escape the notice of whatever malevolent spirits dwelt up here.

Stupid, fanciful notions, she told herself, yet she couldn't help jumping every time a floorboard creaked or the wind outside moaned loudly enough to be heard even in this windowless void. By the time she reached the far end of the attic, her heart was pounding painfully in her chest, and her palms had turned damp, her fingers cold.

A quick glance at the accumulated dust told her she wouldn't find what she sought back here. Everything looked as if it hadn't been touched since her grandfather had ordered it brought up here and abandoned more than sixty years ago.

As she carefully picked her way back—the narrow planks were often warped and carelessly set down so that here and there a hole gaped, threatening to trip her and send her plunging through the ceiling of the rooms below—she could have sworn that something followed her. The one time she dredged up the courage to look around, nothing was there. It was only her imagination that saw El lurking in the darkness while a pool of hot blood formed at his feet.

Forcing away the absurdly childish fears, Kate dragged a stool out of the mess and plunked it down in front of one of the trunks set nearest the stairs. Nothing she'd looked at had borne her mother's name or seemed the least bit familiar, so this was as good a place to start as any.

A chilly draft slipped through the open stair

door to curl around her feet. No light came from below, yet she couldn't bring herself to shut the door and seal herself in this temple of the dead that her grandmother and great-grandfather had created up here.

Wrapping herself in the wool blanket she'd brought up with her, Kate settled on the stool, pried open the rusting hasp of the trunk, and bent to look inside.

Three hours later by her watch, an eternity later by the stiffness in her back and the coldness in her fingers, Kate reluctantly shut the fifth trunk she'd explored and got to her feet. The blanket slipped off her shoulders as she pressed her hands to the small of her back and stretched, trying to work out the ache.

Nothing. She'd found absolutely nothing. Packets of bills and canceled checks dating back thirty years and more, newspaper clippings of obituaries for people she'd never heard of, stacks and stacks of *The Saturday Evening Post* and *Ladies' Home Journal* and, to her surprise, a large box of *Ranch Romances* that must have been the cook's, but nothing that might have been her mother's and nothing that was of any use to her. She'd gone through everything, every bill and clipping and magazine, without finding anything of any value. The only consolation was she hadn't fallen asleep or suffered any delusions like the one last night in Gertrude's bedroom.

Her head was pounding from tension and the strain of trying to read by a single lantern's light. It hadn't helped that flashes of her confrontation with El had insisted on intruding. She'd had to fight to keep her attention on her search and not on replaying everything he'd said over and over again.

Even though she'd warned herself that the search might take days, possibly even weeks, she hadn't really believed it. She'd wanted it to be easy, wanted to find at least some clue to the necklace's whereabouts with her first real effort. That she hadn't was far more discouraging than she'd expected.

"Don't be a fool," she muttered. "Nothing's ever easy. *Nothing.*"

Her voice sounded oddly flat and lifeless in the chilly silence.

Shivering, she gathered up the blanket and the sputtering lantern and groped her way down the steep, narrow stairs. A quick wash in the icy water from the tap—Ruth had always been as much a stickler for cleanliness as her grandmother—brought her awake with a painful snap. The last thing she wanted was to antagonize Ruth further by leaving her with all the work of preparing the midday meal. It would be the main meal of the day, and that meant there was much to do.

She didn't remember the butchered chicken

until she walked in and found it lying on a platter set beside the big enameled sink. Her stomach churned at the sight and threatened to revolt altogether when she spotted the pinkish pool of blood mixed with water that had formed under the carcass.

El had already gutted and cleaned the bird—the gizzard, liver, and heart were set in a separate bowl to the side—but there were still some more pin feathers and the stubs of some of the tougher quills to pull out. And the carcass to cut up, Kate reminded herself, clutching a queasy stomach.

She'd always known where the food on her plate came from—hard not to when you lived on a farm, even at Grand House—but this was different. This time it was El who'd done the killing with such efficient violence, El whose face floated in front of her closed eyes, grim and forbidding.

Desperate for something to distract her from that gutted carcass, she checked the fire in the stove, then added more wood. It had been a long time since she'd last stoked a stove like this, but she found she hadn't lost the knack of knowing how to arrange the wood so the ash wouldn't choke the fire. The coal stoves in the rest of the house used to provide extra heat were easier to manage, but Gertrude had always insisted that wood be used to cook her food, and Ruth clearly hadn't wanted to change.

Kate watched as flames caught the new wood, but what she saw was El swinging an ax above his head, then bringing it down with teeth-rattling force. El, coatless in the wind, the fires within him hot enough to defy the cold. El, tying a loop of cord to the barren branch of a cotton-wood.

With a choking gasp, Kate forced away the un-wanted images and slammed the iron lid back into place.

"That you, Katherine Mary?" Ruth called from somewhere down the hall.

Guiltily, Kate tossed the lid handle aside. "Yes, Aunt Ruth. I—I thought I'd start potatoes boiling, if that's all right with you."

Footsteps answered her, coming closer. Ruth paused in the hall doorway, big hands disdain-fully propped on her bony hips, eyes hostile as she studied the room. Without saying a word, she crossed to the stove, elbowing Kate aside so she could lift the lid and check the fire.

Kate watched, unspeaking, as she poked at the flames, then added another piece of wood.

Ruth shoved the lid till it dropped into place, then pointedly hung the handle from its hook. "If you'd ever had to work growing up, you might have learned how to manage a fire. Pity Gertrude never made sure to teach you something useful."

The spiteful words stung. There'd been noth-ing wrong with the fire, and they both knew it. If anything, Ruth had just made it too hot for proper cooking, but Kate wasn't about to mention that.

When she remained silent, Ruth snorted in disgust, backed off an argument she would have relished.

"At least you can peel potatoes and set them and the chicken to boil. Even a fool can manage that. And clean that chicken properly. You can do that, can't you?" she demanded, looming over her threateningly.

"Yes, Aunt Ruth. I can do that."

Kate had to fight to keep from backing away. Ruth was several inches taller than she was, bigger boned and heavier. Stronger, too, despite her age. Years of hard, physical labor had endowed her with a raw strength that only advanced age or illness would take from her. Shelving books for a living couldn't begin to compete.

"There's canned tomatoes. Gar likes those. With the chicken and potatoes, that'll do."

"Yes, Aunt Ruth." Boiled chicken, boiled potatoes, stewed tomatoes. Kate's stomach churned at the thought of the tasteless fare.

Ruth eyed her suspiciously. "Don't act so meek, girl. I know you. You're lazy and sneaking and sly and you think everybody owes you something, but you're not meek and never have been."

Kate felt her shoulder muscles twist into painful knots. Ruth had always terrified her. The woman had been a second pair of eyes for her grandmother, always watching, always disapproving. Whenever Ruth had complained of something she'd done, Gertrude had been more than willing to ring a chorus of blame. Now that Gertrude was gone, Ruth seemed ready to do the destructive work of two.

"What? Nothing to say?"

Ruth eyed her with contempt, but Kate refused to rise to the bait. She doubted she could have gotten the words past the sudden constriction in her throat if she tried.

The courage—or had it been merely desperation?—that had enabled her to stand up to Ruth yesterday was gone. That frightened her. Not twenty-four hours at Grand House and already the place and the people in it were winning.

"Fine, then," Ruth said with a dismissive snort. "Keep quiet. As long as you do your work, I don't care. I don't imagine there's anything that you've got to say that I would want to hear, anyway."

In the end, Kate didn't boil the chicken. It had been difficult enough cleaning it; she found she couldn't bear to cut it into pieces, too. The image of El spinning the thing, then snapping off its head was still too vivid. Instead, she larded it with strips of bacon as she'd seen Gertrude's cook do, then baked it in a stove that was still too hot.

118

Ruth took pleasure in pointing out the over-cooked parts.

"If you'd boiled it like I said, this wouldn't have happened," she said with satisfaction, conveniently ignoring her husband's obvious pleasure in the crusty, bacon-flavored skin.

Kate kept her head down and her attention on her plate. It didn't stop her intense awareness of El, who was sitting on her right, silently and methodically working his way through the food on his plate.

He'd washed at the outside pump before coming in. His coal black hair had been wet at the edges and droplets of water had clung to the beard that was already beginning to show, despite his morning's shave. She'd had to busy herself with cutting her meat into bits to stop from brushing off his chin and jaw.

Despite the heat from the stove, traces of dampness still lingered around his hair line. She could see where a few strands were plastered to the side of his neck, just beneath his ear. The back of his collar was damp, too. Her fingers itched to straighten the rumpled flannel so it lay a little more smoothly.

I'm thinking of making love to you.

Her mouth went dry and her palms damp, remembering.

If El was suffering from the same kind of physical awareness, he gave no sign of it. Since he'd walked in that door, he hadn't met her gaze once and hadn't said a word more than he absolutely had to. If he could have, she suspected he would have taken his meal somewhere else entirely. But Ruth would have demanded to know why, and El wasn't fool enough to risk that, no matter how little he wanted to be sitting here with her now.

". . . clean the parlors and the study and dining room."

Kate glanced up as Ruth's harsh voice forced its way in over her thoughts, demanding attention.

"Those rooms haven't had a good cleaning since long before Gertrude died," Ruth continued disapprovingly. "The minute the house was mine, I fired those lazy good-for-nothings who'd been taking her money and doing nothing for it."

Her gaze narrowed to fix on Kate. "Now you're here, you might as well do something useful. And while you're at it, you can make some bread this afternoon."

That brought Kate's head up. "What?"

"Bread. That stuff you've got set at the side of your plate that you haven't even touched. Wasting good food like that when people, hardworking people, are going hungry . . . it's a crime. An absolute crime."

"But—"

"Use the potato water."

"The potato water?"

"That's what I said. The water the potatoes boiled in. You saved that, didn't you?"

"No," Kate admitted, bewildered. "I threw it out, just like you did last night."

"Threw it out!"

Gar dropped the chicken leg he was sucking on, startled by the sharp words. Ruth didn't even notice.

"I didn't know—"

"That's no excuse, missy! Potato water makes good bread, gets it rising right. Or didn't you know that, either?" When Kate remained silent, she added nastily, "I suppose you have *your* bread delivered? All neat and tidy and wrapped in a paper bag so it won't get dirty. Isn't that the way they do it in the big cities?"

"I been to the big city," Gar announced. "All the way to Chicago, even. Got lost. Twice!" He laughed at the memory. The grease from the chicken that he'd managed to smear all around his mouth glistened in the light.

Ruth and El ignored him. Kate's heart twisted in her chest.

"I get my bread from the shop around the corner," she said, forcing her attention back to Ruth. "And I can't afford to have my groceries delivered. No one I know can. As for the bread . . . I don't know how to make bread. I never learned."

Ruth snorted in disbelief. "Never wanted to, more like."

Kate flushed, but stubbornly held her tongue. She'd wanted to, all right. She'd wanted to do a lot of things, but Gertrude had never let her do anything but polish the silver or carry her Bible or sit on a stool at her feet for endless, aching hours reading from some suitably grim book. She would have preferred to feed the chickens and slop the pigs, but Gertrude had said that sort of thing wasn't suitable for a Mannheim. More than once she'd wanted to shout back that neither were icy baths, or a cold, uncomfortable bed in a cubbyhole intended for a servant, but she'd never found the courage to say it.

Sometimes it had seemed as if her grandmother wanted to ensure that she would always be dependent, fit for nothing but being the meek little girl who did as she was told. She wasn't allowed to associate with the servants and farm laborers, and Gertrude had always claimed it was too much work to run her into town for any of the social activities that other girls her age engaged in, even girls from farms that were a great deal farther from town than Grand House was.

It hadn't mattered that Gertrude always had the newest, biggest car in the county, or that she was always more than willing to be driven into Mannville so she could remind everyone else that she was the mistress of Grand House and the richest woman in five counties. That was Gertrude Mannheim. Petrol was too expensive to waste driving her granddaughter into town for frivolous things like a Friday movie with friends, and the hired men were always too busy to stop what they were doing to take her, even if they were doing nothing much at all.

It was only when she'd started looking for work in New York that Kate had realized just how little she *was* fitted for. She couldn't cook or clean, she had no training that would fit her to be a teacher, and she was far too shy to be a successful secretary even if she could have learned to type. The only thing she was really good at—the only thing she'd *ever* been good at—was reading, which was why she'd been so relieved to read the help-wanted ad that said the proprietors of the J. Daniel Bookstore were seeking a knowledgeable clerk to shelve and assist customers in their selections.

It had been a perfect shelter for her, right from the start. All those years of devouring every book she could find, from the classics that lined the shelves in her great-grandfather's study to the pulp novels that cook had secretly been fond of, had finally paid off. She knew the books, and she'd found, to her surprise, that it wasn't quite so impossible to learn how to deal with the public as she'd thought. Although that might have been because folks who read a lot tended to be solitary types themselves, people with whom she felt she had something in common, even if they never spoke of it.

Despite the friends she'd made, she still led a rather solitary life. After ten years, she knew her customers' names and almost nothing about their private lives. Gertrude had always said it was rude to pry, and she'd never had the courage to break through the natural barriers that always existed between customers with money and the people who served them.

The store had survived the crash of '29—barely—but the effort to keep afloat had been too much for the aging owners. Now that Lily Daniel was failing, her stomach slowly being eaten away with the cancer that was killing her, Jonathan wanted to get out. They had offered her the first chance to buy the business. It was a good deal, even in these hard times, but Kate knew the offer had been more a gesture of friendship than because the Daniels really expected her to be able to come up with the necessary money. They'd given her a week to say yes or no, and two months to get the money together once she'd startled them by barging into their office and shouting—she, who never shouted!—that, yes! she wanted to buy the store.

At first, she'd thought she could manage with a loan and her meager savings as a down payment. But the banks wouldn't even talk to her. Loan money? For such a marginal business? And to a *woman?* Some had been more polite than others, but the answer had always been the same: No!

After her last turn down, she'd dragged herself home, discouraged, and started making a list of other bookstores in New York that might be willing to hire an experienced clerk who worked hard and cheap. That was when she'd remembered the diamonds.

To begin with, she'd thought the memory was nothing more than wishful thinking, but the more she'd dug down into some of those memories she'd tried to hide away inside her, the more she realized that her mother had considered the diamonds her ticket to freedom, too. She vaguely remembered Sara rambling on one night about the places they'd go and the things they'd do once she got the diamonds back.

Sara had never found the diamonds or her dreams, but Kate was determined that *she* would have both, no matter what obstacles Ruth put in her way.

If only El hadn't been here! If Gar had been himself, it wouldn't have mattered so much. But Gar was nothing more than a wreck of the man he'd once been, and El—

She wasn't going to think about El, she told herself. Not that way. Not when he was less than three feet away and she was so achingly aware of him. If someone had asked, she might almost have reported the number of silky black hairs on the back of the hand nearest her. She was no artist, but she could have drawn the way his fingers curled inward when he was relaxed, the angle of each knuckle, the ropy veins beneath the skin that shifted with every move of the bones beneath . . . and she wouldn't have needed to look to do it.

"Can't bake bread," Ruth muttered, disgusted. "Next you'll be telling me you can't sweep, either."

No, she wouldn't tell her that, Kate thought, dragging herself back to the conversation at hand. She also wouldn't tell her about all the disasters, large and small, she'd suffered through until she'd learned to take care of her own clothes and her small apartment. Those daily humiliations were part of the past she was determined to keep buried forever.

Ruth heaved a long-suffering sigh. "All right, then. I'll make the bread—I won't risk wasting supplies to help you learn—but I'll expect you to do the rest of it. As your payment for your food and for staying here."

Before Kate had a chance to object, El broke in, as calmly as if he hadn't heard a word of what had gone before.

"I'm due to go into town tomorrow," he said without bothering to look up from his plate. "Got to take the milk in to old man Proctor, pick up some more grain."

The edge of Ruth's mouth lifted in a sneer. "See that hussy down at the Depot Cafe. *I* know. Don't think you're fooling me, because you aren't and never have."

He did look up at that. Something hot flashed in his eyes. "Maybe."

Ruth was the first to look away.

His gaze dropped back to his plate. He pushed a bit of potatoes atop a piece of meat, ate, swallowed. "There anything you need while I'm there?"

Ruth sniffed. "I wouldn't have. Now there's another mouth to feed, though, I suppose I'd best give you a list. And Gar was asking for some jam this morning. You can get a jar or two of that. Mind you," she added, her hostile gaze swinging around to Kate, "none of the fancy stuff. Some folk may be used to it, but Gar and me, we'll settle for whatever's cheapest. That's always been good enough for us."

She shot a triumphant glance at Kate, making sure her point had gotten across, then shoved to her feet. "I'll go get Gar washed up. Once you've got things cleaned up in here, you can get that bucket of cleaning things that's out on the porch. With three parlors, the study, and the dining room to do, there'll be plenty to keep you busy."

Kate didn't bother to protest. It wouldn't have

done any good if she had. She didn't offer to help with Gar. She didn't need El's warning glance to know the offer wouldn't be appreciated.

She tried not to think about what might lie between El and a hussy down at the Depot Cafe, and failed.

Chapter Seven

The instant Ruth had led a shuffling Gar away, Kate pushed her plate aside.

"You didn't eat much." They were the first words El had directed to her since they'd parted in the barn. "As much work as Ruth has planned for you, you'd do well to eat, keep your strength up."

"I'm not her servant!" Kate tossed her napkin down on the table beside the plate. It was one of the coarse, cheap napkins her grandmother had kept for the servants' use, and the edges were fraying. The fine linen ones were no doubt still tucked away in that monstrous carved bureau in the dining room, properly starched and ironed, unsullied. "If Ruth wants someone to clean this place, she'd better be prepared to pay for the service."

He cocked his head a little, his expression as uncommunicative as ever. Once, she'd thought she could see behind the mask he showed to the rest of the world. Now, she wasn't so sure.

"Why don't you suggest it?" he said. "Maids in Mannville are earning up to fifty cents a day, plus meals. Or so I've heard."

She gaped at him, dumbfounded. "Be Ruth's *hired help*? Have you gone mad?"

He shoved his plate away, too. His was empty. The fact might have given her some pleasure if she hadn't known that he'd never paid much attention to the food he ate. Since he'd had to endure Ruth's cooking all those years while growing up, it was probably just as well.

"Why not work for her?" His right eyebrow lifted mockingly. "What's wrong with wringing a few dollars out of her now she's rich?"

"Thank you, no! It's one thing to help out around here, quite another to put myself in her power like that."

For a moment, he simply stared at her, unspeaking, the air between them weighted with all the things she hadn't said. Then, softly, but with steel beneath the words, he said, "You already have, Kate. The minute you got off that train in Mannville you put yourself in Ruth's power. You know it as well as I do."

Because he was right, and because she didn't want to admit it, she started clearing the table.

Her chair grated on the floor like chalk on slate when she shoved it back.

El stood, too. He carried his plate and Gar's messy one to the sink and dumped them on the drain board. For an instant, she thought he was going to offer to help with the washing up and couldn't decide whether it would be safe to stand that close to him or not.

Instead, he refilled his mug with coffee from the pot on the stove and sat back down at the table. He dumped in some sugar, took a tentative sip of the thick, black brew, then tilted back in his chair until he was balanced on only the two back legs. The casual, masculine move would have earned a sharp lecture from Ruth if she'd seen him.

While he sipped at his coffee, she scraped the food scraps into the covered bucket under the sink where the slops for the pigs were always kept, then dragged out the big tin wash basin and dumped that in the sink. Steam billowed when she filled it with hot water drawn from the boiler in the basement. The old pipes groaned and whined as she drew enough cold water to make the temperature bearable.

As she worked, she could feel El's eyes on her. He didn't speak, made no effort to press his outrageous proposal on her, yet she would swear she could hear the idea ticking over in his head. That and more she probably didn't want to know about.

She couldn't help thinking of how easy it would be to pack up her few things tomorrow morning. He'd probably leave right after breakfast, early enough that she might still catch the first train going east. If the connections worked out just right, she could be back at her job next Monday, with more than enough time to find another job if she had to.

As if he could read her mind, El finally spoke up. "If you don't want to work for Ruth, you could go into town with me tomorrow."

Kate couldn't tell whether the sudden tightness in her chest was from relief or regret.

"If we leave early enough, you could catch the first train out," he added as if it were the most reasonable thing in the world. "You'd be back in New York in no time."

She scraped at the old tin baking pan she'd used to cook the chicken and cursed a little under her breath. Bits of skin and flesh seemed to have welded themselves to the bottom. Next time, she'd remember to grease the thing first.

Every nerve ending was alive with her awareness of him. Three feet or three thousand miles, it didn't matter the distance between them. She'd always been aware of him and probably always would be.

The admission was enough to make her knees

tremble. Rather than give in, she attacked the cooking pan with renewed fury.

"You wouldn't even have to tell Ruth if you didn't want to," he said, mistaking her silence for uncertainty. "I could get your bag out for you without her ever knowing."

"I'm not going." It came out more a breathy little grunt than real words. No wonder she'd had a hard time getting that chicken out of the pan. The burned stuff was welded on. She wasn't sure she'd ever get it off.

His chair came down on the floor with a thump. She'd swear she could hear the soft scrape of his clothes as he leaned forward across the table. He'd be wearing wool under the flannel and denim, she knew. And under the wool, warm, bare skin that held the scent of him and the flavor.

"Well?" he demanded. "What do you say?"

She flung the pan and the old knife she was using back into the water and spun around to face him. "I'm not going."

The instant the words were out, she knew they were the right ones. She was staying for as long as it took to find the diamonds, no matter what.

Or until she was forced to admit that they didn't exist and never had.

They exist something within her insisted. They *had* to exist. Her stomach churned at the thought of her future if they didn't.

133

All she said was, "I'm not leaving Grand House until I've found what I came for."

"Your mother's things." He said it with a sneer, challenging her to tell the truth.

"That's right."

Because she had to do something with her hands and the pan would have to soak some more before she had a chance of getting it clean, she grabbed up a tea towel and began furiously rubbing at the glasses and plates she'd tipped upside-down on the drain board to dry. Twice she almost dropped something because her hands were shaking so.

El didn't offer to help, thank God. She might have thrown something at him if he had. She didn't dare risk having him that close.

The anger was a live thing in her, a good thing. She wasn't often angry. She didn't often dare to be.

Drying the dishes gave her the chance to watch him, study him. The anger gave her the courage.

He wasn't watching her. His head was lowered, his unreadable gaze fixed on the depths of the mug he held as if he thought he could find a few answers written there. She didn't think she wanted to know the questions.

If he was aware of her studying him, he gave no sign of it. She wouldn't have expected him to. He'd always been able to hide whatever he was thinking or feeling. As much as she'd loved him, all those years ago, there were times she'd wanted to hit him, to scream and tear at him and keep on screaming until he lowered those protective barriers that divided them. He never had. She never had. She'd never found the courage, not after she'd stood in the wreckage of her shattered dreams and he'd refused to offer one word of explanation or comfort.

Yet watching him now, she could feel the anger seep out of her and a familiar, yearning ache fill its place.

Here in the kitchen with pale, clear winter sunlight creeping through the dusty windows, he didn't seem quite so dangerous or intimidating as he had in the shadowy barn this morning. The light muted the hint of silver in the unruly black hair and softened the hard angles of his face, making him more human somehow, but no less desirable.

Once, she'd loved him passionately, and he'd loved her. Once, they'd talked of leaving Grand House together, of building a life somewhere far away where no one knew them and no one had ever heard of the name Mannheim.

A dead girl had taken that from them. All of it.

Kate watched as he stretched to reach the coffee pot, then poured the last, thick, bitter dregs into his cup. He didn't bother with a towel to protect his hand from the hot metal handle, just moved quick and sure, too centered on his own thoughts to notice anything else.

She'd pleaded with him once to run away with her. They'd been lying together in the tumble-down wreck of a barn on the tumble-down farm Gar had worked from the day he'd married Ruth. The afternoon had been hot, and the air was soft against their bare skin, cooling the sweat from their lovemaking.

If she closed her eyes, she knew she could still smell the scent of him, potently male, and the sweet scent of the hay that had made their bed. The old wool blanket they'd spread beneath them had been scratchy, she remembered, though she hadn't really noticed that then. She hadn't noticed much of anything but him at first, him and the way he made her feel and the fire he lit within her.

But the fire cooled, as it always did after they'd made love, banking down to a safe, comforting heat that warmed without threatening to destroy her. In his arms, with his strong, broad chest pressed tight against her breasts and her belly rubbing against his, she'd asked him to run away with her. It had taken her weeks of thinking, planning, to work up the courage to ask. They'd been lovers for almost two months by then. It had seemed forever, and not nearly long enough for her to believe it was really real.

"Let's leave now, El," she'd said, half choking

on hope. "Not next week or next month. *Now,* before anyone can stop us."

She could still remember the way his arms had tightened around her when she'd suggested it.

As clearly as she remembered the physical aspects of the moment, however, she couldn't remember his exact words. Perhaps she hadn't wanted to. She'd been so sure he'd agree. She'd never been sure of anything, sometimes not even his love for her, but she'd been sure he'd agree to that.

He hadn't. He'd said they needed time, time to prepare, to put a little money aside, said he couldn't leave Gar right then, not with harvest coming on. She'd argued, pleaded, cried. She'd seen the misery in his eyes—the pale gray eyes through which she'd thought she'd looked into his heart—but nothing she'd said had made him change his mind.

The next day he'd been arrested and charged with the murder of Louisa Bannister. Eventually, he'd been released for lack of evidence, but by then she was living in a shabby, overcrowded boarding house in the Bronx and desperately looking for work. By then, there were twelve hundred miles between them and wounds so deep they'd scored her heart and made it bleed with every beat.

She'd thought then that she would never see him again. She'd tried to tell herself she didn't care, but ten years of tortured dreams and wordless longing had proved her wrong.

She didn't know what she felt for him now. The physical need for him was still there, sharp and hot and vicious, inescapable as death. Everything else was bewildering confusion, her present emotions too tangled with the emotions of ten years ago for any of it to make sense. In Grand House the past was inexorably tied to the present. Like varnish over wood, it covered everything, staining and blurring what lay beneath.

As if he could read her mind, El looked up from the depths of his coffee mug. His eyes locked with hers, but there was no longer any heart behind them. Not that she could see at any rate.

Abruptly he drained the mug and got to his feet. It took six steps for him to cross to her—she counted every one of them with a pounding heart. The heavy pottery mug clanked against the sides of the wash basin as he dropped it in, adding one more thing for her to wash.

When his hands clamped around her shoulders, she flinched, but stood her ground. When his lips crushed down on hers, they tasted of bitter coffee and man.

This time she didn't moan, didn't sway into him or try to push him away. She just stood there while he took and took and took and the blood roared in her ears.

The more she refused to yield to that demanding mouth, the angrier he became. His hands crushed her shoulders, grinding her bones together.

"Damn you," he snarled when he wrenched away at last. He sucked in air, let it out. "You should leave while you have the chance."

"I'm not leaving."

"Then you're a fool."

She didn't try to answer that. She was afraid he might be right.

It was only her imagination that she could still hear his footsteps crunching across the ground outside long after he had gone.

Eventually Kate gave up trying to clean the baking pan and hid it away at the back of a utility cupboard overflowing with abandoned junk on the back porch. She considered sneaking back to the attic, but decided to give in to Ruth's demands and do at least a little cleaning in some of the rooms on the main floor, first.

But only *some* of the rooms. She didn't have to clean *all* of them, or clean them all that well.

The thought didn't bring any comfort.

She'd planned to search those rooms anyway if her hunt through the attic yielded nothing. Cleaning and dusting and polishing were as good a cover for searching as she could think of, and Ruth had handed it to her, just like that. Truth was, she didn't really have a choice.

Ruth owned Grand House now. She didn't dare provoke Ruth, Kate reminded herself, reluctantly dragging an oversized bottle of lemon oil down from a cupboard shelf. She couldn't risk being shut out of Grand House before she'd found the diamonds.

All good, sensible reasons for doing what Ruth had asked. Yet as she rummaged through the bins and cupboards on the porch gathering dust cloths, dust mop, and a bucket to put the cloths in, Kate's stomach twisted into tighter and tighter knots. Her fingers trembled as she fastened one of cook's huge old aprons around herself.

She *really* didn't have to clean *all* the rooms. If she had to, she'd clean the grand parlor and the dining room, which took up the entire east half of the first floor, even though she doubted her grandmother would have hidden the diamonds in either of those places. She'd clean the butler's pantry and her great-grandfather's study on the opposite side of the central hallway. She'd clean the second-best parlor at the front of the house that Ruth had converted to a bed and sitting room for her and Gar. But that was it. That was more than enough. Even Ruth wouldn't demand she clean every little inch. She'd give up the search before she'd turn into the woman's servant, paid or not.

It was easy to be brave and determined when she was shivering on the porch, yet as she passed the butler's pantry, she couldn't help edging to the far side of the hallway. It wasn't far enough.

Out of the corner of her eye she could see the open door of the small parlor sandwiched between the pantry and her great-grandfather's study. She could see the massive, velvet-covered chair that Gertrude had always sat in, and the stool she'd always been relegated to. She saw the dark wallpaper and the dark furniture and the heavy brass chandelier that her great-grandfather Mannheim, so Gertrude had told her more times than she could remember, had brought all the way from Vienna.

Just the sight of it was enough to make her heart pound faster.

She forced herself to walk past. One step. Two.

Three feet beyond the door, she could go no farther. Head bent, shoulders hunched, she held onto the bucket and dust mop as if they were a lifeline from another world, fighting against memory. The back of her neck twitched as if a hundred spiders skittered across her skin.

It was just a room. A small, dark, over-furnished room, nothing more.

It was the room of her nightmares and had been ever since she was nine.

Helpless, her breathing quick and shallow, Kate turned back to the open door.

Nothing had been removed from the room. Nothing had changed. Enough light swam through the drawn shades to show every chair in its accustomed place, every table still cluttered with the useless, expensive things Gertrude had loved. The carpet on the floor was still covered with blood-red roses, and the paintings on the wall were still cloying and dark and filled with the dying children and suffering, repentant women that had been so much in vogue a half century earlier. The high ceiling here seemed lower, though, dangerously lower, dragged down by the weight of her great-grandfather's chandelier.

The room had originally been intended for the use of the ladies of the house, a quiet, intimate place that was all their own. Before Sara's death it was hardly ever used, since Gertrude preferred the grand parlor at the front of the house. She'd believed that anything less was unworthy of a Mannheim.

Only after Sara died had Gertrude transferred her allegiance to the smaller ladies' parlor. She'd made it a point to sit there whenever she wanted Kate to read aloud from some long, gloomy tract on the wages of sin or the punishment meted out to undutiful children. There had been a lot of long, gloomy tracts over the years, and even more hours spent listening to endless lectures on the way her mother had died and never-ending reminders that she was her mother's daughter, and a bastard.

Kate still had nightmares in which she was trapped in that narrow, over-furnished room. In the dreams, the door was always locked, the windows shuttered and barred as if the room were a prison cell and not a simple parlor. From every corner she heard voices—sharp, malicious voices murmuring of sin and damnation and the retribution to be heaped on the heads of the sinners. She cried out for someone, *anyone* to let her out, but no one ever came. The louder she called, the more frantically she pounded on the door, the smaller the room became until it was so small it squeezed out all the air and crushed her.

She always woke from those black dreams sweating and gasping for breath. The only way she could get to sleep afterward was to turn on all the lamps in her little apartment to drive away the shadows. The lamps, but never the overhead lights. Never, ever those.

Trembling and afraid to risk Ruth seeing her in this state, Kate ducked into her great-grandfather's study.

Fool! Fool, fool, *fool!* In all the hours she'd spent thinking about Grand House and her return, she hadn't once thought of that small parlor. Had tried *not* to think about it. Which was just more foolishness. Gertrude was dead, and the last thing Ruth would want was to sit there listening to her drone on for hours reading out of some depressing tome. That sort of thing had been Gertrude's way of making her do penance. It wasn't Ruth's.

She drew in an unsteady breath, then another, deeper one, and felt her heart slow to a more normal pace. With no thudding pulse to deafen her, she could hear the house whispering, a tiny creak here, a little moan of shifting timbers there, each sound virtually inaudible unless you were listening for it.

As though roused by the whispers, the high, paneled walls of the study began to contract, sighing and pressing in from every side just as the walls of the ladies' parlor squeezed her in her dreams.

She backed up a step, and then another, and another, until she backed right into the paneled wall behind her. The bucket thumped against the wood, rousing a dull echo like the tolling of a bell.

The paintings on the walls—grim hunting scenes of death and violence—peered down at her, the dead, glassy eyes of the slaughtered deer and fox and pheasants suddenly alive and wickedly knowing. The very air seemed to drain away, taking the light with it.

Kate spun, trying to get away. The door had swung shut behind her.

Dust mop and bucket fell from her nerveless hands, clattering on the floor.

The clangor jarred her back to her senses. She gasped and slumped forward against the paneling, trembling. The polished wood was cold against her brow, smooth and comfortingly normal.

Stupid! She pounded the dark wood with her fist. Stupid! Stupid! *Stupid*! The door had swung shut because it wasn't hung quite straight. It had always done that, and always when you least expected it. The dead animals in the paintings weren't real, and there were no dark spirits here to harm her because they didn't exist.

She spun back to face the room and found a dead fox staring out of a painting. Defiant, heart pounding, she glared back until the fox was once more mere daubs of paint on canvas. With that, the room regained its normal size. The air came rushing back with an almost audible *pop*.

Reassured, and slightly dizzy, she retrieved the dust mop and bucket, and quietly slipped back into the hall. She moved quickly, but with care. The only sounds she could hear were her own footsteps, muffled by the Bokhara runner in the hall and the muted sounds of the house itself.

When she reached the open door of the second-best parlor, Kate hesitated, then decided not to tiptoe past. If Ruth caught her, she'd accuse her of being up to something unpleasant. But she couldn't quite bring herself to walk right past, either.

In the end, she shifted the dust mop to her other hand, then walked up to the open doorway, hand raised to knock. One glance and she let her hand drop. Ruth, her back to the hall, was standing at one of the west-facing windows, silently staring out at nothing, oblivious to the house and everything in it.

Curious, Kate studied the room. Despite its generous dimensions, it was too small for all the furniture crowded in it. Rather than pick and choose from what was there, Ruth had simply squeezed everything closer together to make room for the things she'd added.

The cheap iron bedstead that had served as Ruth and Gar's marriage bed for more than thirty years had been set up against the far wall, close to the fancy coal stove that made this, with the kitchen, one of the few rooms in Grand House that were ever really warm during the winter. A second, narrower bed stood just beyond the first. Ruth's bed, she had no doubt, eyeing the worn quilt and the age-yellowed sheets drawn taut over the mattress. It was the neat, sterile bed of a caretaker and nurse, not a wife.

Gar was there, almost lost amid the jumble. Head drooped on his chest, hands curled loosely in his lap, he was slumped in an old chair set near the stove, snoring gently. The chair had been one of his favorites, Kate remembered, and winced at the sudden pain in her heart.

He didn't belong here anymore than she did. Not even here, in the one room Ruth had chosen for their own. Gertrude was dead and buried, but she stilled ruled in Grand House. Except for the shabby beds and the battered old chair, which had been crammed in wherever they could be made to fit, everything here reflected Gertrude's tastes, Gertrude's choices, Gertrude's life.

Ruth might own Grand House, but she was no more its mistress than the hapless maids she'd fired when she'd taken possession. Like a visitor who wasn't quite sure of her welcome, she'd fitted her life around the edges of whatever Gertrude Mannheim had left behind. It was, Kate thought sadly, an awkward, ugly fit.

Her gaze swung back to the stiff, silent figure at the window.

Ruth Skinner was a big woman—tall, broad shouldered, and raw boned—yet the room made her look small and worn and insignificant.

What must it be like to be her? Kate wondered. Still mentally and physically strong, yet trapped in this sitting room day after day with the wreck of a man she'd loved, perhaps still loved. To have everything . . . and absolutely nothing that mattered.

147

Kate shuddered. She'd never liked the woman, yet she couldn't help pitying her. It must be bitter as gall to spend your life dreaming of what you could not have, then suddenly have it all only to watch it crumble into dust in your hands, to know that you were still, somehow, on the outside looking in.

Instead of giving her the power and respect she'd always craved, Grand House had become a prison from which Ruth would never escape.

None of your business, Kate chided herself, silently moving away before Ruth could turn and see her.

Yet as she set down the bucket inside the door of the grand parlor, she couldn't help thinking of Ruth and the way she'd stood at that window, staring out. With the gardens dead, the fields long since abandoned, there wouldn't be anything much to see. Beyond that window the land ran away flat and straight to where the sun set, spilling over the edge of the horizon without so much as a tree or house to stop it.

Slowly, scarcely noticing what she was doing, Kate plucked a cloth out of the bucket and started dusting.

Years ago she'd dreamed of following that departing sun. She and Elliott had talked of it sometimes, spinning fanciful tales of what they'd find out there and all the things they'd do. One time they'd talk of Denver, another of Arizona or

Nevada. Sometimes they talked of going all the way to California.

She'd teased him about becoming a movie star. He'd talked of buying land of his own, or of starting a business. He'd be rich, he'd told her once, eyes shining at the thought. He'd build a fine, big house of his own and fill it with beautiful things, better than anything in Grand House.

He would have gone on, spinning his dream bigger and bigger and bigger, but she'd stopped him by clamping her hand over his mouth with a panic-fueled fury that had startled them both.

"Don't talk about a house like that," she'd said. "Don't *ever* talk about a house like that. You talk like that, you even *think* like that, and one day the house will own you instead of the other way around."

He'd never mentioned it again.

In the end, when she'd finally left, she'd fled toward the rising sun, and she'd gone alone.

Ruth checked on her twice. She didn't say anything either time, just stood in the door of the big parlor eyeing the room and Kate and the work that she'd done.

Caught between resentment and remembered pity, Kate kept her tongue between her teeth and kept dusting. There was a lot to dust.

Unfortunately, there was nothing to find. She hadn't expected there would be, yet she couldn't repress a sigh of disappointment when she'd flipped the last edge of the last rug back into place and tossed the last cleaning rag back in the bucket with the rest.

At least there had been no half-waking dreams to plague her this time, no phantoms quarreling before the big, marble-fronted fireplace. She hadn't expected there would be. The parlor was just a parlor. It wasn't a place where the past seeped from the walls to catch her unaware.

She wasn't sure that was better, though, because the tedious, physical work had left her with far too much time for thinking—and all her thoughts centered on El. Memory teased her by dragging him from shadowy corners, or turning the faintest hint of draft into his breath on her neck and cheek, or making her remember the feel of his hand on her arm when she brushed against something. Even concentrating on the bookstore she dreamed of owning wasn't enough to dislodge the scent and feel and taste of him from her mind.

Despite her aching head and back, Kate decided to dust the entry, as well, and have done with it. The shallow room was really little more than a baffle to keep the North Dakota winds from racing through the central hall and chilling the house. The only furnishings were a carved wooden hat stand and a shallow marble-topped table shoved against the wall beneath the mirror she'd seen through the front door when she arrived.

It was the mirror that caught her unaware. She glanced up and found herself staring at a stranger. In the age-dulled glass she looked old, worn, her features dragged down by weariness and defeat.

Slowly, Kate laid down her dust cloth. It was just the mirror, she told herself. This unhappy creature wasn't her. Surely it wasn't *her*.

Her hand trembled as she stretched to touch the dust-filmed surface. The other woman raised her hand to meet her. Fingertips touched, but Kate felt only cold, hard glass.

It was the mirror that was at fault. She wasn't this old, this worn, this unhappy. She *wasn't*.

With an unsteady finger she traced the line of the reflection's cheek and mouth. No smile came in response.

Her skin pricked with a sudden chill, making her shiver. To heck with the dusting. She'd done enough for the day.

She let her hand drop and turned away. It was cold in here, and she was tired and under stress, that was all. She *couldn't* be that sad creature in the mirror.

Yet as she bent to retrieve the cleaning rag she'd dropped, she caught a startling image out of the corner of her eye. Heart pounding, she spun back to face the mirror.

The same unhappy, wide-eyed woman she'd seen a moment before stared silently back. There was no one and nothing else. Even the big door behind her seemed dim and distant, lost in the depths of the old mirror.

There was no one but her in the chilly entry.

Yet for an instant, for the space of time between one heartbeat and the next, she could have sworn she'd seen her mother's face reflected in that mirror, too.

Chapter Eight

To Kate's dismay, one day followed another until a week had passed, then two, without her finding any diamonds.

She hadn't found much that had belonged to her mother, either—a locket with her own baby picture, the photograph curling at the edges and turning brown with age; a few clothes, all too old and out of fashion to be of use to anyone; a worn copy of *A Child's First Book of Verse* with "This book belongs to Sara Mannheim" and the date, August 1891, written in a looping, childish scrawl on the inside cover. Her mother would have been ten when she'd written that. The thought had brought tears to Kate's eyes as she'd traced the fading ink. She'd put the book with the locket at the bottom of her suitcase and hadn't looked at them since.

The most important find was a clipping from a New York newspaper dated March 12, 1901. The photo showed a tall, stern-looking man dressed in formal evening clothes with a young and pretty woman at his side. The man was her great-grandfather. The woman was her mother.

Sara had been dressed in an elegant, off-the-shoulder party gown, and she'd been wearing the diamond necklace. The caption read, "Mr. Charles Gordon Mannheim and his granddaughter, Sara Mannheim, at a ball recently held at the Rockefeller mansion. Miss Mannheim wears a stunning diamond necklace that was a gift to her from her grandfather on the occasion of her sixteenth birthday."

There wasn't anything else, but it was enough to prove the necklace had existed. If she found it—no, *when* she found it! Kate reminded herself—the clipping would be hard proof that the diamonds were hers, not Ruth's, no matter what Gertrude might have said.

She found nothing else, but she refused to admit that there wasn't anything else to find, that Gertrude, out of anger and spite, would have burned or given away everything else. Kate hadn't realized how much she'd counted on finding *something*. But so far, there was nothing, no journals, no letters. Nothing that would have helped her understand her mother and what had happened, all those years ago.

There were still a few trunks left in the attic she hadn't investigated, Kate reminded herself, giving the worn linoleum of the kitchen floor a vicious scrape with her scrub brush. She still had five of the eight bedrooms on the second floor to explore. And if all else failed, there was the basement.

She'd hoped she wouldn't have to search the basement. Just the thought of that cold, damp, virtually windowless hole made her flinch.

At least she wouldn't have to clean it. Even Ruth wouldn't expect that. She'd insisted on her cleaning everything else.

It had taken two weeks of hard work, but Kate had dusted, swept, polished, and scrubbed her way through every room on the main floor of Grand House. She hadn't intended to do half that much, but Ruth had been adamant: If she wanted to stay in Grand House and look for her mother's possessions, Ruth had said, she would have to earn her keep, and earning her keep had meant cleaning. Everything.

Ruth, bristling with distrust, watched her constantly. The older woman had taken to popping up at odd moments, checking to see what she was doing, prowling through a room after she had finished as if she were counting every porcelain figurine and fading silken pillow.

Kate had tried to ignore the woman, but as she'd worked her way from room to room, she'd gone from resigned to resentful to angry. Dusting was one thing, washing windows and scrubbing the floors on her hands and knees quite another. In two short weeks she had become exactly what El had said she would—Ruth's unpaid servant.

Just thinking of it made her straighten, then toss the brush back in the bucket. Dirty water slopped over the rim and onto the freshly scrubbed floor.

To hell with it, Kate thought sourly, and got stiffly to her feet, swearing softly. Curses, she was finding, were a far more accurate expression of her feelings than any ladylike "darn" could ever be.

She wiped her hands—chapped, now, from all the work—on her apron, then dug her fingers into the muscles at the base of her spine and arched backward. The kitchen was big, but it seemed three times bigger when you went over it inch by inch on your hands and knees.

One good thing had come of this enforced servitude: She'd found a useful way to work out her growing anger. At Ruth's nagging insistence, the second time she'd tackled the grand parlor Kate had carried the smaller rugs outside to beat them. Now, she almost looked forward to having more rugs to beat or draperies to shake. Physical violence, she was finding, could be dangerously appealing. Almost . . . addictive. It made her feel stronger, tougher than she really was.

At times like this, when her head throbbed and her back hurt and her knees ached, she felt as if she could defy the Devil himself.

Still grumbling, she moved the bucket, then used the folded scrap of towel she'd knelt on to mop up the slopped water.

At least the work let her search for the diamonds unmolested. By the time she'd finished cleaning the main floor, she had poked into every nook and cranny, searched every cabinet and drawer and shelf, handled every box and jar and plate right down to the last sherbet spoon and pickle fork. If the diamonds had been in any of those rooms, she would have found them.

All she'd found was dust.

She'd even gone through the ladies' parlor, but only after she'd opened every curtain and lit every single lamp except the chandelier. Her spine had tingled and her stomach churned the whole time she was there, but she'd forced herself to be as thorough and careful as she'd been in every other room.

The room had yielded nothing. The minute she was sure there was nowhere left to search and absolutely nothing to be found, Kate had drawn the drapes, snuffed the lamps, and firmly shut the door behind her. She'd made sure it stayed shut ever since.

With the downstairs finished, she'd reluctantly started on the second floor. The second time around she searched Gertrude's room from ceiling to floor and every inch in between. Nothing, not even a repeat of the troubling dream she'd had the first time she'd explored.

None of the other bedrooms offered much hope. They'd hardly ever been used, and it wasn't very likely that Gertrude would have hidden anything in them, anyway. Her grandmother had liked to keep her treasures close to her, which was the only hope Kate had that Gertrude hadn't locked the diamonds away in some bank vault, out of reach forever.

Regardless of her chances, Kate was determined to search every one of the over-furnished bedrooms. Every single one of them. And after them, the servants' rooms on the upper floor, though she had even less hope of finding anything there than she did of her chances on the floor below.

The thought of searching El's room made her sweat. She tried not to think of it too often. Tried not to think of him.

Might as well try not to breathe.

For two weeks, Elliott had kept his distance. Work, he'd said, though Kate wasn't sure how much work one cow and a few pigs and chickens could possibly be. He'd finished chopping up the old elm. The wood was stacked in a bin at the back of the porch where it would be easy to get to no matter what the weather. Out in the yard, there was nothing left except a stump and a lot of scattered wood chips. Without the tree's protective bulk, Grand House seemed smaller somehow, more vulnerable.

Until the steady *thwack thwack thwack* of his ax was gone, she hadn't realized how edgy the sound of it had made her. Without that sound at the borders of her awareness, it was easier to forget how hard and cold his eyes had been that first day, and how his hand had felt when it had closed around her throat.

Easier to tell herself she wasn't still afraid.

Her fingers trembled, just a little, as she fished the scrub brush out of the bucket and wrapped it in the bit of old towel so it wouldn't drip on the floor. She could feel her heart pounding as she carried the bucket and brush out to the back porch.

Ruth's insinuations about the woman at the Depot Cafe troubled her. El had gone into town twice since then, taking milk and eggs, returning with mail, meat to set in the ice house to freeze— never a problem at this time of the year—and groceries to add to the stock in the pantry. He never spoke of what he'd done or whom he'd seen, and never again offered to take her with him.

That last violent kiss he'd claimed still burned along her nerve endings. She dreamed of it, but wasn't sure if the dreams were more fantasy or nightmare. She wasn't sure she wanted to find out.

And maybe that was the third thing about all this work for which she should be grateful—the more hours she spent at this drudgery, the easier it was to stop thinking, stop remembering.

The scrub brush went on a sagging wood shelf. The old towel—dirty now where she'd mopped up the water—she hung over a rope strung across the porch. The other cleaning rags she'd hung there earlier were already frozen so stiff they crackled when she touched them.

She didn't need Elliott in her life. What they'd once shared was over, part of the past she was determined to put behind her.

Except she couldn't forget. Sometimes she lay awake for hours, staring into the dark, trying not to remember how his mouth had felt on hers, trying not to remember the heat of him and the way he'd held her against him. As if he'd *had* to hold on. As if he'd needed her as much as she, in that moment, had needed him.

She tried not to think of that, either.

She needed to try harder, Kate grimly reminded herself, emptying the bucket out the back door. The dirty water arced away in a smooth brown curve and hit the frozen ground with a splash. The puddle it made would be frozen quickly enough.

She eyed the steely sky and shivered, yet

Thrill to the most sensual, adventure-filled Romances on the market today...

FROM  LOVE SPELL BOOK

As a home subscriber to the Love Spell Romance Book Club, you'll enjoy the best in today's BRAND-NEW Time Travel, Futuristic, Legendary Lovers, Perfect Heroes and other genre romance fiction. For five years, Love Spell has brought you the award-winning, high-quality authors you know and love to read. Each Love Spell romance will sweep you away to a world of high adventure...and intimate romance. Discover for yourself all the passion and excitement millions of readers thrill to each and every month.

Save $5.00 Each Time You Buy!

Every other month, the Love Spell Romance Book Club brings you four brand-new titles from Love Spell Books. EACH PACKAGE WILL SAVE YOU AT LEAST $5.00 FROM THE BOOK-STORE PRICE! And you'll never miss a new title with our convenient home delivery service.

Here's how we do it: Each package will carry a FREE 10-DAY EXAMINATION privilege. At the end of that time, if you decide to keep your books, simply pay the low invoice price of $17.96, no shipping or handling charges added. HOME DELIVERY IS ALWAYS FREE. With today's top romance novels selling for $5.99 and higher, our price SAVES YOU AT LEAST $5.00 with each shipment.

AND YOUR FIRST TWO-BOOK SHIP-MENT IS TOTALLY FREE!

IT'S A BARGAIN YOU CAN'T BEAT! A SUPER $11.48 Value!

Love Spell  A Division of Dorchester Publishing Co., Inc.

Get Two Books Totally
F R E E —
An $11.48 Value!

▼ Tear Here and Mail Your FREE Book Card Today! ▼

PLEASE RUSH
MY TWO FREE
BOOKS TO ME
RIGHT AWAY!

Love Spell Romance Book Club
P.O. Box 6613
Edison, NJ 08818-6613

couldn't bring herself to go back in the house. Not quite yet.

El was out here someplace. Working, he'd said.

Keeping as far away from Ruth and Gar as possible, Kate thought. *And far away from me.*

It wasn't the best of days to be outside. The old bunkhouse was gone, burned down in a cooking fire after a laborer fell asleep while fixing his evening meal, or so Ruth had said when she'd asked. The unheated barn and outbuildings provided shelter from the wind, but not much else in the way of comfort.

They'd had snow twice these past two weeks, flurries that blew in on the edge of an icy wind out of Canada, then left as quickly as they'd come. The snow those flurries had left never lasted more than a day or two, but the storm hovering on the horizon now promised a more serious threat.

Still shivering, Kate retreated to the kitchen. She'd forgotten how much she hated winters on the open prairie.

Winters in New York could be miserable, but the wind didn't get on her nerves the way it did here. There, a storm swept in and buried the city, then moved out. Here, the wind could howl for days on end, rising to a roar, then backing off, fooling you with a lull right before it came raging back, driving a killing snowstorm before it.

Once, when she was ten or so, they'd been

snowed in for more than a week. The men had strung ropes between the house, the bunkhouse, and the barns and chicken coops and pens so they could find their way out to the animals and back. Even those lifelines weren't always enough.

A neighboring farmer had become disoriented when his rope guidelines were buried in the snowdrift that formed while he was tending his animals. He'd tried to find his way back to the house, and couldn't—in the heart of a storm like that, a man couldn't see his hand in front of his face, couldn't hear anything but the wind roaring in his ears.

The farmer had frozen to death less than twenty feet from his kitchen door, then been buried in the drift that formed over him. They hadn't found his body for almost a week. His wife, trapped in the house with three small children to care for, hadn't dared go out to look for him.

Kate shoved aside the awful memory and tried to concentrate on the work still to be done. She was adding another piece of wood to the stove when Elliott, shoulders hunched against the cold, swept in on a blast of frigid air.

"Cold enough to freeze the tits off a boar," he grumbled, stamping his feet to get the circulation going. "We'll have snow by tomorrow."

He unwound the muffler looped around his neck and hung it up with his coat and hat, then crossed to the stove. As he stretched his hands to the heat, he sighed with satisfaction.

"Day like this, a man learns to appreciate a good fire."

"Coffee?" Kate didn't wait for an answer, just filled a mug and dumped in sugar.

She watched, fascinated, as his big hands curled around the heavy mug, watched as he drank and the muscles of his throat worked as he swallowed. It was such a simple act, giving a man a cup of coffee, yet there was a comfortable, domestic intimacy in it that roused a yearning in her that was almost painful.

"Ah. That's good," he said, lowering the mug at last. "Better than that godawful stuff Ruth brews, and a hell of a lot better than mine."

The praise made her relax a little. This was the first friendly exchange they'd had since he'd kissed her, two weeks before. She tugged on her apron to straighten it and wished she'd tidied her hair.

"The secret is to make just enough, then make more when you want it. The best coffee in the world would taste like sludge if it sat on the stove half the day."

At least the apron hid her dress, a drab but sturdy wool one that she'd pulled out of the closet the day after Ruth had first set her to cleaning. After a few days' use, it had finally stopped reeking of mothballs. No sense ruining her two good dresses when there were so many others she'd had to leave behind ten years ago.

His eyes met hers across the massive stove. "Guess I should say I've enjoyed your cooking, too."

The sudden warmth in her cheeks was from the stove, Kate assured herself. The wood she'd added was finally starting to burn.

"Anything would taste better than Ruth's cooking."

"There's that," he said, and grinned.

Kate couldn't help smiling back.

She'd almost forgotten how. The warmth of it spread through her like heat from the fire, thawing the cold spots.

"I'm making stew for supper. Stew and cornbread."

His smile faded. "I won't be here for supper."

"You're going into town? Again? And on a day like this?"

He nodded, then his gaze dropped, shutting her out again. "Got some milk and eggs for old man Proctor."

"How much milk can you possibly get from one cow? And at this time of the year, too!" The words came out sharper than she'd intended. That instant of shared understanding made his sudden withdrawal seem all that much harsher.

"I promised him. And Ruth likes the extra income."

And there's that hussy down at the Depot Cafe, Kate thought, and felt the stab of pain. Every week he'd gone into town, and every week she'd tried not to remember Ruth's accusation, and failed.

"It's a long way into town just to sell a few gallons of milk and a couple dozen eggs," she said instead. "Why don't you just feed whatever we don't need to the pigs? That's got to be more profitable than paying for the gas in to town and back. Especially with what Mr. Proctor's paying you. The only person in this county that's stingier is Ruth."

El's mouth thinned. He refilled his cup then slowly, deliberately, added sugar and stirred. The *clink clink clink* as the spoon struck the sides of the mug sounded uncomfortably loud.

"There are . . . other things I have to do," he said at last, reluctantly. He struck the spoon against the rim so sharply, the mug rang like a muted, angry bell. "Things that can't wait."

Things that are none of your business. He didn't have to say it.

Kate rubbed her hands up and down her arms, hugging herself against the ice in his voice. If that shared smile had warmed her like fire, his distance now chilled her as much as the winter wind outside. She glanced out the window at the dull gray sky.

"What if that storm comes in before you get back? What will you do then?"

He shrugged, still refusing to look at her. "There are lots of folk along the way who'll take in a stranded traveler."

"But will they take in *you?*" she asked, wanting to hurt.

That brought his head back up. He met her angry gaze with a piercing one of his own.

"Some will," he said after a moment. "Not all, but some."

"Guess you'd better hope those are the ones you're closest to if you end up walking."

He took another drink of coffee rather than respond to her.

Tell me. The words all but screamed inside her head. *Tell me about that woman at the cafe. Tell me what you're looking for, where you've been and where you're going. Tell me the truth you refused to tell me ten years ago when I begged you.*

She didn't say a word. The distance between them had never seemed greater than it did right now, and she hadn't the slightest idea how to bridge the gap. She wasn't even sure it was safe to try, yet the need to understand this man she'd once loved, to understand what had happened, and who he had become, and why, was like a hunger deep inside her, gnawing at her heart.

"I'll stoke the furnace before I leave, take care of the animals," he said. "If I don't get back—and

I sure as hell expect to—Ruth can help you with them, show you what to do."

Kate nodded. She couldn't speak. All the things she wanted to say were jammed so tight and hard in her throat that she couldn't get them out.

His gaze slid down her body, slowly, assessingly. Making her blush.

His mouth curled in distaste. "At least you won't have to worry about ruining your clothes."

The blush burned away in a rush of fury. "Just what do you mean by that?"

He slammed his cup down on the table. "Dammit, Kate. Two weeks in this place and look at you! Your hair's a mess. You've dirt on your face, and you're dressed like a . . . like a damned Okie living on others' castoffs. And that apron!"

With another curse, he threw up his hands and stalked away. Halfway to the back door he stopped, then turned around and stalked back. This time he came around to her side of the stove.

"Didn't I tell you it was a mistake to stay?" He was almost shouting now. Like a boxer gauging the reach to his opponent, he leaned toward her. "Didn't I warn you about what would happen if you did?"

Kate clutched her arms tighter around herself, but held her ground. She wouldn't let him scare her off. She wouldn't let herself long for the impossible, no matter how often her thoughts turned that way.

"I told Ruth I'd pull my weight, and that's just what I'm doing."

"You're turning into her drudge, *that's* what you're doing. Look at you! Look at your hands!"

Before she could stop him, he'd pried her fingers loose and claimed her hands. She tried to wrench free and couldn't.

"See? Cracked and rough as sandpaper. And look, some of the cracks are starting to bleed. Here. And here and here." His thumbs brushed over the small wounds, making her wince.

"I found a can of Bag Balm," she protested. "I've been using that."

"Well, use some more." His thumbs skimmed across the center of her palms. Her nerve endings danced, though not with pain.

There was nothing in his face or rough touch to show that he knew what he was doing to her. What he could do to her without even trying.

With a snarl, he let her go. "If it were up to Ruth, you'd wear your hands to the bone. And you wouldn't say a word about it, would you?"

The last he almost spat in her face. Kate couldn't stop herself from tucking her chin in and leaning away, but her feet were glued to the floor. She didn't back up an inch.

"Of course you wouldn't!" He paced away, stomped back. "And you know why you wouldn't?" he demanded. "Because you're crazy enough to think you can find what you came looking for. But let me tell you something, you can't. You hear me? You *can't*. Just ask me. I *know!*"

There was madness in his eyes, mixed with the fury. The fury came from deep within him, driven by more than just his anger at her and her present state, and that frightened her more than all the rest put together.

This time she did step back. One step, two, then she whirled to put half the kitchen between them.

Her fingers closed around the edge of the sink as she stared out the window at the approaching storm. Her chest heaved, her lungs laboring to drag in air.

A butcher's knife lay on the drain board where she'd left it, intending to sharpen it when she'd finished with everything else. She could *feel* it even as she forced her gaze to fix on what was passing outside the walls of Grand House.

Her very awareness horrified her.

"Hell!"

The exclamation sounded as if it had been wrenched from him. She didn't turn to look.

He came across the kitchen to her, his every step deliberate, cat-light and dangerous. Still she refused to face him.

His hands closed over her shoulders. "Kate,

I . . . I'm sorry. I didn't mean to hurt you."

This time his words were as gentle as his touch, but she was afraid to trust that gentleness. Since she'd come back, every time El softened to her, she somehow ended up regretting it.

"It's just . . . I don't like leaving you here like this. Alone, with no way out, no one to help you if something were to happen."

That brought her around, bristling in anger.

"Who's going to hurt me? Gar?" she mocked.

A shadow darkened El's eyes. She could have sworn he flinched.

"Maybe," he said. "Even if he didn't mean to, Gar could hurt you."

"He wouldn't!"

"He *might*," El said, fiercely. "And that's more than enough to scare me." Again he leaned closer, so close she could feel his breath on her face. "It ought to be enough to scare *you*."

"Don't be a fool!"

He jerked back as if she'd struck him. His gaze skimmed down her face to her lips, her chin, her throat, then back up. His jaw hardened.

"God forgive me," he grated as he let his hands fall away from her shoulders. "I already am."

When he turned away, he left her shaken, her legs barely able to support her.

Keeping his back to her, he snatched up his forgotten mug of coffee and drank in great gulps. The *thunk* as he set it down again made her jump. He took a deep breath, let it out, then took another, even deeper. His hands worked, opening and closing as if he were trying to ease the tension in them.

Still without turning, he asked, "Do you know how to stoke the furnace?"

Kate blinked. "No."

He flashed an inscrutable look over his shoulder. "Then you'd better learn."

He was across the kitchen and had the pantry door open before he realized she hadn't moved. "Well? Are you coming?"

"But . . . why?"

"If I can't get back tonight, you might need to know."

"But surely Ruth—"

"To hell with Ruth," he snarled. "I'm showing *you* how. *Now*."

The arrogance of the order roused her own anger. "All right."

By the time she reached him, he had pulled up the heavy trap door set in the pantry floor. A metal latch set in the opposite wall held it open. A chain slipped over a hook for extra security.

Kate eyed the gaping black hole at her feet, then the massive wood door propped against the wall. Her stomach squeezed. The steps turned at a right angle about four feet down, then disappeared into the darkness below. The chill, dank air carried the scent of rotting wood and mice and other things she didn't care to identify.

There wasn't much down there, she knew—the furnace; the coal bin, which was filled from a chute at the side of the house; dozens of shelves laced with spider webs where the cook had once kept jars of homemade relish and canned fruits; and a warren of windowless rooms and useless cubbyholes where the household's castoffs had been tossed. The place had given her nightmares when she was a child. The thought of being trapped in that musty, rotting darkness made chills run down her spine even now.

"You'd better leave the trap door open," she said. "I'm not sure I could open it by myself if I had to."

El looked up from lighting a candle in the tin lantern that was always kept handy. "What about the things stored in the pantry?"

"I can get around the edge here if I'm careful." She tried not to think of what would happen if she wasn't. "I'll lock the pantry door so Uncle Gar can't get down there if he goes wandering."

One dark eyebrow arched, but all El said was, "Follow me. And watch your step."

Chapter Nine

The stairs were claustrophobicly narrow and steep, and the wavering light from the lantern made the shadows treacherous. There was no handrail.

As she followed El down, Kate waged a war between her good sense, which said she ought to keep her hand on the wall for safety, and her horror of touching the chilly wall of stone and crumbling mortar. It wasn't damp, but there was something about the slick, uneven stones and grainy mortar that made her think of ancient mold and dreadful things, lurking in the dark.

She couldn't stop an almost explosive sigh of relief when they reached the bottom and she stepped onto the hard-packed earthen floor.

"You go down those stairs like you know every

one of them," she said, taking refuge in sniping at El.

He shrugged. The lantern light multiplied the gesture, making it seem larger and more threatening when it was a shadow on the wall. "I go up and down them twice a day, morning and night. You get used to it after a while."

Kate shuddered and glanced back up the stairs. The light from the kitchen seemed impossibly golden and far away. "That's something I *never* want to get used to."

"If you'd take my advice and go back to New York, you wouldn't have to."

Each word scraped across her skin like sandpaper.

She forced herself to turn away from that beckoning light and focus, instead, on the darkness that lay ahead.

"Why don't you just show me how to feed the furnace," she snapped. "The sooner we can finish here, the happier I'll be."

Again he shrugged, but this time what she saw was the man himself, not the shadow. He didn't look any smaller or less intimidating than the monstrous shape that slid along the wall behind him.

"Whatever you say." He gestured toward the end of the black tunnel that stretched before them. "It's this way. And watch your head. There are some big spider webs down here and a couple of low beams."

She couldn't help it. Kate walked the rest of the way with her shoulders hunched and her head tilted to keep a wary eye on the shadows in the floor joists overhead.

The tunnel was, in fact, a narrow hallway cut with doorways here and there on either side. There were no doors in the openings, but the lantern light wasn't strong enough to do more than hint at what lay beyond. Down here, the smell of damp and rot was thick, filling her nostrils like a heavy fog.

The stone walls on either side, designed as supports for the weight of the three massive stories of the house above, were solid—plastered in places, rough-surfaced in others, cold and damp wherever she touched. She tried not to touch too much, but the uneven surface of the earthen floor made her stumble sometimes and reach for support.

She had to fight the urge to grab the back of Elliott's shirt and hang on for dear life. As it was, she kept so close she stepped on his heels twice.

The third time, he threw a warning look over his shoulder and growled at her. Something about giving him enough room to walk, though she wasn't sure of the exact words. Her heart was pounding so hard it drowned out everything else.

When he abruptly halted, she ran right into

him. His back was broad and strong and warm, solidly comforting. If he hadn't turned around right then, she might have grabbed hold and never let go.

"Sorry," she said, backing off.

"If you'll give me a little room, I'll light a couple more lanterns," he said with exaggerated politeness.

Kate backed up another couple steps. "Fine. Great. That's a good idea."

At the other side of the room, she could see the dim outlines of the furnace, a hulking mass of metal that didn't do all that much to keep Grand House warm despite the tons of coal it consumed each winter. Dusty, soot-blackened air ducts snaked away from it to disappear among the shadows overhead. More pipes connected it to the boiler that sat beside it.

From somewhere deep in its innards she could hear, very faintly, the sound of a banked fire burning. Red-gold light leaked out through a grate to hint at what went on within.

It looked, Kate thought grimly, like a sleeping Medusa that only a fool would rouse.

El seemed to have no qualms. He brought down an oil lantern that dangled from a hook screwed into one of the joists, then handed her the smaller lantern he'd brought with them.

"If you'll just hold this?"

Again the dangerous politeness. Kate didn't

say a word, just held the little lantern high until he'd gotten the second one going and returned it to its hook.

The brighter light made her blink and look away.

"There's another couple lanterns here, and then we'll . . ." El's voice faded into a grunt as he reached for a second lantern hung from a beam a few feet away.

Curious, and a little braver now that she could see, Kate edged over to the nearest gaping doorway and raised her lantern. Even without El's bulk blocking the light, she couldn't see that much.

Propped against the wall closest to her was a jumble of what looked like old doors and ripped, sagging screens. Boxes, some stacked so tipsily that their contents seemed in imminent danger of falling out, filled the far end of the narrow room. Their musty smell would be enough to discourage any but the most foolhardy from investigating their contents. Cheap, broken chairs, wobbly stools, a rusting bedstead, and some indiscernible oddments filled the rest of the space.

From somewhere at the far side she caught the scrabble of clawed feet and a tiny squeak of protest. Kate's nose wrinkled with distaste. Mice. She wasn't afraid of them, but she didn't much like them, either.

If all the other rooms and corners down here

were like this, there was no sense even trying to look for a hidden diamond necklace. It wasn't going to be found unless you burned the whole place down around it.

Relief swept through her at the thought.

She moved to the next opening and once more lifted the little lantern.

Crude board shelves lined the walls here, most of them warped and sagging, all but a few bare of anything except dust and more spider webs. The shelves broke their disorderly march around the room for two things only: the door and the window set in the thick stone wall opposite.

The window was almost useless. The dirt-grimed, web-shrouded glass devoured the light instead of reflecting it back. Even in the brightest daylight it probably wouldn't admit more than a trickle of illumination from outside. From this distance, the catch looked so rusty that you'd have to break it to get the window open. Once opened, about the only thing that would pass through that narrow aperture was fresh air. A child or small woman might crawl out, but a grown man would probably find himself stuck if he tried to do the same.

It wasn't the window that interested her, however, but the room itself. This was one of the few places in Grand House in which she'd ever taken real pleasure.

From the time the first vegetables started coming on in early summer until the first hard frost killed off the last of them, Cook was always busy canning and cooking and preserving, and this was the place where she had stored her treasures. By October, every shelf in this room had groaned under its weight of well-filled jars.

Memory pricked—of herself dutifully carrying down jar after jar stuffed with the bounty from Cook's kitchen. The basement hadn't seemed so grim and frightening back then, and the promise of the savory treats that lay ahead had kept her scurrying to Cook's commands.

There had been sweet corn relish, Kate remembered, and jars and jars of pickles, both dill and sweet. There had been canned tomatoes and carrots, pickled onions, canned pears and peaches, applesauce and apple butter, half a dozen different kinds of jellies, strawberry jam, and raspberry jam, and still more corn relish, not so sweet this time.

A huge wooden barrel had stood in the corner, Kate remembered. Every fall it was filled with apples. By the first of summer there was nothing left but black, wrinkled lumps, but in between there had been apple pie and apple strudel and sweet, crisp apples that snapped when you bit into them.

She lifted the little lantern high. Looking. Remembering.

She'd forgotten there were some good memories connected to Grand House, too.

The light reflected off dull glass in the far corner where spiders had buried the shelves under thick, gauzy shrouds. A few jars remained, their contents unidentifiable after all these years and, in some cases, probably deadly. A couple of other shelves held broken boxes, rusting tools, and strange oddments whose purpose had been forgotten long ago. The rest was dust and ten years of disuse.

Kate sighed and lowered the lantern.

So much for fond memories.

She turned to find El not five feet away, staring at her, his expression set, his eyes unreadable in the semi-dark.

"Whatever you're looking for, Kate," he said softly, "you're not going to find it down here."

"I'm not looking for anything. Just—"

"Your mother's things. I know." Disgust mixed with the scathing irony in his voice. "Don't bother lying."

"I've never lied to you!"

"The truth can carry a lot of lies inside it, Kate," he said softly, like a lover whispering secrets that only two could share.

Her breath caught. She forced it out.

"So can silence, Elliott," she said clearly, so every word would cut like a knife.

He just stared at her for a moment, then abruptly turned away.

She had to force herself not to run after him.

With a muttered curse, he snatched up a pair of worn leather gloves.

"Use the gloves," he said, "even if they are too big. Otherwise, you'll spend an hour afterward trying to scrub coal dust off your hands. It's hell to get out, especially when it gets under your nails."

"El—"

He picked up the short-handled shovel that was leaning against the side of the coal bin.

"Don't try to heap the shovel with coal. You won't be able to lift it. Better to take a little at a time than risk hurting your back or spilling coal where you don't want it."

"Elliott!"

He glanced at her, then looked away.

"Pay attention, Kate," he growled. "The sooner I get on the road, the sooner I'll be back so you won't have to worry about how to keep from freezing to death tonight."

"All right," she sighed, resigned. There wasn't any use in arguing. How did you tell a man about your memories of jars of fruits and vegetables when he refused to say one word to light the darkness that lay between you and him? "Show me how to feed this monster."

"Right." He turned back to the hulking furnace

as if turning to a lover. "Here's the fire door. Make sure you've got the gloves on when you open it. The handle will burn you if you don't. Here's the damper. Turn it like this if you want more air to get to the coals so they'll burn hotter, back like this if you want them to last longer. The ash falls through here. You won't need to worry about cleaning that out, even if I don't make it back tonight."

Step by step he walked her through the process of stoking the furnace, then checking the big boiler that provided hot water to the house. The furnace wasn't all that much different from the coal-burning stove upstairs, yet somehow the whole process seemed a great deal more intimidating.

It's just bigger, that's all. Kate told herself. *I'll get used to it if I have to.*

Yet even as she went through each step under his disapproving supervision, her attention was on him, not the work.

He was standing so *close*.

"Not like that!" he snapped when she added more coals to the flames. "Heap them in the center. Don't let them fall against the sides like that. You'll waste too much, otherwise, because it won't burn properly.

"You're giving it too much air," he said when she closed the damper down. "If you want it to last through the night, you won't let it burn that hot that fast.

"God! Don't open *that* valve!" he shouted. "This is an old boiler. If you get it that hot, you'll blow up the whole damned house!"

By the time she finished, she was ready to throw gloves, shovel, and ten pounds of coal at his head.

"I don't know why it matters." She slammed the shovel against the wall of the bin. "There's never enough heat in my room, no matter how hot you make it, and Ruth and Gar have their own stove. Why do you even bother?"

"Damned if I know." He snatched up the gloves where she'd thrown them on the floor. "And for your information, without what heat you do have, your room would be damn near the same temperature as the weather outside. Would you prefer that?"

She started to snap out a retort, but bit back the words and heaved a sigh, instead. "No, I wouldn't prefer that."

He frowned, unimpressed by her sudden meekness.

"Oh, God, Elliott!" she cried. "Why are we always quarreling? Can't we ever put the past behind us long enough to at least be civil with one another?"

He stared at her, his eyes so deeply sunk in shadows that it was like looking into a well. A deep and dangerous well that had warning signs posted all around.

For a moment, she didn't think he was going to answer her, then: "You can't put the past behind you, Kate. I'm learning that. No matter what you do, it's always there, biting at your heels."

The words had a hollow sound to them, as if they came out of that same dangerously deep well.

He frowned down at the gloves he still held, then abruptly tossed them on the floor by the shovel and bent to adjust something on the boiler. When he stood again, the expression on his face had shifted, grown more distant.

"Sometimes," he said, "I think the only way to get rid of the past is to burn it down around you. You can't just walk away. I've tried that, and it doesn't work." His gaze swung back to her, coolly assessing. "I suspect you tried it, too, with not one damn bit more success than I had."

Kate nodded reluctantly.

"But burning it . . ." He paused, savoring the words, and smiled.

The smile sent a shiver down her spine.

"It would be easy to burn this place down, Kate. Did you ever think of that? How easy it would be?"

She stared at him. "Burn it down? No." She shook her head, trying to shake off the images his words roused in her head. "No, I never thought of it."

His lips curved in a mocking smile. "Really? You *never* thought of it? Not even once?"

Again she shook her head, but the word that slipped out wasn't the one she'd intended. "How?"

"How?" The mocking smile grew fiercer. "You want to know how?"

She stood there, mute, almost dizzy with the thought of it. A world without Grand House. A way to wipe out all visible traces of the past, just like that.

Say no! a voice shouted in her head. *Yes! Yes! Yes!* screamed another, just as loud.

El looked as if he heard the voices just as clearly as she did. His gaze skewered her so she couldn't move. The voices' clamoring made it impossible to speak.

"There are several ways to do it," he said. Lightly, as if he were chatting of the weather in a lady's parlor. He pulled on the gloves again, opened the firebox door, and stared at the fire within.

"One way is to stoke that fire till it's almost choked with coal. Three times as much as you just added. Four times, maybe. Then you open up the dampers all the way so it can suck in all the oxygen it wants."

He turned the handle to lock the furnace door

shut, then adjusted the dampers down even farther, so just enough air got to the coals to keep
them burning. The light that seeped from the
heart of the old furnace cast his face in a molten
gold tinged with devil red.

"Once you've got a really hot fire going, you
keep stoking it. More coal. Lots more. Keep that
fire up hot and high. So high it roars."

A moment ago the fire in the heart of the old
furnace had been no more than a soothing mur-
mur, but Kate would swear the sound of it grew
louder with each word El spoke, so loud she
could hear the deep bass rumble in it, like the
rumble in the throat of a big, hungry tiger eyeing
its next meal.

"Eventually the fire will get so hot that something will overheat. The flue maybe. All that coal
tar stuck to the sides of the flue would catch fire
the instant things turned too hot. If you hadn't
cleaned it for awhile, you'd have a roaring fire in
no time. And from there the fire would spread.
There'd be no stopping it, once it got going."

His eyes closed, as if he were savoring the images his words had aroused. His mouth lifted in
a small, secret, satisfied smile. "So easy."

He drew the vowel sound out, savoring that,
too.

And then his eyes flew open and latched on
her. "Houses burn down every year for just that
reason, Kate. Did you know that?"

Again Kate shook her head.

"It's true. That kind of fire burns so hot there's nothing left but ashes afterward."

El's voice caressed the words, a lover to the object of his adoration.

"And then there's the boiler." He swung to study the boiler, and smiled. "Have you ever seen the damage a big boiler like this can do when it gets so hot that the water turns to steam? No? Well *I* have. The explosion could rip a hole in the side of the furnace, right through that heavy cast iron plate. The fire would come tumbling out, so hot that whatever water's left in the boiler couldn't possibly put it out. And with five tons of coal right there for it to feed on . . ."

His eyes glittered with the reflected light from the firebox.

Kate choked on a sob, and ran.

He was right behind her on the stairs, every step groaning under his pounding weight.

"Kate! Kate! For God's sake, *Kate!*"

She had almost reached the servants' stairs when he grabbed her arm and pulled her back around to face him.

"Don't touch me!" She pounded on his chest, kicked at his booted feet. "Let me go!" Tears branded her face.

"Stop that! Kate!" He shook her, hard. "Stop it! Do you hear me? *Stop it!*"

Kate sucked in air, then forced herself to go

still and stiff. His fingers were digging into her arm like metal clamps. Vaguely, at the back of her mind, she knew she'd have bruises there, and didn't care.

The line between them was so clearly drawn that neither one could miss it.

"I'll only ask this one last time, Kate. Will you go into town with me? Now, so you can leave before the storm comes in?"

His eyes were the flat, angry gray of that same approaching storm, and they made her just as cold.

Her mouth suddenly went dry.

"No," she said.

He swore, then let her go. "Damn fool. You damned, bullheaded fool. I hope you won't regret it."

So do I.

She didn't say a word as she wrenched open the door to the servants' stairs, then let it slam shut behind her.

Her footsteps echoed hollowly in the stairwell as she took each step, feeling her way upward in the dark.

Chapter Ten

Kate was checking on the ham and potatoes she'd made for supper when El brought the old truck around to the kitchen door three quarters of an hour later.

She would have walked away and left the food to burn if it meant she could have avoided him, but Gar was with her, slumped in his old chair by the stove, impatiently picking at the quilt Kate had tucked around his legs. She didn't dare leave him alone. According to an exasperated Ruth, who'd dumped him in Kate's care for a while, he'd been fussing all morning, restless and easily irritated with everything around him.

At the sound of the old Ford's engine, Gar's head came up. "Who's got the truck out on a day like this?"

Before Kate could stop him, he'd thrown the

quilt aside and shakily gotten to his feet. "That El? It's El, isn't it?"

Kate took his arm, steadying him. "That's El, Uncle Gar. He has some work to do, but he'll be back. Don't you want to sit down? See? Right here. Here's your favorite chair."

He irritably brushed her aside. "Been sitting the whole damn day, missy. Oughta get out and help the boy. See what's what. He's too young to be left on his own for long, you know."

With surprising strength, he broke free of her hold on him and shuffled toward the door.

Kate grabbed his sleeve just as he swung the door open. The cold air hit them like a wall of ice.

"Uncle Gar—"

"Get your hands off me!" he snarled, turning on her. "Leave me alone!"

She fell back, startled.

An instant later he was out the door. "El? El! Don't you go fooling around with that truck, boy! What have I told you about machinery like that? Gotta know what you're doing!"

Kate grabbed the nearest hat and coat off the rack on the wall and rushed out after him.

Gar was already halfway to the old Ford truck parked outside the back door, its bed loaded with half a dozen large, battered milk cans. El hadn't noticed them come out—he was hunched over the right front fender, tinkering with something under the folded-back hood while the engine patiently chugged.

"Come on out from under there, boy!" Gar shouted, thumping on the raised hood with his fist. "Didn't you hear me yelling?"

"What the hell?" A scowling El emerged from under the hood. At the sight of Gar, his jaw dropped. "Uncle Gar! What are you doing out here?"

"What do you think? Got work to do! Can't sit around staring at the wallpaper all day now, can I?"

He grabbed the handle for the hood on his side, then snarled when he couldn't budge it. "Damn machine. Oughta've greased those hinges a week ago."

Kate edged up beside him, uncertain how to deal with this sudden, angry energy. "I brought your coat and hat, Uncle Gar. See?"

The old man glared at her, teeth bared.

"Damn fool women. Won't leave a man in peace. If it ain't Ruth nagging about one thing, it's Gertrude nagging about another. Even got the damned maids coming after me! Well, I won't have it! Do you hear me? I won't have it!"

He pounded on the truck's open hood as he shouted, starting a metallic clanging and ringing that echoed off the stones of Grand House.

Kate nervously backed out of reach. This was

a side of Gar's dementia she hadn't seen, and it frightened her.

El seemed unsurprised. While Gar ranted, he set down his tools, turned the engine off, then calmly walked around the truck to the old man's side.

"I couldn't agree with you more, Uncle Gar." He took the coat Kate handed him, then held it out for Gar. "Want your coat?"

"My coat?" Gar frowned at the garment. "That ain't my coat."

"Sure it is. It's the new one Aunt Ruth bought you, remember? I don't even want to think about how much she'll fuss if she hears you left it lying around like that."

"Humpf," said Gar, reluctantly letting El slide the coat over his arms. "Women!"

"You can say that again," said El, buttoning it up.

"Women!" Gar roared, and thumped the hood again.

El laughed. After a moment's startled thought, Gar joined in.

"I'll go get Aunt Ruth," Kate said, almost in a whisper.

El nodded, but didn't take his eyes off Gar.

"Don't forget your hat." He plopped the hat—one of his own and far too big—atop Gar's balding head.

Three minutes later, when Kate followed an

anxious, scolding Ruth out the door, the two men were peering at the Ford's engine as if it were one of the seven modern wonders.

"Gar?" Ruth called, hurrying toward them. "Are you all right?" When Gar, irritated, turned to glare at her, she threw up her hands in disgust. "You old fool! What do you think you're doing out here?"

"Working, what do you think I'm doing?" Gar snapped back.

"Catching your death of cold, that's what."

El got the full force of her temper.

"Why didn't you bring him in? You know he's too sick and weak to be out in the cold like this."

"He didn't want to come," El said mildly, folding his arms across his chest and propping his hip against the truck. "And right now, he's not in the mood to be persuaded about anything he doesn't want to do."

A dangerous glint in his eyes belied the mildness of his tone.

"You should have dragged him in, then! He'll get his death of cold standing around out here like this with nothing to keep him warm but a coat that's too small and a hat that's way too big."

"Don't fuss, woman." Gar gave her a poke in the shoulder that made her stagger. "I'm not coming in. El and me, we're going to town."

Despite the fire in his tone, he was paler than before, and his hands were shaking badly.

There was a hint of pleading when he turned back to El.

"You're going to town with me, aren't you, boy? Be good for you to get out, and I can use the help. You work hard enough"—he leaned closer and lowered his voice to a conspiratorial whisper—"I'll buy you some ice cream over at the drug store. Double dip. What do you say?"

"No one's going anywhere, Gar." Ruth wrapped her hand around his arm and tugged, trying to get him moving toward the house. "You don't need to, either."

"The hell I don't!" Gar wrenched his arm away. He was really agitated now, his anger driving his frail body more than Kate would have thought possible.

"There's that old sow I promised to Mr. Daigler," he said, giving Ruth another poke. "And the eggs." Poke. "Haven't taken the eggs in since I don't know when." Two hard pokes that made her wince.

"Said I'd take him the sow, and that's what I'm going to do." He was turning downright truculent, his jaw set hard as a mule's.

He reached for the handle on the hood again. This time when he couldn't budge it, he gave a little jump in an effort to drag it down by the sheer weight of his body. With a rusty groan of protest, the hood moved downward, throwing him off balance. He staggered, slipped, but refused to let go.

"Damned rusty heap. I'll show you!" he panted. His whole body shook as he gave another heave.

"For Heaven's sake, Gar!" Ruth cried, grabbing hold of him. "Let go of that thing!"

"No!"

"Ruth!" said El, trying to pull her away. "You're just making things worse."

"I'll make you some fresh biscuits," she wheedled. "You'd like that, wouldn't you, Gar? Fresh biscuits with some of that nice strawberry jam El got the last time he was in town?"

"No time for jam." Gar's agitation was turning into a shuffling dance as he tried to drag the hood back down. "Gotta get to work. Got that sow to deliver. Can't spend the morning eating."

"Gar—"

Pushing Ruth aside, El put his arm around the old man's shoulders, steadying him. The contact seemed to reassure the old man, calming him enough so he let go of the hood.

"You're right about that sow, Uncle Gar," El said casually, turning him so he couldn't see the truck. "Want me to help you get her loaded?"

"You bet. You and me, we'll load her, won't we, El?" Gar sagged against the younger man, breathing heavily. The fire in his eyes was dying out, leaving only empty ashes.

"Sure, Uncle Gar. Sure, we'll load her. But, you

know what? I'm sort of hungry. How about we have something to eat first? You wouldn't mind waiting a bit while I have something to eat, would you?"

Gar looked about him, blinking in confusion. "Eat?" he said in a fading voice. "Is it time to eat?"

He could barely drag his feet as El, one arm still wrapped around him for support, slowly led him toward the back steps.

"Better put him to bed first," Ruth said, hurrying ahead to open the door. Her face was a study of anger, resentment, and fear, the three so mixed that she probably didn't know what she was feeling.

Hot tears stung Kate's eyes and the cold bit deep, but she waited until she was sure they would have left the kitchen before she followed them in.

According to Ruth, Gar fell asleep immediately. To Kate's relief, Ruth wanted to keep an eye on him so she took her meal in their room. The older woman's frustrations and fears would burst out sooner or later, but Kate would much prefer to have it later. She couldn't cope with lectures and ranting right now.

El refused to talk and claimed he didn't want anything to eat. He'd stop at the Depot Cafe, he said. Right now, all he wanted was to get on the road.

What he wanted was to get *away*. He didn't say it, but Kate knew that was what he was thinking. She knew, because it was what she wanted, too.

A few more days, she told herself as she sliced the ham she'd fixed for four. A week, maybe, but not an hour more. If she hadn't found the diamonds by then, they weren't going to be found and there wasn't any sense in lingering. She had to get back to New York to tell the Daniels that she wouldn't be able to buy the store after all. And then she'd have to find a job.

Her savings were paying the rent on her small apartment while she was here and not there, working. But her savings wouldn't last for long, and without the diamonds . . .

She wouldn't think about what would happen if she didn't find them. She didn't have to. If she couldn't buy the bookstore, then there wasn't much to look forward to but jobs like the one she held now. Quiet, safe little jobs in a bookstore, if she were lucky, or an office if she weren't. Jobs that brought in just enough money to pay the rent and her expenses, with a little, a very little, left over for an occasional treat and to put aside for emergencies and her old age.

The prospect didn't please her much, but then, when had life ever tried to show her a future that did?

At the thought, Kate gave a particularly vicious slice to the ham. The knife hit the bone and twisted so that both ham and knife slid off the plate onto the counter, spilling the cut slices in the process.

Kate eyed the mess in disgust, then grabbed the ham by the shank bone and slammed it back down on the plate, stacking the cut meat in an untidy heap. While she was woolgathering, she'd sliced almost all of it, which meant she wouldn't have the big hunks of ham she needed for the pot of ham and beans that Ruth had planned for tomorrow. And that meant Ruth would scold and fuss and blame her for everything, including Gar's inexplicable tantrum earlier.

The urge to sink the knife into something other than the ham was tempting.

From outside came the grinding sound of an engine that adamantly refused to start.

She frowned at the mess on the plate in front of her. Grab a bite at the Depot Cafe, would he? Hah!

When she stepped out the kitchen door a few minutes later, securely bundled in her coat and a wool muffler and with two towel-wrapped packages in her hand, the hood on the truck was once more folded up like wings, and El was bent over the exposed auto's guts, swearing.

Unwilling to interrupt him, she quietly walked

around to the front of the truck and leaned in to see what he was doing.

El jerked away and banged his head on the hood. "Damn!"

He backed out, rubbing his head and cursing. "What in hell are you doing, sneaking up on a man like that?"

"I'm sorry. I—I brought you a couple of ham sandwiches." She held out a bundle. "And some coffee in a tin flask," she added, holding out the other. "As late as it is, I thought you might want them."

He looked at her. Then he looked at the bundled sandwiches, frowning.

"I'll just put them in the cab. Here on the seat, where you can get to them easily."

It was safer not to look at him. Safer not to let him get too close a look at her.

She squinted at the sky instead. The gray clouds that had hovered on the horizon since morning were growing, moving closer. They'd be here by nightfall, maybe sooner.

"Do you really think you ought to go, as late as it is?" she asked. "That storm's looking awfully unfriendly."

She could feel his gaze on her. The skin at the back of her neck prickled in response.

"I don't have a choice, Kate." He started to shove past her to climb into the driver's seat, then hesitated, as if he didn't dare get too close.

She pretended an intense interest in the milk cans.

"It's just—I have some commitments, Kate. Things I *have* to do."

"Like see that woman at the Depot Cafe?"

She hadn't intended to say it. For a moment, she thought he was going to deny it. But the moment passed. He cursed, low, under his breath so she couldn't make out the words, and slid behind the wheel.

"That's why you're going, isn't it?" Kate persisted. "Because of *her*."

It was like picking at a wound where a scab was starting to form, but she couldn't help it. The thought of El and some strange woman who worked in a cafe gnawed at her like a hungry rat.

He didn't look at her, just stared straight ahead through the windshield at absolutely nothing.

"Her name's Della," he said at last, forcing the words past gritted teeth. "And she's not the reason I'm going into town."

"You're not going for the milk, either."

His hand slammed down on the wheel. "Dammit, Kate! Just let it go, will you?"

She flinched as if he'd hit her.

He forced his hand to uncurl from around the steering wheel, then deliberately focused on pulling out the choke, just so, a quarter of an inch, then a little more. Satisfied, he mashed his thumb down on the starter and pulled the throttle out. The old truck coughed, spat, then grumbled to life.

Kate blinked back tears. She would cry for Gar and what was lost. She would even cry for Ruth. But she would not cry for this.

Yet she couldn't let it go, either. That newformed scab was almost gone. She could feel the blood welling just below.

"Don't forget the sandwiches," she said. "And be careful with the coffee. All I could find was an old tin flask. The top sticks a little when you try to unscrew it."

He cursed again, then slid back out from behind the wheel and shoved past her. She thought he would go back to tinkering with the engine, but he just stood there, staring at her instead.

"What? Why are you looking at me like that?"

His eyes narrowed in suspicion. "You've been crying."

"The cold out here makes my eyes water, that's all."

"No, you were *crying*, Kate. Your lids are swollen."

Kate gave a silent curse. She'd splashed cold water on her face, trying to erase the telltale traces of those tears. She should have checked in a mirror to make sure she'd done the job right.

"It has nothing to do with you. I—I was crying for Gar."

El raised his grease-smeared hand as if to

touch her, hesitated, then let it fall, defeated.

"Fight with me all you want, but don't let them see you cry, Kate," he said fiercely. "You hear me? Don't *ever* let them see you cry."

Before she could catch her breath, he'd plunged back under the hood.

"I'll be done in a minute," he threw over his shoulder. His voice was sandpaper rough. "If you're still so damned set on staying, you might as well get back in the house instead of freezing to death out here."

Kate spent more fruitless hours burrowing in the attic and emerged to find the sun had set, and the wind had risen again. This time it brought snow. She could hear the icy pellets hitting the kitchen windows.

El still hadn't returned. She couldn't hear a sound from the second-best parlor where Ruth and Gar were.

Her head throbbed; her body ached. She longed for her warm, comfortable bed in her tidy little apartment in New York. Twelve hours' sleep sounded just about right, then breakfast at Jerry's diner around the corner, where coffee was a nickel for endless refills and a plate heaped with eggs and bacon and freshly baked biscuits cost fifteen cents on a Sunday.

Unfortunately, New York was twelve hundred miles and four days' travel away. The best she could hope for tonight was that dinner would be over quickly so she could escape to her bed and to sleep.

She should have known better than to hope.

El finally returned just as she was setting the table for dinner. She heard the truck clattering past, the sound of it almost drowned beneath the whining of the wind and the scratching of the snow against the windows.

He blew in a few minutes later, bringing the wind and a heaping armful of firewood with him. He kicked the door shut, then dumped the wood in the box beside the stove.

"Dinner will be ready in a few minutes," Kate said, keeping her head down so she wouldn't be tempted to look at him.

"Thanks," he replied.

He didn't say a word as he stripped off his coat and hat and gloves and hung them on their hooks, then came to warm his hands at the stove. When Ruth led a shuffling, bewildered Gar into the kitchen, El pulled a couple of crumpled dollar bills and some coins out of his pocket and slapped them down on the counter. Ruth didn't ask for any other accounting, and he didn't offer any.

Dinner was a grim affair. Ruth was silent and hostile. Gar, still drawn and pale from his outburst that morning, chattered about the prob-

0

lems he'd had with that old tractor, then, in the middle of a sentence, drifted into silence. He hadn't spoken a word since.

Kate forced the food down, one dry, tasteless bite at a time, and wondered what Della was like. If she'd had the diamonds, she could have gone with him. How far away would she have gotten by now? Fifty miles? A hundred? Two?

Her head ached, a dull throb that made it hard to think and turned her vision blurry. She felt like she could sleep for a month if only she had a warm, comfortable bed. The best she could hope for tonight was not to be crushed beneath the extra blankets she'd have to add to keep from freezing.

El kept his distance and his thoughts to himself. He didn't linger afterward, just took his coffee and an oil lamp upstairs without so much as a word of goodnight.

Ruth caught her watching him leave.

"Don't go sniffing after him, missy. He's trash. Always has been, always will be."

Kate bit back a retort. El didn't need her to defend him, anyway.

She picked up El's plate and set it atop her own, hoping Ruth wouldn't notice all the food she'd left uneaten. "I'll wash up the dishes, Aunt Ruth. If you want to settle Gar—"

"Sit." Ruth spat the word, as if she were speaking to an unruly dog. "Gar's happy where he is, and I want to talk."

Gar was, in fact, frowning at the bread he'd squashed into an unrecognizable lump, puzzled, and a little resentful that it should have changed shape without his realizing it. Pinning one edge of the balled up bread to the table with his thumb, he tried to peel back the edge of crust buried in the wadded mess.

Kate set the plates down, then sat. Good doggie, she thought sourly, but took care not to let the emotion show on her face. She didn't have the heart for a fight.

"So, what do you want to talk about, Ruth?"

Ruth eyed her, then frowned at the sludgy dregs in her coffee cup as though she sought some guidance there.

"You're a Mannheim, Katherine Mary," she said at last. Her mouth pinched a bit, as if the words had a sour taste to them. "You may be a bastard, but you're still a Mannheim. Like your grandmother." She paused. "Like me."

Like my mother!

It was a silent shout, but it incited the demons in Kate's head to pound even harder. All she said was, "That doesn't count for very much in New York."

"Well it does here!"

Kate said nothing.

Ruth glared. When Kate still refused to respond, she glanced at Gar, then abruptly shoved her cup away.

"You're a Mannheim," she said again, her mouth curling with distaste. "If things had gone differently, you might have inherited Grand House instead of me."

Kate repressed a shudder. She couldn't imagine anything more horrible.

"I don't begrudge you the house or anything in it," she said. "All I want is what's mine. Nothing more."

"Which is little enough. Sara Mannheim never had anything her mother didn't give her in the first place . . . except you."

That last was said with a sneer that would have drawn blood if Kate hadn't already been armored against it.

Ruth was wrong, in any case. Gertrude hadn't given Sara those diamonds. They were a gift from Gertrude's father to his only grandchild.

Kate thought of that strange dream she'd had in her grandmother's bedroom that first night, and shivered. In an effort to control a wayward daughter, Gertrude had taken what was never hers to begin with.

It wasn't the only thing she'd stolen from those around her. Gertrude Mannheim had been a soulless thief, and they were all still paying the penalty for her greed.

"Gertrude didn't much like having a bastard

for a granddaughter, you know," Ruth continued implacably.

"I know."

The bald admission brought the older woman up short. She eyed Kate with disfavor. "Gertrude was a proud woman. Your mother shamed her and dirtied the Mannheim name."

"And for that I was treated like dirt under Gertrude's feet my entire life," Kate shot back, stung.

"What cause do you have to complain? You had a roof over your head and food on the table, didn't you? And all those pretty, expensive clothes? Gertrude took care of you in spite of your mother and what she did."

"Or because of it. After all, what pleasure would Gertrude have gotten out of playing the martyr if she couldn't constantly remind me of what she'd suffered? If I hadn't been around, she wouldn't have been able to tell me, over and over again, how good she was to take me in."

She eyed Ruth with distaste, wanting to hurt. "You ought to understand what it was like, Ruth. You were always the poor relation, too. The only difference was, Gertrude took you for granted because she'd always had you to kick around. I was just a more recent novelty."

Every word came from the heart, but Kate didn't much like the bitterness they left on her tongue. She squeezed her eyes shut, fighting against the throbbing in her head and the sick feeling in the pit of her stomach. All that was in the past, and cutting at Ruth would accomplish nothing but to make relations between them even more difficult. She lived for tomorrow now, she reminded herself, not yesterday. She had to.

When she opened her eyes again, it was to see an unexpected glint of understanding in Ruth's hooded eyes, and of pain. Her words had stabbed far deeper than she'd intended, and they'd drawn blood.

Ruth sagged. The anger and resentment drained out of her like oil out of a lamp, taking all color and light with them. Her skin took on a grayer cast. Her face turned gaunt; the wrinkles looked deeper suddenly, the bones beneath more stark. She seemed older somehow, and tired with a weariness that went bone-deep. She seemed . . . defeated.

Gertrude's legacy, Kate knew. From the day she'd been taken into the household, Ruth had been the unwanted poor relation who was tolerated because she could be put to work, because she was loyal, and because the rest of the world would admire the Mannheim generosity for taking her in in the first place. There had been no love all those years ago, no more than there had been when Sara had reluctantly returned to Grand House with her small daughter.

In that moment of shared memory, Kate's anger died. She had escaped Grand House. Ruth hadn't, and never would.

Chapter Eleven

For a long moment Ruth didn't speak, didn't even seem to realize anyone else was there. Kate could tell by the changing shadows in her eyes when she came back to an awareness of the present.

She drew in a deep breath, then roughly tugged the bodice of her sober gray dress into place.

"I didn't ask you to stay so we could quarrel, Katherine Mary." It was as close as she was ever likely to come to an apology. "I asked you because—because Gar and I—"

Ruth glanced at her husband. Gar had abandoned the wad of bread and was now simply sitting there, a frail, broken old man silently staring at nothing at all.

Something in Ruth stiffened. The anger flooded back.

She swung back to Kate, her expression fierce. "I won't leave Grand House to a Carstairs. Not to that arrogant son of a—Even if he's related to Gar, I won't do it. I won't do that to Gertrude Mannheim's memory."

She paused, drew in an unsteady breath, let it out. "But I will leave it to you."

"What?"

"There are conditions, however."

Kate stared at her blankly. "Conditions?"

"That you stay here, help me take care of Gar and the house. You do that, I'll leave everything— Grand House, the money, everything. I'll leave it to you in my will."

"But—" Kate stopped, trying to gather her wits. "If you need help, why don't you just hire Gertrude's old servants back?"

Ruth flinched. "I can't do that. They . . . they upset Gar."

She couldn't quite meet Kate's eyes as she said it.

"Someone else, then," Kate persisted. "It can't be that hard to find someone suitable, someone he'd like. Not with times as hard as they are now and so many people looking for work."

The last thing she wanted was to spend her life immured here at Grand House. The place and the things it contained had warped her grandmother and tormented Ruth. It had destroyed her mother. It would destroy her if she remained.

But she couldn't tell Ruth that. Not now. Not while Ruth's defenses were down.

Not while she herself still had so much to lose.

"I could help you advertise, if you like," she said instead, groping for a way out that wouldn't hurt Ruth's pride. "You could try people out for a couple of weeks, maybe a month, see if they upset Gar—"

"No!" Ruth shook her head. "No, not that way. It wouldn't matter who you found, they wouldn't suit. Gar wouldn't like it."

Kate glanced at the old man. He'd fallen asleep, head bent, his chin on his chest. A thin ribbon of drool trailed from the corner of his mouth. Her heart tore. This gaunt, shrunken, confused old man wasn't her beloved Uncle Gar. Her Gar—Ruth's husband—had gone away someplace, never to return, and left this fragile shell behind.

She thought of his violence this afternoon and wanted to weep.

He hadn't gone away entirely, after all, she realized. This morning, that *was* her Gar who'd cussed and argued and tried to hurt. The difference was, when he'd cried out from the gray, amorphous prison that held him, anger was the only voice he had left.

"Gar's only happy with family," Ruth persisted. "He likes me to take care of him. He trusts me." She leaned forward, intent, determined to make

211

her point. "He trusts *you*, Katherine Mary. He'd be happy with you. That's important, you know. That he be happy."

"Yes, of course," Kate murmured, distracted.

"It—It wouldn't be for long." Ruth blinked and for a moment Kate thought she caught the glint of tears. "A year maybe. Maybe more. Maybe . . . less. Doc Hodders won't say. Though what that fussy old fool knows . . ."

Ruth gave an angry shrug. Kate kept silent.

"It probably wouldn't be all that long until you'd have it all," Ruth continued. Her voice was rough now, to hide the emotion beneath. "I'm seventy-three. Gar's seventy-five, and you see how . . . how frail he's become—"Kate pretended not to hear the catch in the older woman's voice—"and how much he needs to have someone watching out for him all the time."

Ruth leaned forward suddenly, stretching to fold her big hand over Kate's.

"He *needs* you, Katherine Mary. *I* need you. I can't take care of him by myself. I *can't*. It's— He—I just . . . can't. Not anymore."

That stark admission had to be one of the hardest things Ruth had ever done. Kate winced, fighting the guilt and love and pity that threatened to swamp her.

"But what about El?"

"El!" Ruth jerked back as if stung.

"He's done so much, and he loves Gar so—"

"He doesn't love Gar." Ruth spat the words. Fury burned away the tears. "And he hasn't done anything he didn't already owe us. All those years of feeding him and housing him, with him wearing out his shoes and growing out of his clothes every time you looked around, and always into trouble. And after what he did . . . !"

She kicked her chair back and shoved to her feet. The scrape of the chair legs across the floor brought Gar awake with a start.

"Ruth?" He looked around blankly, disoriented. "That you, Ruth? Something the matter?"

He tried to stand, but forgot to push the chair back first. For an instant, he hung there, awkwardly caught between the chair and the table. Panic bloomed in his eyes.

"Ruth? *Ruth?*"

Ruth was around the table in an instant. "I'm here, Gar. I'm here," she soothed, holding onto him even as she pulled his chair away. "You're all right."

He clung to her, stumbling a little as he fought to regain his balance. "Ruth."

"Yes, Gar. Ruth. Don't worry. You're all right."

"Where's El?"

Ruth's mouth thinned. "He's not here, Gar. I'll help you, all right? Let me help you."

"But where's El? I got to tell him—"

"Later, Gar," said Ruth tiredly, leading him away. "Whatever it is, you can tell him later."

It was a long while before Kate found the strength to start clearing the table.

Like leaves in a whirlwind, Kate's thoughts spun and danced and went nowhere. By the time she put away the last fork and dried the dampness from the sink, she felt lightheaded. Weariness dragged at her, yet her thoughts refused to stop churning.

Talking to Ruth tonight had given her a new perspective on the woman . . . and on herself. She'd thought she'd escaped Grand House even if Ruth had not. Now, she wasn't so sure.

For ten years the place and the people in it had stalked her dreams and cast their shadows across her waking thoughts. But when the Daniels offered her the chance to buy the bookstore, her first thoughts had turned back here. Even when she'd tried to find another way out, the house and all it represented had loomed at the back of her thoughts.

If she left now and never looked back, would she free herself from the invisible chains that had held Ruth prisoner for so long? *Could* she? Was there was no other way to claim the future except through this constant, unsettling confrontation with the past?

With deliberate care, Kate dried her hands, then folded the worn dish towel and hung it from its hook. Every motion, every step cost an effort.

She added more wood to the kitchen stove, then closed the dampers so the fire would burn through the night and there would be coals hot and ready for breakfast tomorrow morning. The simple action took the last drop of her energy.

Maybe she should just make up a pallet over there in the corner. If she asked, El would help her drag down a mattress and the blankets and sheets and pillows. One trip, maybe two, and she'd have everything she needed.

It would be warmer here. Light from the banked fire would seep around the edges of the iron lid over the firebox to shove the shadows back to the farthest corners, where they belonged. There'd be music in the comfortable hiss and sigh as the fire worked its slow way through the night's supply of wood. The wind would still be there, at the back of everything, but it wouldn't be the only thing she heard.

She'd never do it. She was Kate Mannheim, and her room was at the very top of the servants' stairs. Right beneath the attic where the weight of dead lives pressed too close.

With a sigh, she sank into Gar's old chair. She'd go upstairs in a minute. She just needed to rest for a bit first. Just for a little bit.

The heat from the stove wrapped around her like a blanket, drawing her down into sleep.

* * *

Claws digging into her shoulder dragged her out of incoherent dreams.

"Wake up. Wake up, you fool!" Ruth gave her another vicious shake.

Kate sat up with a jerk, wincing at the stiffness in her neck. Cold air swirled around her ankles.

Ruth's fingers dug deeper. "Why didn't you stop him?"

Blinking away the fog of sleep and dark dreams, Kate stared up at the woman. "What? Stop who?"

Cold air. Her brain finally started to work.

"Is Gar gone? How could he get out?" She thought of Gar as she'd seen him that first day, hatless, shoeless, with not even a sweater between him and the winter cold. Panic touched her. "The door was locked. I swear the door was locked. I checked."

"You checked." Ruth's face twisted in a furious sneer. "You fell asleep and let him escape. If you hadn't been sleeping you could have stopped him."

"Why didn't *you?*"

Ruth backed away. The harsh words that had risen to Kate's tongue died unspoken. It wasn't fury she saw in the older woman's eyes, but fear. She got to her feet.

"I'm going after him." Ruth snatched her coat from the hook, grabbed the lamp from the table. "Get Elliott. Go get Elliott."

An instant later she was gone. The door slammed shut behind her, sealing out the cold and the wind that had swallowed Gar.

Fear sent Kate flying up the stairs, heedless of the dark. She stumbled, had to grope, but found the right door somehow.

"Elliott! El! Come quick! Uncle Gar's gone! Hurry!" She pounded on the heavy wood, desperate. "Please, El! *Hurry!*"

She almost fell into El's arms when he wrenched the door open.

"Gar's gone?" he demanded. *"Outside?"*

Kate nodded dumbly. The lamp light cast the room behind him in gold, but he was all grim, black shadow. It was her own fears that made him seem bigger, more dangerous than she remembered. His shoulders seemed to fill the doorway.

His hands clamped around her arms like a vise. "When? How long ago?" His voice rose. He shook her again. "How long has Gar been out there?"

"I don't know. I fell asleep in his chair by the stove. The door was open. Ruth says—"

"Hell." He shoved her away, headed toward the stairs. "Stay here. Do you hear me? Stay here!"

"No! I'm coming with you!" Her shout was met by silence. He was already gone.

She found him in the kitchen lighting a lantern. He didn't look up.

217

"Get some water boiling," he said. "He'll need tea. Strong, hot, sweet tea to get him warm. And blankets. Heated blankets. Check the fire in the parlor, make sure it's going strong. And light another lantern, will you? There's a hook outside the kitchen door where you can hang it. Maybe if he sees that, he'll come back on his own."

"I'm going with you. Three can search a larger area faster. You *need* me." She was already dragging on her coat when El grabbed her, dragged her hard against him.

"Damned fool. You're not going anywhere." His words ripped at her like ragged teeth. "You have to be here in case he comes back. He's done that before. Slipped past us, snuck back in."

She tried to pull away. His grip tightened. She could hardly breathe, couldn't think. El's furious gaze held her pinned like a bug on a board. Her heart hammered in her ears, deafening her.

"Whatever you do, don't trust him. Do you hear me, Kate? You never know what he'll do. You don't know what he *can* do. If you—"

"El! You're hurting me!"

He let her go so abruptly she staggered.

For an instant, he stared at her as if she were a ghost come to haunt him, then he turned away and, snatching his coat from its hook and the lantern from the table where he'd left it, shoved past her without a word of apology.

At the door he stopped, turned back. "And, Kate?"

"Yes?"

His eyes burned. "Be careful."

Chapter Twelve

Be careful.

As she scurried about putting the kettle on to boil, hanging the light by the back door, stoking the fire in the second-best parlor, fetching blankets, El's words echoed in Kate's mind. Be careful? Why the warning? What had he meant? She wasn't the one stumbling around in the dark and the cold looking for Gar. Why was *she* supposed to be careful?

The house offered no answer. Her heart had none to give.

El had frightened her. He still frightened her. Ruth she had always understood, but El eluded her. There was more to his hostility than old anger at her betrayal, and more to his warning than mere caution. But what?

More important, where was Gar? And why hadn't they found him by now?

Troubled, she busied herself wrapping hot bricks in towels and tucking them into Gar's bed. This close to the stove, the room was almost tropically warm. The heat made her dizzy, but she didn't dare damp down the fire. Gar would need every bit of warmth when they found him.

If they found him.

She pushed down the horrible thought with a shudder and tried not to think of that poor farmer, dead in a snowdrift a few short yards from his back door.

They'd find him. Neither Ruth nor El would rest until they'd found him. He was an old man and weak. He couldn't go far.

But what if he'd fallen? What if he couldn't hear them calling him, or couldn't answer if he did? They had no way of knowing how long he'd been gone. Ruth hadn't even said whether he was dressed, or if he was wearing shoes. He didn't have a coat or hat—both were still hanging on their hooks in the kitchen. How long could a frail old man like Gar survive in the cold?

Kate's hand trembled as she smoothed Gar's pillow. She felt so . . . helpless. So horribly useless.

"No."

The single word, spoken on a dying whisper, brought her head up with a snap.

"No. No, no, no."

Kate spun about. There was no one there.

"No."

This time so faint she could hardly hear it. She squeezed her eyes shut, fighting down panic.

It was the wind, nothing more. The wind that had long ago found every crack and crevice in this old house.

Or her imagination, Kate chided herself, drawing a deep breath and forcing her eyes open. The room was silent save for the muted crackling of the fire behind the closed stove doors.

To hell with Elliott and his orders. She was going to help search for Gar. Better that than sitting here idle and letting her mind play tricks on her.

As she opened the door to the hall, a cold draft swirled past, making her shiver. The light from the kitchen lamp seemed brighter than it had before.

She was halfway down the hall when she realized the light wasn't coming from the kitchen but the open door of the ladies' parlor.

Kate stopped dead in her tracks.

There was no one in the parlor. No reason for anyone to be there. Not now. There was no Gertrude to force them to sit there, hour after hour, and Sara—

Frightful images exploded in her mind's eye—
black memories and scraps of nightmares.

Her heart raced, threatening to burst through
her ribs. Air lodged in her lungs, making her
chest hurt. She couldn't breathe, but she would
swear she could hear Grand House breathing
around her, a slow in-out susuration like that of
a beast of prey, hunting.

"El?" she called. It came out more of a squeak.
"Aunt Ruth?"

A thump was her only answer.

"Uncle Gar?" It had to be Gar. He'd wandered
back. He probably didn't even know where he
was.

It was just a room. That's all it was. A room
like any other.

Kate forced her feet to move.

The first thing she saw was her grandmother's
chair, the big, ugly, red damask chair where Gertrude had sat for hours, forcing her to read from
all those endless books on sin and damnation.
And there was the stool. Her stool. Her penance,
part of the price she'd paid for her mother's sins.

And there was Gar. Still dressed in the rumpled shirt and trousers he'd worn that morning,
he was standing beside the small table, where
he'd set the kitchen lamp, peering into the dark
above him. His face was drained of color and so
pinched with cold his cheeks were cavernous
hollows. His eyes peered out of black holes

drilled in his skull. In the lamplight they were devoid of color or life, and utterly mad.

"Uncle Gar!"

Gar gave no sign he heard her. His head was tilted back, his mad gaze fixed on the chandelier that Kate's great-grandfather had brought all the way from Vienna.

Kate didn't look at the chandelier. She couldn't move out of the open doorway, couldn't bring herself to step over that sill. Not even for Gar.

"Uncle Gar?"

"Pretty Sara. Pretty, pretty Sara," Gar crooned, staring up at the chandelier. "What are you doing up there, Sara? You're not supposed to be there. That's not right. Not right at all."

Kate's stomach clenched. She clamped her arms across her belly, fighting nausea. The floor rocked under her feet.

Be careful, El had said.

But this was Gar. Good, kind, befuddled Gar. He wouldn't hurt her. It was her own fears, her memories of this room and what it had contained that held her like this, pinned and helpless.

Fears and memories, nothing more. Her mother wasn't here. They'd cut her body down from that chandelier and carried it away long, long ago.

Screwing up her courage, Kate forced herself to step into the room.

"Uncle Gar? Are you all right? Do you want some tea?" Her voice was too high and tight with strain, but Gar wouldn't notice, or care.

At the sight of her, his face lit up. "Sara! There you are!" He took a shuffling step in her direction, hand out as if to welcome her. "You scared me. You shouldn't do things like that."

Kate forced herself to take his hand. It was icy cold but still big and rough and surprisingly strong. The rest of him was shrinking, folding in on itself and disappearing, but Gar's hands were the hands she remembered.

All except for the cold. Gar had never been cold.

He clasped his other hand over hers, holding her in a vise.

"Like what, Uncle Gar? What shouldn't I do?"

"Fool me." The mad, washed-out eyes glittered in the light. "I thought you were hanging from the chandelier."

A strangled sound came from Kate's throat, like the sound a small animal might make when it was caught in a trap.

If Gar noticed, he gave no sign.

"Why were you hanging from the chandelier, Sara? You didn't look very pretty that way. Not at all like my pretty Sara. Your face. And your tongue sticking out like that . . ." He frowned. "You scared Kate, you know."

Kate tried to pull away, but his grip on her

225

hand tightened. "Poor Kate. Poor, poor Kate."

His frown deepened to a fierce scowl. He leaned forward until his face was only inches from hers. His breath was sour and unpleasant. His skin smelled of old age and decay.

A corpse would smell like this, Kate thought, frightened, trying to tug her hand free of his. Her mother had smelled like this before they shut her in her coffin and buried her in the hard, cold ground.

She tugged harder, frantic now, desperate to get free.

Gar didn't like it, but her tugging was so insistent he finally let her go. "You shouldn't frighten Kate."

"No." The protest strangled in her throat. Kate clamped her hand over her mouth to stop the sobs. Tears stung her hand. She hadn't felt them fall.

If Gar noticed the tears, he gave no sign of it. He cocked his head, brows furrowed in puzzlement, his eyes gone vague again. This close she could see the washed-out blue of his irises, the dirty yellow of the whites. But she couldn't see Gar in there. Not anywhere.

"Kate?" he said, the furrows easing. "Kate!" Smiling again, as if nothing had happened. In his confused mind, perhaps nothing had.

He gently patted her arm, still smiling. "Pretty Kate. My pretty, pretty Kate."

The tension in Kate's chest eased a fraction, letting her breathe again, but only just.

She could feel the weight of the chandelier pressing down above her. It would crush her if she let it. She couldn't let it.

Her hand trembled as she touched Gar's arm. "Let's go, Uncle Gar. I've got some blankets warming I'll make you some tea."

"Tea," said Gar, a hopeful light in his eyes.

Whatever had driven him earlier was gone, the energy it gave him dissipated, leaving him weaker than ever. He was shaking with cold and curling in on himself, almost too tired to stand.

"Come on, Uncle Gar." Kate wrapped her arm around his shrunken shoulders, nudging him toward the door. She had to fight against the urge to stoop. She could *feel* the weight of that chandelier pressing down on her, harder, heavier, crushing her without remorse.

"Hot tea, Uncle Gar," she said. "Hot tea and a fire."

With Gar tucked into the brick-warmed bed, still fully dressed, Kate checked the fire in the coal stove, then went to brew some tea and call Ruth and Elliott back. The old man would probably be asleep before she took the teapot off its shelf. He didn't have the strength to get out of bed, let alone wander away a second time tonight.

The instant she stepped out of the over-heated

227

parlor into the chilly hall, she shivered. The far end of the hall seemed a mile away, lost in shadows.

Halfway down the hall, the door to the ladies' parlor still stood open. Lamplight spilled from it, staining the Bokhara runner in the hall a dull red-gold, then turning a tarnished black when it reached the dark wood floor at the farther edge.

She had to fight not to squeeze against the opposite wall as she walked past.

Enough light escaped around the closed doors of the kitchen stove to let her see to light another lamp. Outside on the stoop, the cold took her breath away. The moon was up, but all she could see of it was a pale silver glow now and then when the scudding clouds thinned enough to let it shine through. The snow had almost stopped, but the wind cut like a razor, blowing what snow had fallen along the ground in front of it, piling up mounds at the side of the house and along the fences, sweeping the earth bare in the open spots.

Though she tried, Kate couldn't see any sign of a lantern's light. If there were voices out there, calling for Gar, the wind had snatched them into silence.

She shouted for Ruth and Elliott, then furiously rang the bell that had once called the farm hands in for meals. The night swallowed her voice, as well, and muted the clanging of the bell.

If they weren't back in ten minutes, she'd try again. It was too cold to wait for some sign that they had heard.

Her teeth were chattering by the time she stepped back inside. She tried not to think of Gar out there in the dark. She tried not to think of anything at all except the mundane details of brewing tea and preparing a tray. Later, when she wasn't so tired, she'd think about what Gar had said and done in the ladies' parlor. But not now. She wouldn't think about any of it now.

She didn't have a chance to. Ruth erupted into the kitchen in a flurry of scolding accusations and demands for information. On learning that Gar had been tucked into bed, fully clothed, she barreled down the hall with Kate in her wake, trying to explain.

Gar was already asleep. Ruth pulled up short beside the bed, eyes wide, breathing hard. She hadn't even bothered to throw off her coat or the rough knit scarf she'd wrapped around her neck. She bent over the bed, murmuring nonsense, anxiously patting her husband's hands and shoulders and cheek, trying to reassure herself he was all right.

He was alive, but he wasn't all right. Drained of the mad energy that had driven him out into the night, he looked shriveled and lifeless. His sparse white hair stuck out around his skull like old, bleached straw tossed by the wind. It was so thin Kate could see freckles and the dark splotches of liver spots scattered across his scalp.

Beneath the wild fringe of hair, his papery skin stretched over the broad brow and around the deeply sunken eye sockets, across the bridge of his nose and the sharp ridge of his cheeks. His mouth was open slightly, his breathing shallow and too fast. In the lamplight his teeth looked long and yellow and ugly.

The tears she'd fought back silently fell now, stinging her lids, burning down her cheeks and sliding over her jaw and down her throat into the collar of her dress, growing colder and colder the closer they got to her heart. She couldn't stop them and didn't try.

"I'll go get the tea. You'll need a cup even if he won't," she said, turning away so Ruth couldn't see the tears.

Ruth ignored her. Without taking her eyes off Gar, the older woman pulled up a chair and took his hand in both of hers. If she noticed she was still wearing her coat, she gave no sign of it. She didn't even look up when Kate walked out of the room.

In the kitchen, Kate drew water, icy cold straight from the well, and splashed it on her face. The shock of it chased away the tears but not the ache that had lodged just beneath her breastbone.

Was there ever any dignity in dying? Or was

death just a brutal thief who stole whatever shreds of humanity a person had drawn around himself, then slunk away, laughing? Could Gar tell her? Did she want to listen if he could?

And what, Kate wondered, might he tell her of her mother's death?

In this morass of doubt and uncertainty, she was sure of one thing only: Somewhere, deep inside the foggy recesses of his brain, Gar knew things she needed to know.

The memory of him in the ladies' parlor lingered like the smoke of his hand-rolled cigarettes once had, biting and acrid. Even when she tried not to she could see him standing there, staring up at the chandelier and talking to her mother, her beautiful, suicidal mother who had died almost twenty years before by hanging herself from the chandelier that had come from Vienna.

What had he seen, all those years ago? Why had he called her mother his pretty, pretty Sara?

And why did her memory insist that he had never seen Sara hanging there at all?

El still hadn't returned by the time Kate had gathered herself together enough to take the tray in to Ruth. The older woman ignored her. She'd removed her coat and scarf, but she hadn't moved from her chair by the bed. The slight rise and fall of the covers was the only sign that Gar was still alive.

Kate set a cup of heavily sugared tea on the table by the bed so it would be within Ruth's reach if she wanted it, then quietly slipped out of the room. Ruth never looked up or acknowledged her presence.

In the hall again, Kate hesitated. The lamp was still burning in the ladies' parlor. There was no reason she couldn't just leave it burning and go up to bed. She didn't have to retrieve it, didn't have to set foot in the room if she didn't want to.

Let Ruth get it tomorrow, if she cared. If she even noticed.

Yet still Kate stopped outside that open door, standing at the very edge of the light, staring into the room beyond, at Gertrude's chair and the stool that had been her penance and the chandelier that hung above them both. Her heart seemed too small for her chest suddenly, inadequate for the job of pumping the blood through her veins. She felt lightheaded and strangely awkward and disjointed, as if the various pieces of her body didn't fit.

She didn't look directly at the chandelier. She knew if she did, she'd see her mother hanging there still, the heavy silk cord from one of the draperies knotted around her neck, her beautiful face twisted and swollen, her neck broken. Kate had seen that vision so often in her dreams that every detail was as clear and precise as it had been on that gray winter day twenty years ago when she'd first walked in and found her mother's body.

She couldn't bear to look down, either. If she did, she was afraid she'd see the three-rung step stool her mother had climbed. It would be tipped on its side, just as it had been then, kicked away when Sara had taken that short, brutal jump into oblivion.

She hadn't been able to use a three-step stool since, could scarcely bear even to look at one.

Why why *why* had Gar been there, talking to the ghost of her mother, crooning to her, scolding her as if she still hung there for all the world to see? What twist of memory had dragged him out into the night, then back to this room and these memories? Why should it be so vivid to him now when he had not, could not possibly, have seen Sara then?

Kate sagged against the wall behind her. Her head spun. She shut her eyes, pressed her fingers to her temples, fighting against the dizziness, but still she saw her mother as she had seen her twenty years ago, an ugly, broken doll dangling from the silken cord that had killed her.

A sob caught in her throat, hot and hard, choking her.

She hadn't cried then, all those years ago. Not at first. Though most of her memories of that time were a frightening, incoherent blur, she could remember being puzzled, knowing something was wrong but not quite understanding what she saw and what it meant, what it would mean in the years to come.

She couldn't remember, now, what had made her stop to look. She'd been running an errand for Gertrude, sent to fetch something—she couldn't remember what—and something about the half-open door of the parlor had caught her attention. She'd hesitated, just as she hesitated now, hovering in the hall at the edge of the light, listening to the silence and the pounding of her own heart.

Eventually she'd worked up the courage to move toward that door, just as she did now.

She remembered resting her hand, here, on the door frame, remembered the feel of the polished wood cool and hard beneath her hand, just as it was now. The room had been warmer then, though. The remnants of a fire had burned on the open hearth where now there was nothing but dull iron and cold brick.

Perhaps it was only fitting that once there had been fire and warmth where now there was only cold and shadows. Hadn't her life been like that ever since?

She stepped into the room. One step. Two. Seeing what was and what had been like two pictures in a stereopticon, the one overlaid on the other until she could not tell which was which, until past dissolved into present, and present into past with no clear border to divide the two.

The lamp had been there, on that table by the fireplace instead of on that carved monstrosity that Gertrude had cherished so, but its light had been the same, a circle of gold that illuminated the scene before her, yet left too many shadows skulking in the corners.

She remembered the step stool—there, tipped on its side where that overblown rose gleamed blood red in the center of the carpet.

She remembered staring, just as she stared now, at the chandelier that had come from Vienna and the limp, broken creature that had dangled from it at the end of that silken cord.

And she remembered—oh, God! how clearly she remembered!—how Sara had stared back at her out of vacant, bulging eyes. Her mother hadn't moved, hadn't spoken. She'd just hung there, staring and staring and staring until Kate had thought she would never see anything else in this world again except those awful, awful eyes.

Chapter Thirteen

Elliott found her huddled on the hated stool, her arms wrapped tight around herself and rocking back and forth, staring at the chandelier while tears streamed down her face unheeded.

He touched her shoulder, gently, as if he were afraid she'd shatter there in front of him.

"Kate? Kate?" he said, and knelt beside her.

In some distant part of her mind she saw the shock and uncertainty in his face, felt the cold that clung to him like an enveloping fog. He hadn't even stopped to take off his coat. His lantern sat on the floor at his feet, warring with the lamp and making strange shapes and shadows dance about the room.

"You're cold," she said, and wondered, vaguely, whether her voice sounded as thin and distant to him as it did to her.

He couldn't be any colder than she already was. The cold held her in its fist, not on the surface, but deep inside where other people were warm and alive. There, right there where her heart beat, she was cold. Cold as ice. Cold as the grave. Cold and dead and lost.

The tears welled up, hot and stinging, threatening to drown her.

"Why? Why did she kill herself?" she wailed, drawing her arms tighter about her and starting to rock again. "Why did she go away and leave me here alone? Didn't she know what Gertrude would do? How angry she would be? Didn't she *care?*"

The words poured out with the tears and the pain, rough, choking, a cry from the heart that had waited too long to be given voice.

He squeezed her shoulder, trying to comfort, but there was no warmth there. None that touched her, anyway. And still the words poured out.

"All these years I've wondered if it was something I did, some fault in me that made her want to go away. It had to be my fault because she was so kind, so good. She wouldn't have killed herself. Not like that. Not where I could find her."

"Kate—"

"I remember how she'd laugh and how delicate her hands were and how the light would shine in her hair when she brushed it out at night. I remember her whispering secrets to me, just before I went to sleep, and getting me out of bed in the morning to hear a meadowlark sing. I remember her teaching me to pick daisies and to look for ladybugs in the grass."

The memories came faster now, easier, sliding on the tears.

"I remember all the other things, too," she said, and tasted gall in every word. "I remember how she used to stand, looking out the window at nothing for hours on end. I remember how Gertrude made her cry and how she'd tell me it would be better some day. But it never was. Not here, not in this house. Somehow, even then, I knew it never could be, and yet I wanted to believe her because she was my mother and she loved me."

In some part of her mind she watched herself and wondered whether she was breaking apart.

She watched Elliott watching her, hollow-eyed and haunted, helpless against her rage and grief.

She wanted, suddenly, for him to hold her, wanted to feel his arms strong and firm around her, keeping out the night. But he didn't touch her, didn't speak, and she couldn't reach out to him. Tucked like this, with her arms wrapped tightly around herself, she was armored against the world. If she opened that armor, even by a crack, if she dared reach for him and he didn't take her in . . .

"I thought I heard her," she said in a small, frail voice. "Here, in the parlor. I thought she was whispering to me. 'No,' she said. 'No, no, no, no, no.'"

She turned, looked up at him, at his frightening, beautiful face so close above hers. The pity she saw in his eyes was more than she could bear, and so she looked away and curled even tighter into herself.

"But it wasn't her, was it?" she said. "It was the wind. Just the wind. No, no, no, no, no," she said, shaking her head back and forth with every negation.

Her voice dropped lower still until it was a whisper, less than a whisper. Until she wasn't sure she spoke at all.

"It was just the wind."

He touched her, then pushed back a wayward lock of hair that had fallen forward over her face. He brushed the curve of her ear as he tucked the lock into place, then ran the tip of his finger down to the corner of her jaw and along the edge to her chin. His touch was feather light, but it warmed her skin and broke through the ice that held her.

She turned, lifted her head to meet his gaze, blinking back the tears that made her vision blur. This time there was something more in those cool blue depths than simple pity. Something that burned, cutting through the ice.

"Elliott?" she said, and felt a flutter of hope within her.

He leaned forward and kissed her.

It was a gentle, tentative kiss, quickly over, yet it lingered on her senses. Beneath the heat of his lips on hers, the ice retreated, freeing her heart.

"Elliott," she said, and leaned into his welcoming arms.

He folded himself around her, drawing her close and safe against his chest. The coarse wool of his coat scraped her cheek.

She breathed deeply, drinking him in. He smelled of snow and sweet hay and something dark and reassuringly male.

"It's all right, Kate," he soothed, rocking her. His voice was as rough as hers, though surely not with tears. Elliott never cried.

"Kate, my sad, precious little Kate," he whispered, holding her closer still. His breath was warm against her brow. "It's all right. I promise, one day it will all be right again."

"How?" She sighed.

"I don't know. I don't know, but I promise it will all come right somehow, someday."

She curled her fingers into the sleeve of his jacket, grateful for something to hold on to. Beneath the layer of heavy wool, she could feel the muscles of his arm flex as his fingers moved against her side, holding her close. There was nothing cold about him now.

His right hand stroked across the top of her head, steady and comforting. Every now and then the rough skin of his fingers would catch a strand of hair. She could feel the pull of it, just for a moment, then his hand moved on, letting her go. His heart beat a few inches beneath where her head pressed against his chest. She couldn't hear it. There was too much between them for that.

She closed her eyes, willing herself not to think, not to hope, but to just *be*, to take the moment and the fleeting sense of rightness that came with being in his arms and let it seep through her, easing the hurts.

Slowly, the icy cold that had gripped her heart let go, one frozen heartstring at a time. The tears dried on her face, leaving her eyes swollen and gritty and her cheeks feeling as if they'd been scraped raw. Her throat was raw as well, and there was a knot of sorrow in the center of her chest as sharp as any physical pain. But Elliott still held her, and for now that was all that mattered.

"Come on," he murmured at last. He rose to his feet, drawing her up with him. "Let's get you some tea. Your skin is like ice."

"Tea would be nice," she said, not wanting to move. She burrowed against him and wished that he had taken his coat off so she could be that much closer to him. Close enough to hear his beating heart.

Only when he reached to blow out the lamp Gar had taken from the kitchen did she remember what had happened and how she'd come to be here.

"Gar's back." She tried to straighten, but didn't resist when he simply pressed her close, refusing to let her go. "He was cold and . . . confused." She refused to think about what he'd said. Not now. She *couldn't* think about it now. "Ruth came and took him and—"

"Then he'll be fine. It's you we have to think of now."

Moving slowly, the lantern in his right hand, his left arm still firmly around her shoulders, he led her out of the parlor and down the hall. He didn't stop to close the parlor door behind them.

The kitchen was brighter than she remembered, more welcoming. The fire in the stove had settled into a muted, contented crackling that invited her in. She could hear the wind howling outside, but it sounded muffled and far away.

"Sit here," El said, pushing her down into Gar's chair.

Kate sat. She didn't have the strength to stand.

The room felt colder and a whole lot emptier when his arms weren't around her.

"I'm going to set some tea to brew," he said. "Then I'm going to check on Gar, all right?"

She nodded, then closed her eyes and sank back in the chair. She'd fallen asleep in it before. Perhaps she'd be lucky and fall asleep now and forget . . . all of it. At least for a while.

Did you dream if you slept sitting upright?

She dreaded going up the stairs to her cold, dark room.

Eyes closed, she sat and listened to the sounds of El moving about the kitchen, of a spoon clinking against pottery, the metallic clank as he set the kettle back on top of the stove. When she heard his footsteps coming across the room toward her, she forced her eyes open.

He'd taken off his coat and rolled up his shirt sleeves. She found herself staring at those sculpted forearms, the big, beautifully shaped hands. She remembered how she had clung to his sleeve, how strong and comforting his hands had felt as he'd held her, stroked her hair.

Remembering, she ached.

Aching, she forced her gaze up to meet his.

His face had gone still and expressionless, his eyes once more coolly distant. A faint furrow in his brow was the only sign that he remembered what had happened, or cared.

With deceptive grace, he squatted by the chair. He rested one hand on the arm for balance and looked up into her face. This close, she could see the tiny lines of color in his ice blue eyes, see the way the hairs of his eyebrows sprang up to curve along the ridge of his brow, see the perfect, masculine arc of his lips and the rough stubble of his beard.

She didn't want to think of what he was seeing.

"I must look a mess," she said, stifling a nervous laugh.

She ran her hands through her hair, trying to bring some order to the tumbled mass, then tugged at the collar of her dress. The collar was damp where her tears had fallen. Her neck felt dirty. She was glad there was no mirror handy—she didn't want to see how she looked, eyes swollen and red-rimmed, cheeks tracked with tears.

"You look fine," he said. "You look . . . beautiful. You've always looked beautiful to me."

She could feel her eyes widen. "Really?"

"Really." He half rose and kissed her brow. "Stay here. Drink your tea," he said. "I won't be very long."

When he left, he took the warmth of the kitchen with him.

Cradling her cup of tea in her hand, Kate tucked her feet up under her, then dragged Gar's quilt over her lap and tucked that around her, too.

El thought her beautiful, and he had kissed her.

The fire in the belly of the stove crackled contentedly as she downed the last of the tea, then set the cup aside.

She curled her fingers into the quilt, but what she remembered was the feel of his coat sleeve and the solid strength of his arm. She closed her eyes and leaned her head against the back of the chair, remembering.

For the second time that night, sleep claimed her.

She woke to candlelight and warmth and an unfamiliar bed. Elliott's scent lingered on the fat feather pillow beneath her head.

A wicker chair creaked. "I thought you'd sleep all night."

She blinked and shifted in the bed, trying to figure out where she was. "El?"

"Yes." He was sitting in a chair pulled up to the far side of the bed, his finger stuck in the middle of a book. She could see the gold lettering on the spine—*Barchester Towers*—and wondered why the sight of it made her want to laugh. Somehow, she'd never pictured Elliott Carstairs reading Trollope.

El slid the ribbon bookmark into place and closed the book, then set it on the bedside table where a fat, white candle burned.

Kate drank in every nuance—the golden light, the fussy tatted linen cloth that covered the dark oak of the table, the dull green of the book's binding. The quiet, distant expression on El's face.

He propped his elbows on the edge of the bed

and leaned forward. "How do you feel?"

She tried to sit up and discovered it wasn't so easy in a plump feather bed like this. It took a heave and a little ungraceful wiggling before she could sit.

Only then did she realize that she was clad only in her slip and chemise and her practical cotton drawers. A moment's startled assessment revealed that even her cotton hose and drab white garter belt had been removed, leaving her legs embarrassingly bare beneath the bed coverings. She grabbed the edge of the sheet and dragged it up to her chin.

At the flush that claimed her cheeks, El smiled. "I thought you'd be more comfortable without your hose and that awful dress. The damn thing must have itched like hell."

"It did." The admission was out before she could stop it. Her blush deepened. "But it was very practical. Good for all the housework."

"No doubt," said El dryly. He stretched to prop another fat pillow at her back. "Better?"

"Yes, thank you," she said shyly.

There was no reason to be embarrassed, she silently scolded herself. El was an adult, and so was she. They'd been lovers once, so this was really quite demure compared to some of the wild romps they'd shared, a few of which had literally been in the hay stacked in Ruth and Gar's old barn.

But we never had a chance to make love in a real bed with feather pillows and fine linen sheets.

Don't think of that!

She dragged her hair back from her face, then tugged the sheet up higher still. "I—I must have fallen asleep."

"You were snoring."

She almost dropped the sheet. "I was not!"

"You were." She'd swear that was a twinkle in his eye, but it had to be a trick of the candlelight. "But it was a very ladylike snore. In fact, I rather liked it."

The twinkle was more unnerving than any angry frown would be.

"You haven't answered my question, though. How do you feel?"

"Fine. I feel . . . fine." It wasn't safe to explore that question any further. She didn't want to think of that small parlor or the storm of grief that had almost devoured her there. "How's Gar?"

El's smile vanished. "Sleeping."

"He looked so . . . old."

"He *is* old."

"Yes." She squirmed, trying to find a little firmer position, one that didn't tempt her thoughts in such dangerous directions.

The squirming only made things worse and reminded her that plain cotton underclothes weren't much protection against physical sensations that were even more dangerous than her thoughts.

She pretended to study the room around her, but as her gaze swept over the dark, ponderous furniture, the small stack of books on the dresser, the flannel shirt that hung from a hook over the narrow closet door, she was acutely conscious of Elliott's steady gaze and of her bare shoulder the sheet failed to cover.

When she was sure that her pulse rate was under control, she let her gaze swing back to El. That was a mistake as well, but she didn't have the strength to look away. There was a hunger in his eyes that was far more dangerous than everything else combined.

"Why did you bring me . . . here?" she asked, and found her mouth had suddenly gone dry.

The smile flashed back again. "Because you're too darned heavy to carry up two flights of stairs. Especially stairs like those from the kitchen."

"I'm not heavy!"

"Hundred and twenty if you're an ounce."

"Hundred fifteen! And that was before I started scrubbing every floor in this house!"

"And trying to eat Ruth's cooking."

She laughed. "That's right."

He settled back in his chair with the air of a man prepared to enjoy a little teasing banter. "I have to confess—I'm a little surprised at how good *your* cooking is. Used to be, you didn't know how to boil water."

"It's amazing what you can learn to do when you have to fend for yourself." She said it lightly, but at her words, a shadow passed over his face.

He leaned forward again, but this time he carefully avoided touching the bed.

"I carried you up here because I was worried about you, Kate," he said gently. "And because I thought you'd be more comfortable here than in those servants' quarters upstairs."

He's tired, she thought, studying the shadows beneath his eyes.

The idea startled her. Somehow, she'd never thought of El as getting tired like other people did.

"Why don't you sit up here?" she suggested, patting the other side of the bed. "You look almost as worn out as I feel."

He laughed, but there was something in the laughter that had her senses on alert. "I hope it's not *that* bad."

"Come on," she urged. Before he could protest, she plumped up one of the extra pillows and propped it against the carved oak headboard. "I won't bite. Honest."

He started to get out of his chair, then abruptly sat back down.

"Coward."

"Good sense isn't cowardice!"

"All right," she said, trying to ignore the sudden fluttering in her stomach. "But I can't see it makes much sense, when you're as tired as you seem to be, to sit up all night instead of stretching out and getting comfortable."

"All right, then." He got to his feet and, after a moment's hesitation, slipped his suspenders off first one shoulder, then the other.

There was nothing sexual in it, Kate told herself. She'd seen lots of her grandmother's hired hands do the same at the end of a long day working in the fields. Yet try as she might to convince herself of it, she could still feel a heat starting in the pit of her stomach that was distractingly sexual and impossible to ignore.

El eased one big shoulder up and around in a circle, working out the kinks, then the other. "Ahhh. That feels good. Sitting in that chair was making me kind of stiff."

Kate plumped up another pillow and piled it atop the first.

El swallowed, then slowly eased down on the very edge of the bed. The big wooden bedstead groaned, almost drowning out the faint squeak of the bedsprings.

He eased over a little more, just enough to get his left buttock firmly planted, then lifted his leg and stretched it out on top of the quilted coverlet. He'd already taken his boots off, but he still wore his socks—bulky, woolen things that couldn't quite disguise the long, elegant shape of his foot.

Kate tried to speak, stopped, cleared her throat, and tried again. "That can't be very comfortable."

He edged one scant inch closer and leaned cautiously back. She'd seen carpenter's rules that looked more relaxed.

Kate couldn't help smiling. Elliott Carstairs never could resist a challenge, but he was fighting this one awfully hard.

"There's plenty of room if you want to put both legs up, you know."

He eased over another inch.

Kate adjusted her own pillows, then settled deeper into the welcoming feather bed. His uncertainty eased her own. She'd been mad to invite him onto the bed with her. If he'd accepted the invitation without a protest, then settled down as a man had every right to in his own bed, she'd probably have grabbed a quilt to cover herself and run for her own room.

But he hadn't settled in, and that, far more than anything he might have said, reassured her.

She still ought to retrieve her clothes and retreat to her room, but she couldn't bear to think of that cold, dark box at the top of the stairs. More than that, she was afraid of the memories that might come once she was alone. Eventually she'd have to face them, but she couldn't bear to yet. Tomorrow would be more than soon enough.

"This room is surprisingly comfortable," she said by way of conversation.

"That's why I chose it. The heating duct that feeds this room rises straight from the furnace." He seemed grateful for the distraction. "That, and it has the longest bed."

That little addition was a mistake. Kate ignored it more easily than she ignored the curl of interest in her belly.

He shifted position, edging back more comfortably onto the pillows and stretching both legs out atop the coverlet while keeping a good, safe distance between them. Kate couldn't help noticing that the tip of his right sock had a hole in it.

"One thing I've wondered about," he said, frowning at his toes, "is how you got out to Grand House that first day. You didn't walk all the way from town, did you?"

She shook her head. "Mr. Simpson was at the station when I came in. He gave me a ride."

"Hod Simpson? I didn't hear his truck."

"He dropped me off on the road. He . . . didn't think he'd be welcome."

That corner of his mouth lifted by a fraction of an inch. "You mean he didn't want to have anything to do with Ruth."

"Something like that."

That fraction of a smile faded. He turned back

to studying his toes. When the toes passed inspection, he cleared his throat.

"New York's a long way from Mannville," he said.

"Yes." In more ways than just distance.

"What do you do there? Where do you work, I mean. How do you earn your living?"

"I work in a bookstore."

"A bookstore? Selling *books?*" He shifted around to face her. The smile on his face was so warm it made her smile, too. "You like that, do you?"

"Yes. Yes, I do. I like it very much."

"You would. I've never known anyone who had her nose stuck in a book as much as you did. Sounds like you landed on your feet."

Her smile faded. "I was lucky. There wasn't much else I was qualified for except selling books."

"But you've done okay?"

Was it her imagination, or was there a trace of anxiety in that question? Had he thought of her occasionally and wondered whether she was all right? Had he dreamed of her as she'd dreamed of him?

"I've been lucky. I like my job, and my employers are kind. I—I have a tiny apartment not too far from the shop." She'd almost said she had a chance to buy the shop. That would have been a mistake. "It's very comfortable."

"You like New York." It was a statement, not a question, yet she sensed he would have preferred a different answer.

"I suppose so." She shrugged, then remembered her bare shoulder and tugged the sheet up higher. "There's certainly a lot of things to see and do."

And it was the coldest, loneliest place in the world when you were all alone.

"Not like here," he said.

"No," she said. "Not like here."

She thought of the empty land that surrounded Grand House. It had been a long time since her world hadn't been bound by brick and glass and stone.

"What about you? Where have you been all this time?"

"Me?" His lower lip thrust out as he considered his answer. "Lots of places. Here, there. New York for a bit, even. Didn't stay long. Didn't much like the place, I'm afraid. Followed the work and eventually ended up in San Francisco."

"California?" Her imagination fired. "I'd like to see California some day. They say it's beautiful."

His eyes warmed at her enthusiasm. "It is. And San Francisco's the most beautiful part of it. There's nothing quite like sailing into that big bay, especially at night when the lights of the city are lit up all across those hills. Like stars snatched out of the sky and pinned there, just to welcome you back."

He turned on his side and propped himself on his elbow. If he noticed how the change in position narrowed the distance between them, he didn't show it.

"You'd like it, I think. Lots of bookstores, good restaurants. Like New York in some ways, but it's still human-sized, and you can smell the ocean there, clean and sharp. San Francisco's got the kind of air that fills you up and makes you glad you're alive even when it's so thick you can't see the hand in front of your face."

From the look on his face, he was there again and the city was welcoming him home.

The thought made her sad, somehow, reminded her of everything that lay between them. Three thousand miles was only part of it, and not the largest part at that.

At least he'd have some place he loved to go back to when he left Grand House again.

That thought made her even sadder, and not a little irritated. She liked New York well enough, didn't she? And what did it matter where he went or whether he was happy there? Soon enough they'd both go their separate ways, and this time there'd be nothing to draw them back, either to Grand House or to each other.

"What kind of work did you do there?" she asked instead. "You mentioned sailing into San

Francisco Bay. Did you work on boats?"

"I did. I shipped out of Boston the first time. Got to California a year later. I still sail a little when I get the chance. These days, though, I work with airplanes."

"You fly airplanes?"

He nodded. "Fix them, too. I—" He stopped, considered whatever it was he'd been about to say, tried again. "There's a future there, no matter what some folks believe. A wonderful future, and I'm going to be a part of it."

Though the single candle was on the table at his back, she could see a light in his face she'd never seen before, an inner joy that burned like a hot, bright flame.

"Airplanes are going to change our world, Kate. They're going to change our very conceptions of space and time and distance. You'll be able to go places you've only imagined, see and do things you've never even dreamed of. Business. Travel. Communications. Farming, even. They're all changing because of airplanes and what they can do. We're making better maps because we can take photographs from the air. We're getting important mail delivered faster than it's ever been delivered. And we're only beginning to understand what's possible."

He laughed and sat up. "Hell, someday we may even fly to the moon. Would you like that, Kate? To fly to the moon?"

She couldn't help smiling. "My imagination doesn't stretch quite that far, I'm afraid. I've read a couple of books about it, though."

"Books! Why settle for books when you can have the real thing?"

His gaze turned to the night-black window where he'd neglected to draw the drapes, but it wasn't the window he was seeing, Kate knew, or the empty land beyond. He was looking at the future he dreamed of, a world far different from the one she knew.

He swung back to face her, eyes alight. "And it *will* be real, Kate. Someday. Already people are beginning to travel by plane instead of train. Someday it will be possible to fly from California to New York in a day, maybe even a few hours."

"A day?" She laughed. "It took me three to get half that distance."

"Three hard and damned uncomfortable days."

"You took the words right out of my mouth. Except for the swearing."

He flashed her a quick, abashed smile. "Sorry. I used to do a lot of my traveling by hopping freight trains. It gets you where you're going, but there's no comfort in it."

"At least a train isn't prone to falling out of the sky and killing everyone on it."

"I got caught in a train wreck in Illinois, once,"

he retorted. "Scared me a hell of a lot more than any plane I've ever crashed."

"You've crashed an airplane?" she demanded, horrified.

"Four, actually. No, five. Never bad. Walked away from every one and was back in the air in a day or two after a few repairs."

He said it as casually as if crashing airplanes were something everyone did now and then. Her stomach churned at the thought of it.

"You should be more careful."

"What would be the fun in that?" That dangerous smile was back. The one that warmed straight through to her heart and almost made her forget everything else. Almost.

"Yet you left all that to come back," she said.

The smile vanished. He swung his attention back to the window. For a moment, she didn't think he was going to answer.

"I didn't plan on being here a week, let alone two months."

"You're going back?"

"Yes. Eventually. Ruth doesn't want me, and Gar—" His hands balled into fists. He stared at them, studying them, then forced them to open again.

What had he said that day in the barn? Something about seeking answers to questions and not finding them.

"There's nothing I can do here that a hired

hand couldn't do as well. And without me to help, maybe Ruth will come to her senses and realize she can't do it all."

She jerked upright, propelled by sudden panic.

"You're leaving? When?" She had to force the words out past a painful constriction in her throat.

He glanced at her, looked away. "Soon."

"How soon?"

"Depends."

"On what?" It doesn't matter, she told herself. But she knew it did.

He shrugged, then deliberately stretched back out beside her. This time, mere inches divided them.

"It doesn't matter, Kate," he said, but there was a roughness in his voice that told her he was lying. "As soon as you find what you're looking for, you'll leave, go back to New York and your life there."

The way he said it, it sounded so flat. Like a judgment from which there was no reprieve.

"And you?" she said. "What will you do?"

She could feel tears starting at the backs of her eyes, but blinked them away.

Again that shrug that was supposed to say it didn't matter when they both knew it really did.

"I'll go back to California. To my life, my planes. Taken all in all, it's a pretty good life."

Kate let go of the sheet, heedless of the way it

fell to expose her shoulder and the neat, unimaginative straps of her slip and the chemise beneath it. She didn't have to stretch far to touch his hand.

His skin was warm, the dark hairs crisp and springy to the touch. She could feel the bones beneath the skin, the leashed strength. Tension thrummed in him like an electrical current in a wire, invisible, but dangerous.

Before she could retreat, he claimed her hand and pulled her down on the bed beside him.

Chapter Fourteen

"Kate," he murmured. "My beautiful Kate."

And then he rolled her onto her back and pinioned her with his body.

The first kiss was swift and fierce, frightening in its hunger.

The second scorched her senses, robbing her of breath and thought. His mouth devoured her. His left hand tangled in her hair, tugging her head back and opening her to his depredations. His right hand claimed her breast beneath the covers.

It was as if the world had exploded.

Ten years fell away like an unwanted garment that is kicked aside and forgotten. They were young again, and hungry, and the world was far away.

All those long, empty nights and haunted

dreams, all those hours spent wandering the streets of New York alone, looking for what she'd had and lost and never hoped to have again—all of that faded and lost its power to hurt.

His mouth burned it all away. His hands promised pleasures without end. His weight pressed her deeper into the feather bed, holding her fast. Quilts and sheets and layers of clothing were barriers to the touch but not to heat or need.

And she needed him, needed the taste and feel and heat of him. Ten years, yet she hadn't forgotten how sensitive he was to a kiss placed just there, at the corner of his jaw. Or how he'd go still for a moment, eyes closed in pleasure, when she licked around the shell of his ear, then breathed out so her breath cooled the wetness she'd left with her tongue.

His hair was coarse silk, long enough to grab so that she could hold him to her just as he held her. His skin, browned by an unforgiving sun, was rough to the touch, and warm. His day's growth of beard scraped her chin and throat and the soft skin above her breasts, mixing pain and heat and sending them skittering down her nerves.

"God, Kate. So long. It's been so long."

She wanted to cry and laugh. Both ended in a gasp as he dragged the covers down and claimed her nipple with his mouth. Through cotton slip and knit chemise, the moist, wet heat brought a hard peak and stirred an answering flash of need lower still, where his hips pinned hers beneath the heavy quilts.

She moaned and arched her back, demanding more.

He shifted from her, then roughly threw the covers off entirely. They made a mountain of tumbled white beside her, a safe, warm wall that held her close against his body.

El reached down and grabbed the hem of her plain, practical slip, then dragged it up. She willingly raised her hips so he could drag it higher—to her waist, to just beneath her breasts—exposing her plain chemise and her practical drawers.

El paused, gray eyes gone stormy. The corners of his eyes crinkled as a slow, sexy smile claimed his mouth.

"That's damned ugly underwear, Kate," he said. Without letting go her slip, he bent and pressed a beard-rough kiss on the soft skin at the side of her navel where a gap between chemise and drawers showed bare flesh.

"You ought to wear silk and lace," he murmured, then slid her chemise up and pressed another kiss at the arch of her ribs.

Her lungs labored for air.

Still smiling, he shoved the garments higher. Up an inch, to the base of her breasts; another inch, and another, up to the aching peaks. The narrow band of lace at the hem of her slip scraped across her nipples, rough as his beard and just as tantalizing.

She tried to sit up so he could pull the garments off, but he pressed her back and claimed a nipple with his mouth. With the tip of the thumb and finger of his left hand, he squeezed and rubbed and tormented the other nipple. The callused fingers were dangerous weapons. His mouth was magic.

The muscles between her legs squeezed tight against a sudden, hungry stab of heat. She moaned and dug her hips in and squeezed tighter still, fighting the animal need for immediate fulfillment.

When she thought she would scream, he drew away, then pulled her up and slid the chemise and slip over her head. He tossed them away without a glance.

"Black lace," he said, and smiled. "Satin would be fine, too. Lots and lots of satin rubbing against that soft skin."

He leaned closer, so close he seemed to fill her world.

"Would you like that, Kate? Smooth, cool satin on your skin, and lots of lace?"

"Yes." She could hardly get the word past all the others fighting for release.

Take me! she wanted to say. *Now. Take me hard and fast. I need you, El. I need you to show me that you want me. That you need me as much as*

I need you. Please, please, please take me.

"Yes," she said instead. It was hardly a whisper, but he heard her, heard all the things she hadn't said.

He smiled and pulled back. His eyes devoured her. He studied her face and the tumble of her hair across the pillow. His gaze slid lower, to the base of her throat, her breasts, her belly. His chest rose and fell with his rapid, shallow breathing.

And then his gaze darkened, his attention narrowed.

Kate would swear they both stopped breathing as he reached for the bow-tied string at the waist of her white cotton drawers.

One gentle, deliberately slow tug. He drew one end of the string up, then let it fall. His finger slid under the half-opened knot and tugged it loose.

The muscles in Kate's abdomen contracted as the backs of his knuckles pressed against her belly. The single layer of cotton between them made the gesture that much more erotic.

She lifted her hips off the bed when he tugged her drawers down. At the simple movement, both of them caught their breath.

The drawers went sailing after the slip and chemise, unlamented.

Neither of them bothered to see where it fell. All Elliott's attention was fixed on her naked body. All her attention was fixed on him, as she watched him watch her.

Never had she known such power.

When she arched back into the welcoming softness of the feather bed, the movement thrust her breasts up and forward. Elliott licked his lips and breathed deeply. When she shifted her hips, his eyes widened involuntarily. When she deliberately moved her legs farther apart, opening herself to him, he stopped breathing altogether.

Heart pounding, Kate touched his gabardine-covered knee.

"You're still dressed," she said, and marveled at the throaty, blatant seduction in her voice.

She marveled at herself. Or, rather, the woman who wore her skin. This wasn't her, this naked, shameless creature who opened her body to El's gaze and gloried in her power over him.

And yet she had never felt so . . . complete, or so sure of herself. For the moment, shy Kate was gone and unlamented. In her place was a wanton who recognized the only truth between them—that Elliott Carstairs wanted her, and she wanted him.

Before she could sit up to help him undress, he'd swung off the bed and out of reach. His fingers, normally so quick and clever, fumbled at the buttons of his shirt and pants.

The heavy plaid work shirt was tossed aside with her underwear. His undershirt followed, then his pants and socks and long drawers. The metal fastenings on his suspenders clattered as they hit the floor.

At the sight of him, gloriously naked, Kate stopped breathing.

His body was no longer that of the slender youth she remembered. El had always been strong, but age and hard work had honed his muscles into a lean, blatantly masculine work of art.

His torso was darkly tanned, the line dividing burnished gold skin from more intimate white riding intriguingly low on his hips. Kate could picture how he'd look, shirtless under a merciless sun, his skin slicked with sweat, and envied any woman who had had the privilege of watching that perfect body as he'd worked.

But seeing him naked like this, his entire body strung tight with wanting her, was a glorious gift. His jutting erection was terrifying. The sight of it, and the thought of the pleasure it promised, sent fire licking through her veins.

It cost an effort to drag her gaze away from that blatant masculine weapon. She blushed to find El watching her as she studied him.

"Do I please you, Kate?" he asked. Softly, clearly sure of her answer.

She nodded mutely, licked lips suddenly gone dry.

He brushed a fingertip over the arch of her

knee, then, lightly, along the swell of her calf.

"Do you want me as much as I want you?" Softer still, yet she could hear the hunger vibrating in him.

"More." She opened her arms, inviting him in. "Please, El. Make love to me. *Now*."

Planting one knee on the bed, he bent over her, rolling her into him. His erection brushed against her thigh, spiking the need churning within her.

With a small, triumphant cry, she wrapped her arms around his neck and pulled him down.

Mouth to mouth, breast to breast, naked flesh to naked flesh—the heat fired her nerve endings and made her muscles clench with need. The mounded covers and yielding feather bed enfolded them, marking the boundaries of a world where only they existed and what was between them was enough to fill a universe.

With little gasps and greedy cries, they kissed, touched, tasted, then ventured further. The dark male scent of him filled her. The skin of her palms and fingers tingled with the feel of him. Her breasts, belly, and legs burned where their bodies met.

She was liquid heat and hope, he all hard strength and passion.

His hands claimed her. His touch seared across the sensitive skin of her belly and down her hip, over the jutting bone, then farther still, down to the clustered curls and the hot, wet secrets they hid.

His fingers plunged into her so abruptly she gasped and arched against the raw sensation that ripped through her.

He swallowed her cries, crushing his mouth down on hers, drinking her pleasure.

She twisted, arching into him, alive with a bright, hot need. Her nails dug into the hard muscles of his back, anchoring her even as she bucked against the insistent urging of his hand and mouth.

Release, when it came, was the flash point of the fire that raged within her. Before it could consume her utterly, he shifted, spread her legs and entered her with one hard thrust.

His cry matched hers. She arched into him, opening herself so he could fill her. For one moment, one brief, aching moment they hung suspended in raw sensation and the overwhelming shock of union.

And then she laughed, and gasped, and thrust her hips even harder against his, urging him on.

He needed no more than that. There was no gentleness left in him, and no mercy. She asked for none, and granted none in return.

All the years of empty, aching yearning burned away as if they'd never been. Her body remembered what he'd once taught it, and demanded what it had been denied so long.

269

He gave . . . everything, shifting to press himself harder against her, slowing to torment and tease her, then driving deep and hard, filling her and sending her soaring higher still. She climaxed, then climaxed again, shuddering at the onslaught of sensation, crying out his name, then sighing as she slid back down.

Her body trembled, yet ached for more. Tears burned her eyes, then slipped free.

He licked them away and murmured her name, over and over again.

"Kate," he said, as if in prayer. "Kate, Kate, Kate. My beautiful, beautiful Kate."

She drew a shaky breath. Her throat hurt, as if something big and grand and dangerous had stuck in it. She wanted to tell him she loved him, and wanted to hear him offer the same gift in return.

Instead, she wrapped herself even tighter around him, willing them to somehow be two halves of one safe whole.

"Don't stop," she said, and wondered whether he heard all the meaning she poured into those simple words.

He groaned and thrust again, then again and again. There was an almost desperate hunger in him now, as if he were afraid she'd slip away if he stopped. As if he wanted it all, and wanted it *now* because he wasn't sure there would ever be another chance to claim it.

She pushed the thought away and simply gave herself, *all* of herself, to what they had in this one bright moment.

When he climaxed, she cried out in joy, held tight while shudders racked his body, then, as the tension in his body ebbed, let go and went sailing after him.

Kate had no idea how long they lay there, his weight pressing her into the bed, their limbs tangled, their bodies replete. Dimly, as if from a great distance, she was aware of shadows dancing on the ceiling, cast by the guttering candle, and of the whispering sighs of the house around them.

Neither shadows nor furtive sighs had the power to frighten her. Not so long as El's strong arms still wrapped around her and his body covered hers. She felt light, unfettered, as if all things good were possible, and nothing bad.

It was only when El shifted onto his side, then pulled the tumbled covers over them both that she remembered she had felt like that once before, and she had been wrong.

They welcomed the dawn with a slow, gentle lovemaking that kept the world at bay a little longer. But not nearly long enough.

"I have to go," Kate murmured. Her head was pillowed on his shoulder, her every sense alive with the taste and scent and heat of him.

"Yes." He gently stroked his hand over her hair, but made no effort to let her go.

"Ruth and Gar will be up soon."

"Yes."

His touch was mesmerizing, but his gaze was fixed, not on her, but on the morning light that was sliding across the ceiling. She didn't have the courage to ask what he saw there.

"In fact, they're probably already awake." Her hand rested on his chest, right above his heart where she could feel its steady *thump-thump*.

"Probably."

"El . . ."

He breathed out—slowly, as if he were letting go of something he didn't want to lose—then reluctantly set her free.

Kate sat. Though she clutched the sheet to her chest, her shoulders were bare. Her tangled hair brushed against her skin, rousing wanton, tempting memories.

She forced the memories aside. A hundred questions tumbled through her mind, but she ignored them, too. What they'd shared these past hours was too recent. She didn't dare examine her feelings, or his, too closely. Not just yet.

El watched her. His piratical good looks seemed even more dangerous amid the mounded pillows and the tumbled, lace-edged sheets.

"I have to go," she said, and slid off the bed. If

she could, she would have dragged the covers with her to hide her nakedness. She snatched her dress off the chair where he'd laid it the night before, then pulled it over her head without bothering about underwear.

His smile when she tugged it into place made her blush, then hastily stoop to retrieve her underthings. After what they'd shared last night, there was something erotic, yet embarrassingly comic about having to gather one's clothes like this.

El didn't offer to help. Oblivious to his own nakedness, he shoved away the covers and sat up. The sight made her blush even more fiercely

"There's one of your socks," he said helpfully, pointing. "And your undershirt, whatever you call it, is over there."

"It's a chemise," she muttered, irritated, as she pulled it from beneath his rumpled pants.

"And that's a slip," he added smugly as she retrieved that, too.

She had to scramble to find everything. Her drawers were half-hidden under his discarded shirt, one sock kicked under the bed with her shoes. The absurdity of it all had her torn between laughing and swearing. Her cheeks stayed hot, though she tried to convince herself it was having to look under the bed that did it and not her intense awareness that she had not a stitch of clothing on under her prim, practical dress.

At the door she looked back to find him watching her. His smile was gone, and there was something in his expression that abruptly robbed the morning of its light.

Barefoot, with her underclothes clutched to her chest, Kate crept up the servants' stairs in the dark.

It was far colder upstairs than on the lower floor, and the sun had a harder time forcing its way through the grimy windows. Kate peered out and found the world encased in white under a dull gray sky.

There wasn't much hot water for her bath, either, and what there was quickly turned cold. Given the confusion of last night, El had probably forgotten to stoke the furnace and check the boiler.

She was in no mood to linger, anyway. In these stark surroundings, all that she'd managed to forget while El had held her came creeping back—Gar, the ladies' parlor, the memories of her mother's death. The images clung like cobwebs, impossible to brush away.

Even the thought of El and what they'd shared last night wasn't enough to drive away dark thoughts. One night of madness couldn't make up for ten years of doubt and recrimination.

Loving him wasn't enough. If he asked her to marry him, she'd have to refuse, no matter what her heart wanted. Marriage—a *good* marriage—

was based on more than love and sex. To work, it needed honesty and trust, too. Without those essential ingredients, they had nothing except lust and longing.

Then again, maybe that was all they'd ever had, anyway.

Kate shivered at the thought.

She was still shivering when she walked into the kitchen almost half an hour later, her hair neatly combed and the buttons on her good blue dress buttoned all the way down to her wrists and all the way up to the throat.

The dress was too good to wear for everyday, but it was the only one with a collar high enough to hide the scrapes on her throat where El's beard had rubbed. Face powder, carefully applied, had covered the marks on her cheeks. At least, Kate hoped it had. The last thing she wanted now was an inquisition from sharp-eyed Ruth.

At her entrance, Gar listlessly looked up from his plate. Kate couldn't bear to face him. His eyes, almost lost beneath the sagging, wrinkled lids, looked haunted.

He didn't seem to recognize her. After a moment's puzzled inspection, he gave up the effort to identify her and turned his attention back to the plate of cold bacon and congealing fried eggs.

Ruth, seated at the head of the table, eyed her

with suspicion. "You certainly took your sweet time getting up this morning."

"I—I didn't sleep well," Kate lied. She crossed to the stove and held her hands out to the welcome heat. She had to force herself to meet Ruth's gaze. Had the face powder been enough to erase the telltale marks, after all? "It's cold up there at the top of the house."

Ruth looked away first. "Don't play with your food like that, Gar. Here, have some more bread and butter."

Kate busied herself adding more wood to the stove.

"Is El up?" She said it casually, as if it didn't matter to her, one way or the other.

"Up and out a half hour since," Ruth said, her attention still on Gar. "Not everyone around here thinks they can sleep to all hours of the morning."

Kate dropped the stove lid back into place with a satisfying metallic clang.

After a moment, Ruth added, "If you stay, you could maybe have one of the bedrooms on the second floor." She made it sound as if the thought had only just occurred to her. "It would be warmer there. In fact, that one right by El's room even has a coal stove if I remember right."

Kate couldn't tell whether there was a jab hidden in there or not. Ruth might suspect they'd been lovers years ago, but she couldn't know about last night, could she?

"I'm not staying, Ruth." The admission hurt, but she'd worked it all out while she was dressing.

Last night she'd been lost, vulnerable, and El had offered the only comfort possible. This morning she'd seen things a lot more clearly, and the hard truth was that nothing had changed between them. She'd give herself another week to look for the diamonds, just until El's next trip into town, and then she'd leave. She really didn't have a choice.

She tried not to think about what could happen in the days until then . . . or the nights.

"I have to go back," was all she said. "I have a job." *But for how long?* a voice in her head demanded. "I can't afford to stay."

"Can't afford to stay! You can't afford to go! And don't tell me you've forgotten my offer, because I know you haven't."

Kate took a mug down from the cupboard. Fixing herself a cup of coffee provided a good excuse not to face the older woman's angry, accusing glare.

"No, I haven't forgotten."

"Well, then? Do you mean to tell me that you'd give up Grand House and all the money that will go with it? For a *job*? Whatever it is you do, you can't be earning more than just enough to pay the rent."

Ruth's thick gray brows collided in a frown. "What *is* it that you do there, anyway? You've never said."

"Because you never asked and never showed any sign you wanted to know."

"I'm asking now."

Kate added an extra teaspoonful of sugar. Ruth's coffee was always thick and black as tar. "I'm a clerk in a bookstore."

"A clerk? In a bookstore? Might as well be a maid! Why would you want to go back to *that?*"

"Because I do." She took a sip and grimaced. To cover the grimace, she took another sip. "My life is in New York now, not here."

So why did it hurt so much to admit it?

The sound of a car pulling up outside the back door made them both freeze. In the two weeks that Kate had been here, they hadn't had one visitor, not even from the closest neighbors.

Ruth glanced at her, then at Gar.

"Give me a moment to get Gar cleaned before you go opening that," she snapped, pulling her husband's plate away in spite of his querulous objections. "Don't wiggle, Gar. You've got egg on your chin, and we have company."

Chapter Fifteen

By the time Kate finally stepped out onto the back porch, Gar's face and hands were washed, his hair combed, and he'd been placated for the loss of his eggs with a hunk of bread and butter. Ruth hadn't even bothered to tuck back the strands of her own iron gray hair that had come free of the net she wore or to straighten the big apron that covered her practical gray dress. It was Gar she worried about, not herself.

The car was a big Chevy. It took Kate a moment to place the tall, reed-thin man who emerged from behind the wheel. When she did, her stomach knotted painfully.

"Sheriff . . . Neumann, isn't it?" she said, grateful that the screens hid her face a little.

The sheriff swept off his hat to reveal a head gone a lot balder than when she'd seen him last, locking Elliott back in his jail cell at the County Courthouse.

If he shared the same memory, he gave no sign of it. "That's right. And you're Miss Mannville, if I'm not mistaken. Gertrude's granddaughter. I heard you'd come back." It didn't sound as if he approved.

"Yes. Won't you please come in?" She swung the screen door wide.

The last thing she wanted was to invite the man in, but good manners required she offer him a cup of coffee and a bite to eat. You didn't keep a visitor standing out in the cold even if he had jailed the man you loved for murder ten years before.

She could have sworn his gaze skewered the back of her head as she led him into the kitchen.

"You can hang your coat and hat here. I'll get you some coffee. After that long drive out, you must be freezing. Town's so far, and cold as it is." She was babbling, but she couldn't stop herself. "Aunt Ruth? It's Sheriff Neumann."

"I can see that for myself." Ruth didn't bother to get up from the table. "What brings you out on a day like today, Sheriff?"

Neumann nodded, unfazed by her hostility. "Mrs. Skinner."

He'd taken off his hat but still wore his coat, which meant he wasn't planning to stay long. His gaze swung to Gar.

A shadow crossed his face. Not shock, Kate decided. Disappointment, perhaps, though that didn't seem right, either.

Gar, oblivious to the intrusion, was industriously tearing holes in his bread, then greedily stuffing the torn-out bits in his mouth, one after another, like a squirrel gathering nuts for the winter.

"Gar?" The sheriff hesitated, then raised his voice. "Mr. Skinner?"

"He can hear just fine," Ruth snapped. "That doesn't mean he'll pay any attention, though. Not while he's eating."

"Oh." Neumann shifted uncertainly. His attempt at a smile came off more as a grimace of distaste. "I heard he'd . . . gone downhill. Didn't realize it was quite so far."

Ruth's only response was a sullen silence.

Neither seemed to notice that Gar had abruptly tossed the bread aside. His gaze was riveted on the sheriff, his face screwed up as if he were straining to remember something that lay just beyond his reach.

Neumann shifted his grip on his hat and scanned the kitchen. "Actually, I came to talk to Elliott Carstairs. He around?"

Kate felt the muscles of her back tighten like ropes suddenly pulled taut.

"Should be," Ruth said. "I don't waste my time

dogging his every footstep. What do you want with him?"

"Talk to him. That's all. Just talk."

"Seems to me you did enough of that ten years ago."

The sheriff's cold gaze locked with her belligerent one. "Some would say I didn't do anywhere near enough back then. Not of talking nor anything else."

Kate couldn't stifle a small gasp of fear.

The sheriff glanced at her in warning, then back at Ruth. "Right now, all I want to do is talk to him."

Ruth heaved to her feet. "Fine. Talk to him. Katherine Mary will get him for you. Right now, *I* need to take care of my husband."

To everyone's embarrassment, Gar chose that moment to be difficult. When Ruth tried to help him up, he kicked over the chair and tried to get free of her.

"Got to tell Elliott," he said, staring at Neumann, wild-eyed. "Got to run. Got to hide."

"Don't you worry about El," Ruth said sternly, trying to draw his attention back to her. "He's not running anywhere."

Gar was having none of it. "Got to. Tell El. Tell him—"

"Gar!" Ruth gave him a shake. "Don't you worry about El. You hear me? He can take care of himself."

"El?" said Gar.

"That's right. El can take care of himself."

The conviction in her voice must have reached through the haze that gripped his mind. With one last wild-eyed glance over his shoulder, he reluctantly allowed his wife to lead him away, still muttering.

Neither Kate nor the sheriff moved an inch until the sound of the parlor door closing at the far end of the hall snapped the tension between them. Their individual sighs of relief came in chorus.

Kate was the first to speak.

"You want some of that coffee while you wait, Sheriff?" She didn't feel any obligation to warn him of the corrosive effects of Ruth's brew. Times like this, there were limits to hospitality. "It shouldn't take long to find El for you."

"No need to trouble yourself, ma'am. I'll find him." Neumann settled his hat back on his head, adjusting the brim just so. "I assume he's out in the barn?"

As if to answer his question, the back door slammed. Heavy footsteps crossed the porch.

"Actually, he's right here," Kate said in relief.

The door swung open violently, and El stalked into the room.

Her relief died the moment she caught sight of his face. Elliott Carstairs was already gearing up for war.

283

He slammed the door shut but didn't bother to take off his coat.

"Neumann. I thought that was your car outside."

"Carstairs." The sheriff met El's hostile gaze with a coolly assessing one of his own. His voice never rose above a polite conversational level, but Kate could hear the steel in it. "We need to talk."

El's nostrils flared. "I don't have anything to say to you."

"There's two ways we can do it," Neumann continued, as calmly as if El hadn't spoken. "We can talk here, sit at this kitchen table like rational adults, or—" his voice hardened, and this time it carried an unmistakable threat—"we can go into town and talk at the jail. Now, which would you like it to be?"

For a moment, Kate had the feeling El would choose the latter. Ten years earlier he might have acted on that preference and dared the sheriff to try to haul him into town. Now, after a moment's struggle, he simply shrugged, then gestured to the kitchen table.

"Take a chair, Neumann. You may be determined to talk, but I'm not going to stand here while you do it." He crossed to the stove. "Want some coffee?"

Neither one of them appeared to notice when

Kate slipped into the servants' stairwell and closed the door behind her.

Almost closed the door. She left it open a crack, not enough to be noticeable, but enough so that she would be able to hear everything that was said if she kept quiet and really listened.

Making no effort to be quiet, she climbed to the second floor, waited a minute, then slipped her shoes off and quietly slunk back down to press her ear to the crack. She couldn't see either man, but their voices came through clearly.

". . . stay away from her, Carstairs. We don't need anymore trouble around here."

Who was the sheriff talking about? Kate wondered, though she thought, unhappily, that she already knew the answer. The mental picture of El leaving his woman friend to take her into his bed a few hours later made bile rise in her throat.

"If Della says I touched her, she's lying." El's denial sounded like the warning growl of a cornered lion.

"She's not saying that, but folks are talking. People don't forget."

"Or forgive." The growl was reduced to an angry, resentful mutter.

"No?" The sheriff seemed to consider that. "Doesn't make much difference, one way or the other. Fact is, you stepped over the line. Any other man, I might overlook it. But not with you. Not with something like this. I can't afford to."

The only response was silence.

A chair scraped against the floor. The sheriff, she thought, but couldn't be sure.

"Whatever your intentions," he said, "I'd suggest you forget it. *And* her. You got to come into town, you do what you have to do, what any farmer would do. But you don't step so much as one toe over the line. You hear me?"

More silence, then the sound of booted feet crossing the floor, the outer door opening.

"Just so you remember . . . I'm watching you, Carstairs. There's still a murder I've got to account for, and one day, maybe one day soon, I'm going to have my man. And when I do, there won't be a hell hot enough to hold him."

By the time Kate had worked up the courage to emerge from her hiding place, the sheriff was long gone, and El had vanished. Though the kitchen was empty, she would swear the animosity of the encounter between the two lingered in the air like smoke, tainting everything.

Even though she knew Ruth would complain of the waste, Kate threw out the coffee on the stove. She needed something strong and hot, but drinkable, and tea simply wouldn't do. Her stomach was churning too much to even think of eating.

The mindless task of grinding more beans, then filling the pot and setting it to perk kept her hands busy while her thoughts raced.

She tried not to think about El and that woman in town, but the images filled her head anyway. El and her, making love. El, angry, violent. Violent enough to frighten her, remind her of his past and of what he was accused. Violent enough to send her running to the sheriff in a panic.

Violent enough to kill?

Kate's heart and soul rebelled against the thought, yet still there was that doubt. Could he kill? *Had* he?

She remembered how his hands had closed around her throat that first day when she'd walked into the yard and the brutally efficient way he'd slaughtered that chicken. She thought of the anger in him whenever she'd demanded the truth, and the way he looked at her, hard and distrustful, as if he were judging her, and, somehow, constantly finding her lacking.

And always, always there was his stubborn, angry silence.

Taken all together, it wasn't enough to condemn a man, but it wasn't near enough to erase all her doubts, either.

Nor was it enough to make her forget how he'd made love to her last night, or how much she'd needed him and how much he'd needed her. For a while she'd been able to pretend that the world had gone away, that it was just the two of them, and the good and honest feelings that had always existed between them that neither had ever found the courage to put into words. But only for a little while because the world and its hard truths and harder doubts had come crashing back quick enough, just as she'd known they would.

And then there was the sheriff—sharp-faced, intelligent, and dangerous. He'd driven all the way out from town to confront El and warn him away. Would he have done that if there hadn't been real cause for it? Neumann might be a small-town sheriff, but he was no fool. Ten years earlier he'd resisted pressure from townsfolk who'd wanted a hanging or, failing that, a speedy trial and swift justice that would eventually put Elliott Carstairs and a rope in their hands anyway. In the end, he'd let El go for lack of evidence, but all that proved was that he was a man who believed in the law, not necessarily in El's innocence.

Ten years had passed, but he clearly hadn't forgotten Louisa Bannister's brutal death, and neither, it seemed, had the people of Mannville.

Her troubled thoughts were shattered by a crash from the front of the house, then a sharply raised voice.

Kate set down her cup and hurried along the hall. The door to Ruth and Gar's room was closed, but as she got closer, Kate could hear voices, quieter now, but still sharp with tension.

She was about to knock when another crash came from within.

"Gar, stop that! Do you hear me? Stop that!" Ruth's voice was shriller than Kate had ever heard it, almost panicked.

Her answer was another crash, then another.

Repressing the urge to simply run away, Kate eased the door open enough so she could peer around the edge, but not so far that Gar could shove past her if that was what he wanted.

The old man stood in front of the fireplace, a porcelain shepherdess held high in both hands. It was one Gertrude had always been particularly fond of, perhaps because it had come from Europe and cost so much. Kate remembered it as a particularly horrid, overwrought thing that was a nightmare to dust. Shards of other porcelain ornaments that had once adorned the mantle littered the floor at his feet.

"Please put it down, Gar," Ruth said, a note of pleading in her voice this time.

Her back was to Kate. She was so intent on her husband that she hadn't noticed the open door behind her.

Gar had, though. His face lit at the prospect of another witness. He glanced back at his wife, then, with a sly, triumphant grin, dashed the shepherdess on the unyielding slate of the hearth. The shepherdess exploded, sending bits of glazed porcelain flying everywhere.

"Gar!"

He snatched another, smaller figurine off the mantle—there weren't many left to grab—and threw that one down, too.

When he reached for yet another, Ruth leaped to stop him. With deliberate malice, Gar threw the figurine at her instead of the floor.

Ruth flung up her hand too late. The figurine struck her on the temple, drawing blood. She cried out, grabbed for the arm of a chair, but slipped on the scattered shards and went to her knees.

Her husband stood on the hearth just out of her reach and smiled.

Horrified, Kate shut the door behind her and, keeping a wary eye on Gar, crossed to Ruth's side.

"Aunt Ruth? Are you all right? Let me help you."

With an angry hiss of pain, Ruth batted her away and struggled to her feet alone. Blood streamed from a cut on her temple and stained her torn skirt where her knees had landed on one of the jagged shards, but she seemed unaware of any of it.

"Get out!" Beneath the blood, her face was a mask of frustrated fury. "Damn you! This is all your fault! None of this would have happened if you hadn't come back. *None* of it!"

"But—"

"Get out! Do you hear me? Get *out!*" Ruth lunged at her, fists flailing.

Bewildered, hands up to ward off a blow, Kate dodged out of reach. "Aunt Ruth? If you would only—"

"*Get out!*"

Kate fled to the only refuge she knew: She went in search of El.

She found him in the stables that, years before, had been converted into a garage. He had pulled the old truck into the concrete-floored bay that had been converted to a workshop and was in the process of gutting the mechanical beast.

He was standing at the workbench now, intently prying into some mysterious marvel he'd wrenched out of the tractor's guts. If he'd noticed her come in or felt the draft of cold air at her entrance, he gave no sign of it.

Uncertain of her welcome, Kate hovered by the door, studying her surroundings.

Grease- and dirt-caked parts were laid out on the floor in some incomprehensible order that only another mechanic would understand. A 1926 calendar with a fading colored picture of the Mannville grain elevator hung askew on the far wall, a yellowing companion to the rusting tools and unidentifiable parts and pieces of metal haphazardly hung on hooks set into the wall. Beneath it, a grease-stained workbench bore more parts and tools that looked as if they might actually be used. A potbellied stove warmed the space, fogging the windows as the wood fire contentedly crackled and snapped and covered the pervasive smell of grease with the sweeter scent of burning wood.

She'd never spent much time here, preferring the living animals to the inanimate machines, but this workshop had been one of El's favorite haunts. He hadn't had much interest in the crops and animals that were the heart of a farm, but he had loved everything mechanical and had driven Gertrude's mechanics to distraction with his constant questions and demands to be allowed to help. It seemed right that he should have come here in search of whatever solace an unspeaking, uncaring machine might offer. Machines, after all, couldn't wound a human heart.

Just the sight of him was enough to start a dangerous, longing ache inside her. She wasn't crazy enough to try to ease that ache, though, no matter what her own heart kept trying to tell her. Even here in a world where she had never intruded there was a tension in him that warned her away.

Earlier, in the kitchen with the sheriff, he'd been hostile and angry. Now he just seemed horribly distant, so far out of her reach that she felt she could have stretched out a hand and touched New York more easily than she could touch him.

He had taken his coat off and rolled his shirt sleeves up to his elbows. His suspenders made a *Y* on his back, emphasizing the width of his broad shoulders and the way his body tapered to a slim waist. His gabardine pants—the same pants he'd flung aside so eagerly last night—fit smoothly across the lean perfection of his hips and down his long, powerful legs. Even the heavy work boots seemed somehow less clumsy when he was the one wearing them.

Last night with its mix of horror and wonder suddenly seemed a hundred years ago.

The thought saddened her and reminded her of the shock that had sent her running to find El in the first place.

Only now that she was here, she didn't know what to say, or what she expected him to do. Ruth hadn't wanted her help. It wasn't very likely she'd want Elliott's, either. And what could he do anyway except tie Gar in a chair until this fit, whatever it was, had passed?

"El?" she said softly. Too softly. He didn't budge.

"Elliott?"

He stiffened at that but didn't turn around. "What?"

"Gar's being . . . difficult." That wasn't what she wanted to say. "I—I think Ruth needs you."

"Does she? Did she say so?"

"No, but—"

293

"Then let her handle it. Gar's her husband, after all."

He still hadn't looked around. He turned the grease-encrusted part he held, peered at something, then set down the wrench he was holding and picked up a screwdriver.

They might as well have been discussing the weather, for all the emotion in his voice.

Kate edged around the truck. "The sheriff's visit upset him, I think. He's . . . throwing things. Breaking all Gertrude's porcelains."

He glanced at her, his expression unreadable, then turned back to his work. "Given Gertrude's taste in decoration, I wouldn't call that any great loss."

The callousness of the remark roused Kate's ire. Abandoning caution, she stomped across to the workbench.

"Did you hear what I said? Gar's upset. He's *angry*. He hit Ruth in the head with one of those figurines, hard enough to draw blood."

El slammed the heavy part down on the workbench so hard the tools rattled. When he finally turned to face her squarely, his eyes were dark as thunder clouds and just as threatening.

"Gar's angry, is he? Well, let me tell you something—*I'm* angry. I'm also bigger and stronger than he is, which makes me a hell of a lot more dangerous. Did you think of *that* when you came running in here?"

Kate flinched and backed up. She couldn't help herself.

"Of course you didn't," he snarled, answering his own question. "Gar gets upset, Ruth gets hurt, and *I'm* expected to settle it all?"

She thought he was going to hit something. Instead, he threw back his head and laughed. The sound vibrated with bitter fury.

"God damn, that's a good jest!" he cried, and drove the screwdriver point first into the workbench like a knife.

Truly frightened now, Kate eyed the still-quivering screwdriver, then the man.

He didn't seem to remember she existed. He just stood there, breathing hard and glaring at the screwdriver, his half-raised hands balled into fists.

"El?" She touched his arm. His skin was hot, the dark, springing hairs insufficient to soften the muscles that were strung tight as steel cables. "Elliott?"

Like a swimmer coming up for air after being down too long, he gasped, then shook himself and sagged against the workbench.

"Hell," he said tiredly. "What does it matter? After all these years, you'd think I'd be used to it, wouldn't you?"

"Used to what?"

He closed his eyes and tilted his head back wearily. "To the accusations. To the way people look at me. To this nagging sense of guilt."

Guilt? Kate felt something in her shrivel.

"Then you did kill Louisa." It came out as barely more than a whisper. It wasn't a question. She felt hollow, suddenly, utterly empty.

And yet the doubt was still there, gnawing at her. Not El. It couldn't possibly be El.

He opened his eyes, focused on her.

"Is that what you want me to say, Kate?" He sounded exhausted. "If I say yes, will that make you happy?"

"Don't be a fool."

"I already am. I thought we proved that long ago."

His pain was almost a physical entity, and it stabbed as deeply through her as it did through him. The bitterness only made the open wounds hurt more.

She stared into his eyes, looking for the truth he'd always denied her. She didn't find it. Though he was so close she could have touched him if she'd dared, he had withdrawn inside himself, safely out of reach.

"You heard, didn't you?" he said. It was an accusation, not a question. "You sat on those stairs and listened to every word we said, Neumann and me."

"Yes." There was no sense in lying now.

His mouth twisted. "So now you know."

"What?"

"That people are afraid of me." He studied her. His lips thinned, curved into a sneer. "Tell me, Kate. Do I frighten you?"

She hesitated, nodded. "Yes."

"Then why do you keep coming back?"

Because I love you!

"I don't know."

He grabbed her chin, forcing her face around to the light. His fingers were strong as steel and just as unforgiving.

Kate started, tried to pull away, but he held her like a trap holds a frightened mouse in spite of the creature's struggles. His eyes seemed to bore straight through to her soul.

With a growl of disgust, he let her go.

"You lie, Kate. You're always demanding the truth from me, yet you won't give it back again."

Tears started in her eyes, but she couldn't say a word because he was right. She *had* lied, while he had simply refused to answer either way. Of the two, whose was the greater crime?

"There's nothing between Della and me." El didn't look at her when he said it. "I just—We talked, that's all. Just . . . talked."

Kate couldn't tell whether he was telling the truth, or lying.

She scrubbed at her chin and cheek where he had touched her and wished she had the handkerchief that Gertrude had insisted a true lady always carried with her. Her fingers came away

297

black. God knew what her face looked like, streaked with grime.

With an effort, she forced her thoughts back to the trouble that had brought her here in the first place.

"None of that matters anyway," she said. "It's Uncle Gar we have to worry about right now, not you and me."

"Uncle Gar!" His gaze fell on the screwdriver. With one powerful move, he wrenched it out of the workbench. The steel point gleamed wickedly in the light.

Kate flinched. "Please, El. For Gar's sake. You *have* to come."

He glared at the screwdriver, then at the truck part he'd been working on as if he expected to find an answer buried under the accumulated grease and dirt. With a snarl, he tossed the screwdriver aside.

"All right, dammit. *All right!* I don't know what I can do, but I'll come."

He wiped his hands on a grease-stained rag, his movements jerky and fierce. When he was done, he angrily tossed the rag aside, then held his hands out in front of him, fingers spread wide. The rag hadn't done much more than take off the worst of the grime, then rub the rest into his skin, but Kate knew it wasn't the dirt that troubled him.

He didn't offer to wipe away the black he'd left on her face.

With a quick check of the stove to close the dampers down and keep the fire burning low and steady, El snatched up his coat and stalked out the door. Kate had to jog to keep up with him as he strode toward Grand House. Neither spoke a word until they stepped into the kitchen and were greeted by the sound of something heavy shattering.

El held up a warning hand. "Wait here."

She was two steps behind him when he reached the closed door of the second-best parlor.

The carnage was appalling. A couple of the figurines had survived with only minor damage because they'd landed on a carpet. The rest were scattered in pieces about the floor like mosaic tiles an artist had flung down and then forgotten.

The man responsible for the destruction stood in front of the windows, a mad smile on his lips and a small, very ugly porcelain terrier in his hands. At the sight of them, he raised the thing over his head, then flung it down, hard.

Instead of shattering, the terrier broke into three pieces. The head ended with the chin pointing skyward and the bulging porcelain eyes, like the eyes of a corpse, blankly staring at nothing.

Like her mother's eyes, Kate thought, and shuddered.

Ruth was slumped in Gar's favorite chair, head bowed, her big, heavy-knuckled hands limp in her lap. Her face was dangerously pale compared to the darkening blood at her temple, and she seemed smaller somehow, as if she were folding in on herself.

She looked, suddenly, old and tired and defeated.

"I kept the lamps out of his reach," she said dully without looking up. "It was the best I could do. I didn't bother about the rest. He wasn't going to stop no matter what I said."

El's heavy work boots crunched on the broken pottery as he crossed to Gar. At his approach, the old man shrank back against the wall, hands up to ward him off.

El stopped three feet away. "You want to tell me why you broke all of Aunt Ruth's decorations, Uncle Gar?"

The old man's chin came up. His eyes narrowed. "They ain't Ruth's. They're Gertrude's. Ruth don't keep useless stuff like that."

"So why did you break Gertrude's things, Uncle Gar?" El was as patient and calm as ever, but there was no warmth in his voice, no gentleness.

Gar glanced over his shoulder as if to reassure himself no one was listening, then leaned toward El and lowered his voice to a theatrical whisper.

"She's a witch, that one. Eat a man alive if you give her a chance. You remember that, boy, and be careful. Stay clear of women who'll eat your soul."

"Gertrude's dead, Uncle Gar. What I want to know now is, why did you break all this stuff?"

"Had to. Had to throw the hounds off the scent."

"What hounds?"

"Neumann. Folks." Gar's face took on a crafty look, like a fox sniffing out danger. "Sheriff was here this morning, boy. You hear?"

El's jaw tightened. Kate could see it from halfway across the room. "I heard."

Again Gar glanced over his shoulder. "Got to run."

"I'm not running, Uncle Gar." El took a step toward Gar.

The old man tensed. El stopped.

"*Nobody's* running," he insisted.

"Got to, boy. Got to get away. Now's the time, while they're still picking through this mess, hoping they're going to find it, wondering which way to go. Got to get *away*."

"Where?"

Gar waved his hand. "Away." His eyes narrowed again. "They can't find a man, they can't ask questions. You hear what I'm saying?"

"I hear, Uncle Gar."

Kate watched them, puzzled. Obviously, Neumann's visit this morning had dredged up memories of Louisa Bannister's murder. Just as

301

obviously, Gar believed in Elliott's guilt and wanted him to run. But why? Was it just the natural confusion of an old man's faltering mind, or had Gar known something he hadn't admitted to ten years ago?

She thought of last night, of Gar's strange behavior that seemed to indicate he'd actually seen her mother dangling from that chandelier even though he couldn't possibly have done so. This morning she'd almost convinced herself it was just his mind playing tricks, that what he'd heard, all those years ago, had somehow become real for him.

Maybe that was all that was happening here, but she didn't think so. El wouldn't be responding the way he was otherwise.

Gar leaned forward, peering into El's face. "You wouldn't tell them, would you, boy?"

"Make him shut up, El!"

Ruth's outburst made them all stare.

Angrily waving aside Kate's offer of assistance, she struggled to her feet. "No sense in listening to that drivel. The sheriff's visit set him off, that's all. He's so confused he doesn't know what he's saying."

El eyed her with unmistakable hostility. "Or maybe he's making a little too much sense?"

"Don't be a fool."

"I already am one. I proved that ten years ago." The bitterness in his voice made Ruth flinch.

Gar was listening to their angry exchange and growing more and more agitated. He was also paler than he'd been a few minutes earlier, and his hands were shaking. Watching him, Kate felt her heart twist.

Stepping gingerly over the strewn bits of porcelain, she worked her way closer to him. Engrossed in their own quarrel, Ruth and El ignored her.

"Uncle Gar?" she said, softly, so as not to startle him.

Gar eyed her doubtfully. "Kate? Little Katie?"

"Yes, Uncle Gar. It's me, Kate." She took his arm. "Why don't you come with me? There's your favorite chair, right by the fire where it's warm. See?"

He looked around, clearly bewildered. The demented energy that had driven him earlier was gone now, leaving him looking frailer than ever. His gaze fixed on El and Ruth.

"What about El?"

"El's fine," she soothed. "Why don't you sit here and wait for him?"

"Got to run," he muttered, but when she tugged on his arm, he shambled after her, slippered feet scuffling through the shards littering the floor.

Beneath his shirt and undershirt, his arm was fragile as a twig. If she hadn't seen his rampage

303

for herself, she'd wouldn't have believed him capable of any of it.

Despite her concern, as she settled him in his chair and tucked a throw around his legs, she found her attention drifting from him to the muted, angry exchange between Ruth and El.

"Just how much do you expect me to take, Ruth?" El demanded. "Your threats won't work. We both know that. And there sure as hell isn't anything left for me to stay for, is there?"

"You have to stay," Ruth insisted, clearly desperate. "He *loved* you."

"*Did* he?"

"He did. He still does. Somewhere in that muddled mind of his, he does. God knows I never understood why," she added bitterly. "It wasn't as if you were the sweet, loving child we'd dreamed of having."

El's upper lip curled. "No, I sure as hell wasn't. But you see, I knew right from the start you didn't want me."

"Gar did!"

"That's what I used to think, too."

"You were like a son to him," Ruth insisted.

"*Was* I?"

"Don't you get sarcastic! He did his best. Him and me both, we tried. God knows you weren't the easiest child to raise, yet not an ounce of gratitude did we get from you for all our sacrificing."

"Oh, I was grateful, Ruth. I was damned grateful. But gratitude wears a little thin when a man's sitting in a jail cell listening to a mob outside calling for a rope."

Kate could have sworn Ruth's face went paler still, as if the last of the blood in her veins had suddenly drained away. When she remained silent, El cursed and turned to go.

The porcelain terrier's head lay in his path. He stared at it for a moment as if he sought to read the secrets hidden behind those shiny painted eyes, then deliberately crushed it beneath his boot.

The sound of porcelain grating against wood as he ground the pieces into dust sent a shiver down Kate's back.

Head up, face frozen in a furious mask, he stalked past her without so much as a word or a glance at Gar, who was cowering in his chair and starting to cry.

Chapter Sixteen

El didn't come in for supper though Kate rang the bell and called his name, over and over again. She didn't go out to find him.

Gar, Ruth had said, was sleeping and would probably sleep through the night. Kate had helped Ruth undress him and tuck him into bed. He'd been difficult to handle, like a confused, fussy child who doesn't know what he wants but is very determined to have it. Nothing he'd said after El's angry departure had made any sense at all.

They hadn't bothered cleaning up the mess on the floor, just cleared a path through the wreckage and left the rest for tomorrow.

It was a cheerless meal. For once Ruth said nothing about Kate's lack of appetite, perhaps because she had none herself. Neumann's visit and Gar's rage lay between them, a mountain they both tried to pretend didn't exist.

When she left, Ruth made a point of shutting the door between the kitchen and the rest of the house. Kate didn't object, even though she was left with all the dishes. She couldn't face going upstairs to her cold, solitary bed just yet.

But she didn't want to be alone, either.

As she worked, she kept glancing over her shoulder, thinking she heard footsteps on the ground outside, a hand on the kitchen door. She wondered what she would say to El when he came in.

He never came.

Kate would swear she could still feel the marks he'd left on her skin as clearly as if he'd branded her with his touch.

Restless, she took the lamp into her great-grandfather's study and scanned the bookshelves, looking for something to read. There wasn't a lot that appealed to her. Charles Mannheim hadn't approved of fiction much. In the end, she took Henry James's *English Hours*, then wondered why she'd bothered. But James's England had the advantage of being far from North Dakota, and his ponderous prose forced her to pay attention to the words on the page, not the doubts crashing around in her head.

She wondered what Ruth was doing and realized she had no idea how the older woman spent her time. Did she read? Sew? She'd never done either when Kate was growing up, but then, she hadn't had the time. There'd been too much to do on the little farm she and Gar had worked for Gertrude and never enough time to do it. But now that all she had to worry about was Gar, how did she fill the long, lonely hours shut up in that overheated, claustrophobic parlor with a man whose mind had gone?

As much as she disliked Ruth, Kate couldn't help pitying the woman. Which was a waste of time: Ruth would far prefer her hatred.

An hour dragged by, then two. There wasn't even the ticking of a clock to keep her company. All Gertrude's clocks had been left to run down, as if her death had drained the energy from the house and time no longer mattered. The house's silence magnified the crackling of the fire and the whisper of each page she turned so that Kate jumped every time a log shifted.

She got up only to stoke the stove and fix herself a cup of tea. Chiding herself for being a fool, she stopped at the windows over the sink to see whether she could catch a light, some sign that El was out there close at hand.

The windows reflected her image and the image of the room behind her but revealed nothing of the world outside. It was as if the world had disappeared and Grand House and all within it had been cut adrift, cast out of space and time to wander endlessly in the dark.

Shivering despite the stove's warmth, she settled herself in Gar's chair and picked up her book again.

Where was El? Why hadn't he returned? Had he left? Had she missed the sound of the truck going past? Or had he slipped past her somehow? Could he even now be waiting for her upstairs, wondering why she hadn't come?

Twice she put the book down, determined to go in search of him. Twice she picked it up again, afraid.

She thought of the book he'd been reading when she'd awakened last night. Trollope still seemed such an odd choice, but Elliott Carstairs had always had the ability to surprise her.

She thought of his room, there at the top of the stairs, and the deep feather bed, and the soft old linen sheets.

She thought of his hands, so strong and yet so gentle. Magic hands with long, shapely fingers that could coax a recalcitrant engine into life, or drive a woman's body to the point where pleasure and pain blended into ecstasy.

But with those thoughts came the memory of his hands wrapped around her throat that first day, his eyes wells of ice and fury.

She pushed that memory aside. Elliott's were not the hands of a murderer. They could not be.

309

She thought of his body naked beside hers and felt a yearning heat start within her.

She loved him. Amid all the confusion, that was the one true thing to which she could cling.

But should she? Was she wrong to try?

Was love really enough for her to ignore every doubt and forgive every failing? Could it really be that easy? Or was she simply deceiving herself because she wanted to believe?

Uncertain, she listened to the silence.

There were no answers in it. She supposed she was a fool for hoping there might be.

Without the wind to torment it, Grand House slept. The fire in the stove beside her had died down—she'd have to remember to add more wood before she went up to bed. The furnace in the basement had gone quiet. She wondered whether she ought to check it since El showed no sign of returning, but she couldn't bear the thought of navigating those narrow stairs or facing that dark, dank basement on her own. Not tonight.

Not even a whisper came from the front of the house.

Any other time, she might have welcomed the silence. Tonight, it set her on edge. It was as if everything had simply stopped and was now waiting breathlessly for whatever would happen next.

*   *   *

Another hour passed. Kate fought against encroaching sleep and James's stupefying prose. El seemed to have vanished off the face of the earth.

At last, she gave in and admitted he wasn't coming. Whatever door had opened between them last night was once again locked and barred, and he was keeping as far away from her as possible. The admission was a defeat as sharp as her fruitless search for the diamonds.

Reluctantly, she stoked the stove and turned the dampers down, then picked up the book, intending to return it to its place. The hall was dark, and no more than a trace of light showed beneath the door of the second-best parlor. But there was light at the top of the grand staircase, faint and beckoning.

Kate studied that faint glow uncertainly. Her first thought was that El had slipped in unnoticed. Her second, that ghosts had claimed the house.

Chiding herself for her foolishness, she set the book and her lamp down on a hall table, then cautiously climbed the stairs. The first door at the top of the stair, the door to Gertrude's room, stood wide, letting lamplight flood this end of the upper hall.

Kate stood in the open doorway, stunned. Ruth had emptied every closet and armoir in the room, then strewn their contents around the room in mad disorder. Drawers had been tipped out onto the floor. Fur coats mixed with high-necked, long-sleeved nightgowns. Beaded evening gowns were half-buried beneath more conservative daily wear. Shoes lay everywhere as if they'd been tried on, one by one, then kicked off and forgotten. At the very top of the mounded clothes on the bed, a fox throw that Gertrude had often worn around her neck glared at the room, its glass eyes virulently disapproving.

Hats were tumbled on the floor or flung atop any convenient knob. A dark red cloche dangled from the top of one of the bedposts. A French lady in a porcelain gown bobbed her eternal curtsey beneath a hat trimmed with pheasant feathers. A broad-brimmed black hat had toppled an unlit lamp off a table and onto the floor. The lamp had shattered, soaking the expensive Persian carpet in oil. The smell of the oil was sharp despite the heavy, cloying scent of perfume that also hung on the air.

On the dressing table, bottles of creams and pots of powder stood open. Powder coated the polished wood and dribbled onto the floor. In the middle of the confusion, a jewel box Kate had never seen before stood open, its glittering contents spilling over the edges and heedlessly scattered on the spilled powder.

In the midst of the disaster, Ruth stood before the cheval glass, preening.

She'd thrown off her usual sensible gray dress.

It lay in a heap on the floor with her sensible underwear and sensible stockings and sensible black shoes, all of them kicked aside and forgotten.

In their place, Ruth wore one of Gertrude's finest gowns, a half-sleeved, beaded silk creation with a low-cut bosom and sweeping train that Gertrude had once worn to some elegant affair at the governor's mansion, then never wore again. She'd stuck an egret plume into her hair and wrapped a strand of pearls around her usual tight, gray bun, then drenched herself in powder and perfume. Rouge made two incongruously bright pink blotches on her cheeks.

The effort to look the *grande dame* had been wasted. Ruth was as tall as Gertrude and almost as full-bosomed, but her body showed the effects of years of hard work and broiling suns. Gertrude's skin had been fine and white and soft, elegant despite the wrinkles that had come with age. Ruth's skin was a blotchy, weathered brown where the sun had touched, a pasty yellow-white where it had not. No amount of powder could disguise the line between brown and white that the low-cut gown revealed, nor could the half-sleeves and elbow-length white gloves hide the ropy muscles under the sagging flesh. Even the gloves betrayed her—beneath the straining white cloth, the gnarly joints of her work-hardened hands showed clearly.

All this Kate took in at a glance. But what caught and held her attention was not the room or Ruth's gaudy finery, but the diamond necklace about Ruth's throat.

She must have made a sound for Ruth jerked around suddenly, head high like a frightened deer sensing the hunter. The diamonds caught the lamplight and reflected it in glittering, white-hot sparks.

"What are you doing here?" she snapped.

"I—" Kate shrugged. Her gaze was glued to the necklace.

"These are *my* things now," Ruth said, drawing herself up to her full height. "My dresses, my shoes, my room. Mine!"

Kate's shoulders slumped. At second glance, she realized it wasn't her mother's necklace; the setting originally chosen by Charles Mannheim was distinctive. Her gaze slid to the jewelry scattered on the dressing table. Nothing there, either.

Ruth jerked back to the mirror. Her eyes were wide and a little wild. She stared at the garish image reflected there as if convinced she would find some answer if only she looked hard enough. Her breathing was unsteady, shallow, and too rapid. The beads on the gown glittered with each rise and fall of her chest.

Her chin came up. "I can do whatever I want," she told her reflection. "It's *mine! All* of it's mine!"

Despite the angry assertion, she tugged at the

gown as if it didn't feel quite right on her, then poked at the plume on her head, trying to adjust it. She succeeded only in knocking it askew. With an angry hiss, she ripped it off and tossed it aside. The pearls slipped, too. She tore them out of her hair, as well and tossed them away. They clattered when they hit the floor, but she didn't seem to notice that anymore than she noticed she'd pulled her hair loose so that it fell in coarse gray hanks about her shoulders.

Ruth turned, seeking a better angle. This time the necklace caught her eye. She leaned closer, tilting her chin this way, then that, fingering the glittering diamonds that flashed hot and white and cruelly beautiful at her throat.

Something shifted in her face. It was like ice breaking apart—first there was a little crack, then another and another until suddenly there was nothing left beneath the powder except pain and raw despair.

With a harsh, almost animal cry, she ripped the necklace from her throat and slammed it against the mirror.

The mirror cracked, then shattered under a second blow, raining shards of silvered glass across the floor.

Alarmed, Kate hurried across the room. Ruth didn't seem to notice. She simply stood there staring at the broken mirror while tears streamed down her face.

"Aunt Ruth?" Kate touched her elbow.

Ruth shook her off tiredly, then pivoted on one foot to scan the room around them.

"Ever since I was a little girl I wanted what Gertrude had," she said, every word weighted with despair. "She had so much, I didn't see why I couldn't have a little, too. A pretty dress or two, a room of my own."

She gave a small, bitter little laugh. "I should have known better. It didn't matter how much they had or how rich they were, they still dressed me in her hand-me-downs and made me sleep in a narrow little bed that hid away under her big four-poster during the day. I didn't get my own room until she turned twelve and insisted that I be removed from hers."

"Ruth—"

"The only thing I ever really had was Gar. He loved me, once," she said, the words bleak as a North Dakota winter.

She stared at the room and the wreckage she'd left, but none of it seemed to reach her.

"They used to say we were like sisters. Did you know that? Like sisters. But I knew better. Gertrude didn't want me here. She didn't want *anyone* who might steal her father's love from her, get some of the attention that was due *her*."

She glanced at Kate, looked away. "That was the best part of the joke, you know. Charles Mannheim never loved anyone but himself, not

even his own flesh and blood. He wanted a *son*.
He built all this not just to show the world what
a rich, important man he was, but to ensure that
his name lived on even when he was dead and
buried. Gertrude knew that as well as anyone.
That's why she tried so hard to please him, to be
everything he wanted her to be, everything he
was."

With the toe of her shoe she nudged a chunk
of broken glass. Kate wasn't sure she even saw it.
Her hand was still fisted around the necklace, but
her gaze had turned inward, back to the past.

"Gertrude's father was the only man who ever
really mattered in her life, but that didn't stop her
from collecting men once she got old enough to
be interested. Whenever an eligible young man
would come around, she wanted him all for herself. She'd get angry if they showed any interest
in me, too. They never saw it, of course, the anger, but she made sure I paid for it afterward.
One way or another, I always paid. She made me
pay for Gar, too.

"I remember the first time I saw him. We were
going into town when Gar came looking for work
one day. I was seventeen and sitting up in front
with the hired hand who was driving us. Gertrude was in the back with her father. I don't
think either one of them noticed him, jumping
back off the road so the horses wouldn't run him

over. But *I* saw him. And he saw me. He smiled, too, and waved."

At the memory, her face softened, grew younger somehow, and happier.

"He was," she said simply, "the most beautiful man I'd ever seen."

Kate scarcely breathed.

"Gertrude spotted him soon enough, of course," Ruth continued, that brief, happy glow fading from her face. "She flirted with him whenever her father wasn't around to see. She liked to flirt, liked to have the boys panting after her even if they weren't rich enough to be taken seriously. But Gar—Gar was different. He was a man, not a boy, and he wasn't interested in being used like that.

"What really made her angry was that he liked me better than her. Me! He started courting me when I turned eighteen. Six months later, he asked me to marry him."

The pain and joy and triumph that were in those simple words stabbed at Kate's heart.

"Gertrude hated it, of course." Ruth continued. By now, she was so wrapped up in her tale that Kate wasn't sure Ruth remembered she had an audience. "She never would have walked out with a mere laborer, not even one as handsome and charming as Gar, but that didn't mean she liked seeing me get him, instead. Nobody else saw it, not even Gar. But *I* knew.

"That's why she talked her father into letting us lease that rundown farm for a dollar a year. Because I was family, she said. Because she wanted to help." She snorted in disgust. "I should have known better, even then. We weren't good enough to stay on at Grand House, but she liked knowing that we owed her and her father for everything we had and every scrap of food on our plates.

"Gar didn't want the place, not even for a dollar a year. I should have listened to him. Things might have been different if I had," she added wistfully.

Kate kept silent.

"He wanted to go away, wanted to see the world. We could go to Montana, he said. Get a job, the two of us together, on one of those ranches out there. And when we got tired of that, he said we could move on, go someplace new.

"I said no. I'd never been anyplace but here. It scared me to think of going away like that, with no money, no guarantee of a job, without knowing anyone at all."

She paused, her gaze fixed on that road she hadn't taken all those years ago. Regret enfolded her like a blanket.

"You want to know what my real sin was?" she asked. "It was wanting to stay here so I could flaunt what I had in front of Gertrude every day. By then she'd married, too, and she was miserably unhappy. And I was *glad* she was unhappy.

"I wanted to stay because I wanted to show her that she could kick me out of Grand House, and she could keep me forever in her debt like the poor relation I was, but she couldn't take my Gar away from me. And God, how she wanted him by then! She wasn't a year married, and she'd have given anything to get rid of her husband, even if it meant marrying a working man like Gar instead.

"You see, Gertrude had made the mistake of marrying to please her father. Her husband was a fool and a spineless weakling, but he had the right breeding and the right connections, and that, along with his willingness to take on the Mannheim name, was all that mattered to Charles Mannheim. Gertrude forgot that *she* was the one getting married, not her father!"

Ruth laughed. It was a mean, mocking laugh, and it made Kate's blood run cold. Ruth turned and looked square into Kate's eyes.

"There were only two things your grandfather ever did that were worthwhile—getting Gertrude pregnant with your mother, then dying young."

She didn't even seem to notice Kate's gasp at the insult.

"I was raised here, grew up here, but I never *belonged* here. Never! But Gertrude gave that puling, miserable excuse for a man everything she'd denied me! And she spent the rest of her life doing everything she could to remind me of that fact.

"If I hadn't had Gar . . ." The words trailed off into nothing.

Her face crumpled. Her shoulders hunched as she folded in on herself, holding the pain of memory tight. The diamonds glinted in her hand, forgotten.

"Oh, my beautiful, beautiful Gar! He was the only one who ever loved me. The only one who was ever *mine*. The *only* one. And she wanted to take even that from me!"

"Ruth! Aunt Ruth? Please!"

"I loved him!" Ruth cried, hugging herself and rocking back and forth. "I really did. He said I didn't. He said all I cared about was Gertrude and this house and all the things I never had, but that's not true! I had *him*! I loved *him*!"

She froze suddenly, blind eyes staring at the horrors in her mind. Her voice dropped to a harsh whisper.

"Was that why he did it? Because of me? Because he didn't think I loved him?"

She swung to Kate, pleading now as more tears gouged paths through the powder unnoticed. "Was it my fault?"

"Was what your fault, Aunt Ruth?"

"Why didn't he realize I loved him?"

"What are you talking about?" Kate asked, bewildered. "What did Uncle Gar do?"

The question hit Ruth like a physical blow. She blinked and shook herself like a sleeper awakening from a horrible dream.

"What did Uncle Gar do, Aunt Ruth?" Kate persisted.

"Nothing. He didn't do anything! *I* didn't do anything! Leave me alone!"

Kate backed away. "I'm sorry. I didn't mean to upset you."

Ruth didn't seem to hear. She glanced around the room, then down at the diamond necklace she still held.

"I'm tired," she muttered, shoving past Kate. "I have to check on Gar."

But she stopped at the door and abruptly swung back. "Bring my jewels, Katherine Mary. They're mine now, you know. I have to keep them safe."

Dressed as she was in Gertrude's ill-fitting gown and gloves and with her hair hanging in lank disarray about her face, Ruth looked like a badly dressed caricature of her cousin. But her face bore all of Gertrude's haughty pride, and her eyes glinted dangerously.

Kate eagerly obeyed. With her back to Ruth, she quickly scrabbled through the contents of the jewel box, then, less happily, gathered the pieces scattered across the dressing table. Gertrude had left what looked like a fairly valuable collection of real jewels and expensive costume pieces, but her mother's necklace was not among them.

"Katherine Mary?"

"I'm coming, Aunt Ruth." Discouraged, Kate blew the powder off a garnet and gold brooch, then tossed it in with the rest and closed the box. "I–I wanted to make sure I got them all."

She tucked the box under her arm, then turned down the lamp on the table.

"Forget the lamps," Ruth ordered impatiently when Kate reached to turn down another. Pointedly ignoring her abandoned clothes and the disaster she'd wrought, she stalked from the room.

Kate snatched up one of the lamps and followed dispiritedly after. Her last hope of finding the necklace was gone now, for if Ruth didn't have it, then it wasn't going to be found.

Ruth, wearing Gertrude's shoes and struggling with the long skirt of her dead cousin's gown, took the stairs slowly, tottering a bit. With each step, the beads on the gown sparkled and flashed in the lamplight.

She stopped at the door to the second-best parlor. She looked truly old suddenly and unutterably weary. "I'll take the jewels now, Katherine Mary."

Kate silently handed them over, then waited until Ruth opened the door to hand her the lamp. The only light in the room beyond came from the stove, and it was too feeble to show more than the shadowed bulk of Gar's bed and the shrunken form huddled under the covers.

Before she could see more, Ruth had slammed the door in her face.

The door to the second-best parlor, not the best, Kate thought, retreating. Even though she was now mistress of Grand House, Ruth had not dared to take the best.

She wearily retrieved the book and the lamp she'd left on the hall table. Her great-grandfather's study seemed colder than it had before, and darker. At least the dark hid all those pictures of dead animals with their wide, staring eyes.

She told herself it was foolishness, something dreamed up by weariness and tension, but she would swear she could feel the creatures watching her as she crossed the room, put the book in its place, then crossed back to the door. Their breath brushed the back of her neck like a cold, dank draft, sending chills down her spine. She almost slammed the door behind her in her haste to be gone.

The hall seemed even darker and colder than before. She was hurrying toward the welcome warmth and light of the kitchen when a sound from the ladies' parlor stopped her.

In the echoing silence of Grand House, she could hear someone on the other side of that door sobbing as if her heart would break.

Kate hesitated. She was tired, she told herself. Weariness was making her imagine things. Yet she would swear she heard crying.

She held her breath and pressed her ear against the door.

It was definitely crying and not some trick of the wind or a fault in her own hearing.

Heart pounding, she turned the knob and cautiously opened the door.

The crying stopped.

Still safely on the hall side of the doorway, Kate raised her lamp and studied the room before her. No one was there.

So why did her skin prickle and a tremor run down her spine?

Old horrors, she told herself. Memories that were the stuff of nightmares, nothing more.

She rubbed her eyes and looked again.

Nothing had changed: The room was silent and empty.

You're tired, she told herself. It's been a long day and you didn't get much sleep last night. Close the door and go to bed.

Instead of heeding her own advice, she walked through the door and into the room that haunted her darkest dreams. The moment she did, the crying started again, softer now, but no less wrenching.

At the sound, her hand started to shake and her legs trembled so much her knees almost knocked together. Before she could drop the lamp, she set it down on the nearest table and collapsed into Gertrude's chair.

"Who's there?"

The crying stopped.

She closed her eyes and told herself she wasn't going mad.

She opened them again and saw Gar standing in front of her.

"Pretty Sara," he crooned. "What are you doing here?"

She started up.

He held up his hands, palms out. "Don't go. I won't hurt you. You know I won't hurt you."

But this wasn't really Gar. It couldn't be. This was a younger man, a man in his prime, dark-haired, strong-limbed, and handsome. A man who looked, she thought wildly, like El. But it wasn't El, either.

This *was* Gar, the Gar she remembered from her childhood. The Gar who had carried her on his shoulders and laughed so long and so loud that the windows shook.

He cocked his head, studying her. His smile was so gentle, so lost and yearning. So . . . hungry.

He took one step toward her, then another.

"Pretty Sara," he said. "I won't hurt you.

She looked into his eyes and saw desperation lurking there.

Again she heard the crying. But this time, beneath the sobs, she heard a frightened chant: No. No, no, no, no, no.

"Pretty, pretty Sara," the younger Gar crooned, and advanced another step.

Kate tried to get up, but couldn't. An icy hand pinned her in place, robbing her of thought and strength and will.

"Don't be afraid. You know I won't hurt you." And then the apparition turned away, fading even as it turned, and became one with the shadows.

"Louisa?"

The sound came from her right, from the deeper shadows at the far end of the room.

"Louisa? Pretty little Lou Lou, are you there?" It was a whisper, faint on the night air, dying away, then rising, becoming more urgent. "Louisa? Love? Are you coming? Come to me, Louisa. Come to me. To me . . . to me . . ."

Another form took shape. Big, broad-shouldered, eminently masculine. It crouched with its back to her, peering into the darkness.

"Louiiiiisssssaaaaa." Breathless and almost too faint to hear. "Sara? Pretty Sara. Kate?"

A sob rose in Kate's throat, but refused to come out. She couldn't remember how to breathe.

It was Elliott's voice she heard, calling for Louisa.

The apparition turned. It had Elliott's face. Gar's. No, Elliott's.

It turned further, shoulders hunched, hands out and curved into huge, grasping claws that could easily choke the life out of a woman and keep on choking.

"Kate?" Another apparition arose between her and the looming, faceless phantasm. It was her mother, and she was smiling.

Kate sobbed and reached for her.

Behind her mother, the monster with the face that wasn't El and wasn't Gar thrust its hands through her mother's heart and squeezed.

Sara's face twisted. Her eyes bulged. "Run, Kate!"

Kate sat there, hands outstretched, staring.

"Run!"

Kate flung herself out of the chair, snatched up the lamp, and fled.

Chapter Seventeen

The servants' stairs were as narrow, dark, and cold as they always were, but she raced up them two steps at a time. She flung open the door to the second floor so hard it slammed into the wall behind. Before it could shut again, she was halfway across the wide central hall.

The door to El's room was shut, a slab of unrelieved black in the darkness. El wasn't there. She'd run to him without thinking, but he had already shut her out.

She glanced at the open door to Gertrude's room at the other end of the hall. Lamplight spilled from the doorway but it did not welcome her. The big, empty hallway was dark and cold.

The silence seemed alive, the shadows more forbidding than ever.

Heart pounding, she raised her hand and rapped on El's door.

There was no answer to her knock. She hadn't expected any. Quietly, with her breath catching in her throat, she opened the door and slipped inside, then slammed it shut behind her. She slumped against the solid oak that divided her from whatever nightmare had possessed her, grateful for its bulk and the support.

The silence of the room enfolded her, welcoming her. There were no voices here and only good, safe memories. Even the shadows seemed softer, more friendly brown than soulless black.

When she could breathe once more and her legs had stopped trembling enough to support her, she raised the lamp higher and studied her surroundings.

Beneath the bed, placed side by side, was a pair of Elliott's shoes. A shirt was neatly draped over the back of a chair, a pair of pants folded on the seat. She could see his shaving kit atop the dresser and a can of tooth powder. Mint flavored, she thought, judging from what little she could glimpse of the can.

From this angle all she could see of the bed was the massive carved footboard and the edges of the comforters poking out on either side.

If she closed her eyes and concentrated, she could even catch his scent, a subtle combination of bay rum shaving lotion and soap and man that made her senses prick.

Little things, but together they built a wall between her and the twisted dreams that lurked on the other side of the door, waiting to pounce.

Though she knew she shouldn't stay, she couldn't bring herself to open the door and venture into the upper hallway or, worse, the claustrophobic stairs that would take her to her own cold, dark room at the top of the house.

She felt safe here, protected. El's possessions were talismans against the darkness and promises of his return. Nothing could harm her here. There was no reason to leave. She *belonged* here.

It was, she realized, Ruth who had taught her that. In her outpouring of pain and shame and regret, Ruth had given her a gift beyond price— she had shown her what was truly important, and what was not.

Ruth had learned the lesson too late, was really only now beginning to understand what she had had, what she had lost, and what she had willfully thrown away.

By wanting everything, she had lost everything worth having. All those years of wanting what she could not have had blinded her to the real value of what was truly hers. Gertrude had had everything, and nothing worth having. Ruth had seen that clearly, and yet she'd kept reaching blindly for what seemed forever beyond her grasp, oblivious.

And then one day she had found herself mistress of Grand House, rich beyond her wildest dreams and queen where she had been a serving maid. Grand House was hers along with all the treasures stuffed inside its walls and all the empty land around it that stretched as far as the eye could see.

But instead of enjoying her new power and wealth, she found herself trapped in a life even more limited than what she had known before. She owned the largest house in the county, yet slept in a servant's bed in a single room that now served as bedroom, sitting room, and nursing ward for two. She owned a fortune's worth of sterling silver flatware, crystal goblets, and the finest china, yet she took her meals at a kitchen table off cheap pottery plates; she dined with a man who dribbled food down the front of his shirt and played with his peas and had to be dressed and undressed and put to bed like a child.

In the end she had won everything, and she had absolutely nothing that mattered because the one true treasure she had had all along was now lost to her forever. Gertrude was dead and there was no one left to appreciate her triumph, not even the man she loved.

The thoughts spun in Kate's head. They hammered at her with an almost physical brutality, insisting she hear the truth: that in the end, love was the only thing that endured, and even that wasn't enough if it hadn't been valued from the start.

Kate heard, and wept.

She loved El, and he loved her. She was sure of it. But they had made the mistake of putting other things before that love—pride, doubt, fear, the shrill accusations of strangers—and because of it, they had almost lost everything that mattered.

But they had a second chance. Somehow, she had to convince El that she was strong enough to face the truth about what had happened ten years ago, no matter how hard that was. And she had to find the courage to fight for what they had, for the love that was strong enough to bind them together despite the years and miles that had separated them.

The truth was simple.

Living by it wasn't nearly so easy, but somehow, someway, they would manage. All they had to do was find the courage to deal with everything that came with it.

Tonight, right now, it was as simple as that.

She set the lamp on the dresser, then moved to the bed and pulled down the covers. Tonight, El wouldn't have to undress her.

With steady fingers she unbuttoned her dress

and neatly laid it over the shirt hung on the chair. One by one she slipped out of slip and chemise, shoes and stockings and drawers. The shoes went under the bed right beside his—she rather liked the way they looked, her shoes and his, side by side like that. The stockings and undergarments she folded and stacked atop his trousers.

Naked, she slipped into bed and pulled the covers up to her chin. The sheets were cool and soft against her skin, and they carried the tantalizing traces of his scent, and hers.

The memory of last night stirred her, but even that wasn't enough to fend off the weariness that seemed to have claimed her limbs and wrapped her mind in cotton wool.

El would come soon. That was what she told herself as she burrowed deeper into the welcoming feather bed. He would come. Somehow, he would know he must because she wanted him. Because she *needed* him.

As she drifted into oblivion, a soft, cool, comforting hand brushed her brow. Kate murmured sleepily, and smiled, and slept without dreaming.

She came awake slowly, drifting up to consciousness like a swimmer emerging from the depths to touch the welcoming light.

El was standing over her, eyes silver and full of mingled doubt and longing.

"Kate?" he said. He shook her shoulder. "Kate! Wake up!"

She smiled drowsily up at him. "You came. I knew you would."

"What are you doing here?"

His question scraped off the remnants of sleep. Clutching the covers to her breast, she sat up.

"The wind's come up," she said, her attention caught by the sharp whine of the wind at the windows. It seemed oddly distant, as if it couldn't touch her so long as she was here, safe in Elliott's bed.

"Another storm's blown in," El said shortly. "I thought it would wait until tomorrow, but it didn't. The wind hit an hour ago. It was starting to snow when I came across the yard.

"Forget the wind. *What are you doing here?*"

"I was sleeping," she said, meeting his gaze squarely. "And waiting for you."

"Kate!" He dragged a hand through his hair, clearly baffled and unsure what to do.

"I love you, El," she said.

It was so simple, once the words were out. She wondered why she hadn't said them sooner.

"I waited for you all night, kept thinking you'd come back, but you never did."

"Kate—"

"I know. I've thought about it all. I don't know what the truth is, El. Maybe I don't want to know. But I do know you're not a murderer."

His eyes narrowed. "How can you be so damn sure of that?"

"Because I love you."

"As simple as that?" The scorn in his voice was sharp enough to draw blood.

She nodded. "As simple as that. I didn't know how simple it really was until I ended up here tonight. I—"

No, she didn't want to tell him about the voices or that dream or nightmare or whatever it was. She didn't want to talk about Gar or Ruth or the past or what lay ahead. She didn't want to talk at all.

Instead, she let the covers fall and opened her arms to him.

"Make love to me, El," she said. "Please. I want you."

He flinched as if she'd struck him, but she could see the hunger in his eyes and the way his pulse pounded in his throat, there at the corner of his jaw.

She drew a deep breath, let it out.

"I love you, El," she said. "I always have. *Always.*"

He might have been able to withstand the temptation if she'd thrown herself at him, naked, but those few words shattered his defenses.

With a small, choked cry, he threw back the covers, then pressed her back down onto the bed.

This time, he was the needy one—he took and

she gave. She gave him everything she had, her heart and soul as well as her body, her hopes for the future and everything they brought with them. She gave him herself, utterly and without reservation.

His mouth devoured her. His touch marked her his. And then, without bothering to undress, he was in her. There was no slowness this time, no gentleness. No effort to please her. Like a man possessed, he drove himself into her over and over again.

His shirt scraped her breasts, rousing pain and lust together. The rough gabardine of his trousers rubbed the sensitive skin of her inner thighs in a harsh, erotic rhythm to match his pounding need. The pain was small, the glorious sense of power that rushed through her greater than anything she had ever known . . . except her love for him.

There was no murmured praise, no laughter. There were no words of love. He simply took . . . everything.

It wasn't enough, because she had more to give. She would have told him that if he hadn't already gone beyond her reach in the throes of his own release.

With a small, joyous cry, she let herself go and once more followed after.

* * *

Snow struck the windows, rattling like pebbles and dragging her back from the half-world that lay between waking and sleeping. Above her, El stirred, then shifted as if to roll off.

Kate smiled and pulled him back.

"Kate," he murmured, half protest and half blessing.

"I love you, El," she said, and gently smoothed her hand over his head. "I plan on telling you that every morning and every night for the rest of my life, if you'll let me."

"Kate, I—"

She pressed a silencing finger to his lips. "Shush. Don't say anything, El, just . . . listen."

For a moment she thought he would argue with her. He didn't, but she could feel the sudden tension in him. She couldn't help it, because it matched the tension in her.

She held him tighter, reaching for the courage to say what had to be said.

"All these years, I never really believed you were a murderer, El. I couldn't, not even when everything seemed to say I was a fool not to. But I couldn't help wondering why you kept silent, why you wouldn't tell me what had happened."

El stopped breathing.

"It hurt, you see, that you wouldn't tell me. But I didn't understand. I—"

He shifted, pulled free of her hold on him. "Kate!"

Blinded by hot, stinging tears that refused to fall, Kate stared at the ceiling. She couldn't bear to look at El.

"Gar killed her, didn't he?" she whispered.

El went silent and very, very still.

"Didn't he, El? Gar killed Louisa."

He nodded reluctantly. "Yes. I can't prove it, but . . . yes, I think he killed her."

"And my mother?" It was hard to get the words past the horrible ache in her chest.

El swore and abruptly shoved himself upright. Kate forced herself to sit up, too.

"Gar killed my mother, too. Didn't he, El? He killed her, then hung her from that chandelier to make everyone think she'd committed suicide.

El grabbed her shoulders and shook her. "Don't think like that! There's no proof that her death was anything except a suicide!"

"No, no more than there's anything to show that he killed Louisa. But *I* know he did it, El." She paused, then added, "And so do you."

He sagged as though she'd hit him, and let her go.

"I've only just begun to understand, to see it clearly," she said, implacable now.

They had to get it all out between them. Here and now, they had to bring all the ugly doubts and suspicions into the open if there was to be any real hope for the two of them in the years to come. However painful, the truth was always better than any lie, no matter how convenient or comfortable.

"Gar probably never meant to hurt them," she said. "But he loved pretty things and laughter, and he loved women, and there wasn't much of either in his life. He was caught between Ruth and Gertrude, and the two of them must have sucked all the joy out of his life."

In the still, ice-clear depths of Elliott's eyes she could see that she was right, that he had reached the same conclusions she had. But there was a deeper pain in him, for he had worshipped Gar and loved him like a father, and his love had made the betrayal all that much more bitter.

"I imagine it started out as a little flirtation," she said. "But somewhere along the line Gar must have pushed things too far, demanded too much. He probably only meant to quiet their protests, but he was a strong man, and he went too far."

El said nothing. Grief etched his features, cold and bleak as the winter storm outside.

"Ruth knew," Kate continued. "I'm sure she did. She protected him. I suspect she was the one who encouraged Sheriff Neumann to arrest you for the murder. Am I right?"

El nodded. "Yes."

He said it so low that Kate almost didn't hear him. She leaned closer, willing him to speak.

"I never even suspected," he said roughly, as

though the words were being wrenched out of somewhere deep inside him. "Not at first. I figured it had been a bum passing through, maybe an itinerant laborer. But there was something in the way Gar acted that made me wonder."

"Yes?" Kate urged softly when he faltered.

"He—" El's hands opened, closed, reaching for the words he didn't want to speak. "He was always looking over his shoulder as if he expected someone to grab him suddenly from behind. And he refused to look me in the eye. That's what really got me," he added bitterly. "That he wouldn't even look me in the eye."

He let out a long breath and closed his eyes against a pain that was as sharp and real as it had been ten years ago when he'd realized the depths of Gar's betrayal.

"So you ran away."

His eyes snapped open. This time she saw anger there, anger that was for her as well as for Gar.

"I left," he said. "I didn't run away. I *left*."

Kate flinched, but refused to look away. She owed him that much, at least.

"Why shouldn't I have left?" he demanded when she remained silent. "You'd already gone. Gar had abandoned me to the mob. The two people I loved and trusted more than anyone else in the world, and you both abandoned me." His mouth worked as he blinked back the tears he would not allow to fall. "Tell me, Kate, what was there left to stay for?"

"I'm sorry, El," she said as tears flooded down her cheeks. "I'm so sorry." Her voice fell until it was barely a whisper. "For both of us."

It wasn't much, but it was enough.

With a rough cry he grabbed her shoulders and dragged her to him. His mouth crushed down on hers. His fingers dug into her flesh.

She didn't care, for in that small span of a heartbeat before he claimed her she had seen forgiveness in his eyes, and need, and a love great enough to bridge the years and heal the wounds that lay between them.

It was a long while before they finally slept, oblivious to the storm that now raged beyond the windows.

"Kate! Kate, wake up!"

Kate muttered and burrowed deeper into the covers, seeking Elliott's warmth.

A rough hand shook her shoulder, then brutally stripped off sheet and coverlets, exposing her naked body to the cold night air.

"Dammit, Kate, the house is on fire! *Wake up!*"

She sat up with a jerk. Elliott stood beside the bed again, but this time he was shouting at her as he pulled on his clothes.

"You have to get up now!" He tossed her dress

at her, then her underclothes, then dragged her from the bed.

"Fire? The house is on fire?" Kate struggled to get her brain working even as she shivered from the cold and fumbled for her chemise.

"Gertrude's room," El explained. He flung one of his sweaters at her. "Put that on, then get the hell out. Do you hear me? Get out of the house!"

Without waiting for a reply, he pulled a heavy wool blanket off the bed and rushed out of the room. Through the open door Kate could see the red-orange glow of fire dancing on the opposite wall of the upper hall and hear the hungry crackling of flames. She could smell smoke.

She threw on her clothes, shoved her stockingless feet in her shoes, then dashed out of the room after him, pulling on his sweater as she ran. She didn't get past the open door of Gertrude's room.

Horror grabbed her, immediately followed by guilt. She'd never gone back to turn down the lamps that Ruth had lit. Somehow, one of them had tipped over, and now the room was engulfed in flames.

Fire roared in the bed and along the walls, licking up the heavy draperies and nibbling at the ceiling. The clothes spread on the furniture provided fuel, feeding the fire's hunger, tempting it to jump from chair to table to floor and back again. It hadn't yet reached the oil-soaked rug at the center of the room, but it would, and once it did, it would be impossible to stop.

El was beating at the flames, trying to smother them under the blanket he'd taken. Ruth, eyes wild, was dousing the bed with water from buckets she'd no doubt filled in the bathroom, coughing and cursing like a madwoman. She was barefoot and dressed only in a flannel nightgown and a long dressing gown that she hadn't bothered to fasten. More than once the flapping hem of her gown almost touched the flames, but she didn't seem to notice.

For an instant, Kate hovered, uncertain, then she darted forward and shoved at the table that stood on the oil-soaked rug. If she could get the rug out—

El grabbed her arm and dragged her back.

"Dammit, Kate," he roared. "I told you to get out!"

"The rug!" Kate pointed, desperately trying to shout over the roar of the fire. "I've got to move the rug! It's—"

In that instant, the flames hit it, roaring in triumph at this new and richer source of fuel.

El tried to drag Ruth out of the way, but she dodged out of reach.

"This is mine!" she screeched, reaching for another bucket. *"Mine!"*

The bucket was empty. With a cry of rage, she tossed it into the fire, then snatched up a rug near

the door and began beating at the flames just as
El had done.

El hesitated, as if debating whether to pull her
away or leave her be. She cursed, then shoved
him aside to beat at the burning rug.

He let her go and dragged Kate out of the
room, instead.

"You've got to get Gar," he shouted. "Ruth said
he's missing again. She doesn't know how long
he's been gone. I don't know where he is, but
you've got to get him, get him out of the house.
Try the kitchen first. He might have gone there."

Kate nodded, but El hadn't waited for even
that much of an answer.

Fighting panic, Kate left him to his hopeless
battle and went in search of Gar.

The door to the servants' stairs stood open. She
hadn't even noticed it earlier. Her heart in her
throat and with one hand brushing the wall for
balance, she plunged down the stairs in the dark.

The kitchen was empty, but Gar had been
there. Kate skidded to a halt, appalled. He'd
stuffed the stove with every piece of firewood he
could find, then left the firebox open and thrown
away the iron lid on top. Flames shot from the
openings, lighting the kitchen like a dozen
lamps. The stovepipe was so hot it was glowing
red.

Before she could move, the sounds of metal
banging on metal grabbed her attention. She

turned, seeking the source of the noise, and felt her stomach twist sickeningly.

The trapdoor to the basement yawned open, and a dim light showed from below.

Driven by the same befuddled fascination with fire that had prompted him to shove so much wood into the stove and that had no doubt led him to meddle with the lamps in Gertrude's room, he'd gone to stoke the furnace and the boiler in the basement. The boiler that El had said could easily explode if it were ever overheated.

Kate found him standing in front of the open furnace, grinning like a madman and feeding the already roaring fire with more coal.

Forcing herself to be calm, Kate touched his sleeve, then grabbed his wrist before he could add another shovelful. "That's enough, Uncle Gar, don't you think?"

He frowned and angrily wrenched free. "No. Got to get it *hot*, girl. Real hot. Only way to keep things warm."

Desperate, Kate snatched the shovel out of his hands, making him stagger. Coal spilled on the floor.

"Dammit!" Gar grabbed for the shovel.

Kate threw it as hard as she could, back into the farthest, blackest corner of the room. It struck a wall, then clattered across the floor.

Gar started after it, but she grabbed him arm and pulled him back.

"You have to come with me, Uncle Gar," she panted, fighting to hold on. Whatever was driving him had given him surprising strength. "Aunt Ruth wants you."

That stopped him. He froze, staring at her, his mouth working as if he were struggling to speak.

"Ruth?" he said at last. He sounded more angry than confused.

"That's right. Aunt Ruth. She says—"

"Damn her!" Gar roared, wrenching free. "Damn her!"

He started toward the stairs, then hesitated, and turned back to the fire. In the angry red glow of the flames, Kate could see tears pouring down his face.

"It's her fault," he snarled, leaning so close she could smell his sour, old man's breath. "It's all her fault. I didn't mean nothing by it. Nothing! I know I shouldn't've touched 'em, but I apologized, didn't I? Didn't I? *Didn't I?*" he demanded, his voice rising higher and shriller with each angry query.

"Yes, yes, of course you did, Uncle Gar," Kate tried to soothe, her own terror building. "But we'll worry about that later, all right? If you'll just come with me—"

"No!" Gar shoved her, sending her staggering backward. Head lowered like a charging bull's, he advanced toward her, still crying, still furious. "To hell with Ruth! Sara forgave me. She understood. And Louisa—"

He stopped, face twisting with remembered fury. "Hell, I *paid* her! Little tart was teasing El, but she was more than ready to spread her legs for money when I asked."

The words hit Kate like a blow, knocking the very air out of her. She staggered back another step, head reeling. She'd guessed, but to hear it from Gar's lips, and like this . . .

Gar kept his distance. Kate wasn't sure he remembered she was there, even though he was staring right at her, eyes wild and glinting red from the fire.

"It would've been all right," he said, low and angrily as if speaking to himself. "It would've been all right if Ruth hadn't gone so crazy about it. Going to tell 'em off, that's what she said. Just tell 'em what she thought of 'em. But she didn't, did she?"

Bile rose in Kate's throat. She glanced at the furnace. The readings on the pressure gauges of the boiler were rising dangerously. Questions would have to wait.

"Come on, Uncle Gar. Let's get out of here."

She got him to the stairs only to find a dull red-orange glow lighting the opening above. Quelling the urge to run, she coaxed Gar up the stairs in front of her.

She could have cried with relief when he finally heaved himself up the last stair and through the trapdoor. Relief turned to horror a moment later when he reached out and slammed the trapdoor shut. She ducked just in time, then heard the *snick* of the latch shooting home.

"My fault!" Gar shouted through the trapdoor. "She wouldn't've hurt 'em if it hadn't been for me. My fault All my fault." The last words faded with his departing footsteps.

"Uncle Gar? Uncle Gar!" Panicked, Kate pounded on the trapdoor with her fists. "Don't leave me here! *Uncle Gar!*"

Nothing. She crouched, then set her shoulder against the door and tried to shove it open. She couldn't even manage to force it high enough to hit against the latch.

Despair washed over her. Fighting against tears, she slumped on the stairs as her legs turned to jelly. Think! *Think!*

An answer came. Almost sobbing with relief, she hurried back down the stairs. The room across the furnace was just as she remembered. The canning jars filled with rotting vegetables gleamed like poisonous, baleful eyes. The window shone dull red in the gloom.

Grabbing up the first heavy thing she found on the shelves, Kate heaved it at the opening. The tinkle of breaking glass was the sweetest sound she'd ever heard. Heedless of dirt and cobwebs,

349

she scrambled up the shelves beneath the windows.

"El! El!" she screamed as she wrapped one hand in the sleeve of his sweater and broke out the remaining shards of glass. *"El! Help!"*

The storm outside grabbed her cries away. Snow swirled into her face, bringing with it the sharp, acrid stench of burning.

And then two strong hands closed over hers and pulled her up and out. She kicked, fighting for better leverage, and heard the shelves break free behind her, sending their burden of castoffs and canning jars crashing to the floor.

A moment later she was in El's arms, sobbing, laughing, clinging to him, devouring his kisses and demanding more.

"Katie. Kate, my beautiful Kate!" he murmured. She could feel his hands trembling. "I looked for you, and when I couldn't find you I thought you'd gotten out, but—"

"Gar! Oh, El! Gar's inside! He locked me in the basement and—we have to get him out!" She couldn't tell him about Gar's revelation. Not now. Not yet. "He was in the kitchen—"

She stopped, appalled. The first-floor windows were still mostly dark, but the second- and third-floor windows were alive with a demon light. Flames sprouted at the edge of the roof. Then a window shattered and hell roared out.

With a despairing cry, Kate wrenched free of

El's hold and dashed around to the back of the house. The wind clawed at her, driving sharp, stinging snow into her face and freezing the tears on her cheeks. Behind her, the fire roared louder still.

She was too late. Though the back porch was as yet untouched, fire had already claimed most of the kitchen. The front door then? Or a window? El would know.

Before she could move, Ruth came rushing up.

"Where's Gar? Did you find him? Did he get out of the house?" Her eyes glittered madly in a face blackened by soot and burned by flying sparks.

"He's still inside," Kate shouted over the wind. "I'll get El and—"

The words were choked off as Ruth's hands suddenly clamped around her throat.

"Where's Gar, damn you?" Ruth shrieked, shaking her viciously. "Where's my husband?"

El grabbed Ruth from behind and dragged her off. Coughing and wheezing, Kate clutched her bruised throat and sucked in air.

"Gar's trapped inside, Ruth," El shouted, holding her as she cursed and bucked against him. "You can't go in there. I barely got out the front door. I'll try to climb through a window, but you can't go in there!"

"Gaaaaaarrrrrr!" Ruth's anguished wail rose

on the keening wind. Tears ravaged her face. *"Gaaaaaarrrrrr!"*

El let her go. "Stay here! Do you hear me, Ruth? *Stay here!* And *you*," he added, pointing at Kate, "keep out of her way!"

Ruth was past him in an instant, running for the back door.

"Ruth! No!" Kate lunged after her, but El grabbed her and pulled her back.

"Gaaaaaarrrrrr!" Ruth cried as she flung the back door open. "I'm coming! Wait for me!"

For an instant she was there, limned against the voracious flames; then she was gone and the door was swinging shut behind her.

With an anguished cry, Kate threw herself into Elliott's arms and blindly pressed her face against his chest.

She didn't see when the porch went, but she heard the triumphant roar of the flames and felt a wave of heat press against her.

And then the boiler blew.

Out of the Shadow

Early August 1934

Kate screamed as they plummeted. She couldn't help herself.

The sky behind them was a merciless, unwinking blue. The world below came hungrily up to greet them as if they'd been away too long. This time, she was sure, it would grab hold and never, ever let them go.

Air rushed past, deafening her, pummeling her senses and snatching her breath away so that her lungs felt as if they would explode.

She tried to scream again and found there wasn't air enough left within her to try.

Behind her, Elliott laughed.

"Watch this!" he cried, and brought the little two-seater bi-plane out of its dive to spiral upward, spinning around and around as they climbed back toward the sun.

"Hang on!"

And again they tumbled over, then plummeted down, the single engine roaring defiance at sky above and earth below.

Kate's stomach climbed into her throat.

Her heart had been lost too long ago to matter.

This time as the hills rushed up to greet them, she laughed. A great, triumphant peal of joy.

God! How she loved this new world Elliott had given her!

At the bottom of their dive, at the very last moment before she thought they would surely crash, he brought the plane's nose up, then leveled out and swung back toward the city that rose on the horizon. The hills of Marin County disappeared behind her as they roared out over the blue waters of San Francisco Bay.

On her right, she could see a dream beginning to take shape as workers fought the bay and the elements to build what would be the world's longest bridge. The Golden Gate Bridge they were calling it, and now, in the morning sunlight, it was truly golden.

The thought of such daring and such a dream brought another laugh tumbling out.

California was everything El had promised it would be: big, bold, brash, and beautiful. And *warm*. If she never saw snow again in her lifetime, it would be too soon.

Besides, there was so much to see and do and learn about right here in her new home. Not that she had as much time to explore California as she would like. El was forever hauling her off on one of his expeditions, taking her along with his paying passengers whenever there was room.

His company, Carstairs Air Services, was gaining a name for itself and, despite the deepening Depression, was growing so rapidly that even El, who thrived on challenges, had a hard time keeping up. He'd just added his sixth plane, a DC-2, to his growing fleet and was already talking about buying a DC-3 when that marvel finally came off the assembly line.

In the year and a half that they'd been married she had crossed the country five times, been up to Canada twice, down to Mexico three times and, once, across to Venezuela. They'd spent two and a half memorable months flying a wealthy businessman around Europe, with a two-week stop in Paris that had served as a second honeymoon. Their first had been cut short when Clark Gable had hired them to fly him to Montana for some hunting and fishing. These days, they had so many contracts with Hollywood stars and studio bigshots that El had added two more pilots and was seriously considering starting a branch office in Hollywood.

Neither one of them was willing to give up San Francisco, however.

Kate craned her neck to see what lay ahead. The city was coming up under their wings. Though El was flying low, she couldn't spot the little house they'd bought a year earlier. It was a rather nondescript little place perched at the top of a hill, but it had views of the city and the bay that took one's breath away.

And they had neighbors. Lots of neighbors. That was the best part. In the past year she'd made so many friends, it made her dizzy just to think of them.

North Dakota and the burned-out shell of Grand House lay half a continent and what seemed a lifetime behind them.

What was left of Ruth's and Gar's bodies had been buried together in a fine oak coffin in the Mannville cemetery, leaving Sara's, Gertrude's, and Kate's great-grandfather's graves to their lonely dignity on the land where Charles Gordon Mannheim had once dreamed of founding a dynasty. Eventually, no doubt, their headstones would disappear into the tall prairie grass.

Kate couldn't think of a gentler, kinder ending.

Only El knew of the gift that had come from the ashes.

The morning after the fire, when the storm had died at last, they'd emerged from the garage where they'd sought shelter to find Grand House a shell of stone and blackened timbers. While El worked to start the old tractor that was their only way out—the truck wouldn't have been able to make it through the drifted snow to the road—she'd picked around the edges of the still-smoldering ruin, huddled under an old blanket El had retrieved from the barn the night before.

She wasn't sure what she was looking for, but something drew her. Peering through the charred openings where windows had once been, or over the rubble of the wall that had collapsed when the boiler blew, she'd tried to make sense of what she saw.

With the three separate fires started in Gertrude's bedroom, the kitchen stove, and the overloaded furnace, and an icy wind to fan the flames once the windows shattered, the destruction had been staggering. What the fire hadn't consumed had been crushed when the roof collapsed through the floors below.

A few odds and ends had survived—a book here, its edges blackened but its pages intact, a porcelain figurine there—but most everything was burned or broken beyond recognition. All was out of reach. Even if she'd been mad enough to trust her weight on what was left of the first floor, the heat would have driven her back—deep in the heart of the ruins, the embers were still hot enough to burn flesh from bone.

Yet still she'd felt compelled to look, to try to

make sense of what she saw. That same compulsion had drawn her around the house to the front and the corner farthest from the boiler and Gertrude's room.

The destruction there wasn't quite as complete. What stopped her was the black, gaping hole where the front door had been. Some freak of the fire had toppled some of the furniture from the upper floors out onto the stone front steps. There was a chair, its cane seat gone, a twisted metal bed frame, a smoke-blackened but otherwise undamaged water pitcher, and the broken shells of a couple of trunks that must have fallen all the way from the attic.

Kate might have passed them by but something, some tug at her awareness, made her stop instead. After a moment's hesitation, she cautiously picked her way over the rubble and up the steps. The first burned-out trunk was fairly easy to reach, but it was the second that drew her as if some voice were whispering in her ear, "There! That one!"

Using the edges of the blanket to protect her hands, she tugged it free, then dragged it to the edge of the steps and tipped it onto the ground. The remnants of old clothes and papers, most burned beyond recognition, had tumbled out in a stinking, smoldering heap.

At the heart of the heap, its gold settings

twisted by heat but still recognizable, was her mother's necklace.

Even now Kate could remember how the diamonds had winked coldly white and pure amid the blackened ashes, like stars trapped at the edges of hell.

For what had seemed like eternity she'd simply stood there, staring, not sure whether she was awake or dreaming. Then a voice—she'd been sure it was a real voice this time—had whispered in her ear, "Take it, Kate. Take it and be free."

She had dug it out of the ashes, then wrapped it in a scrap of wool torn from the edge of the blanket and tucked it in her pocket, where it had stayed through the long, difficult days that followed, a promise for the future and her mother's last, most precious gift.

After some judicial hemming and hawing, El had been declared Ruth's heir. Suspicions lingered about his role in Ruth and Gar's deaths, as well as in Louisa's, but for the most part they had been quieted when El had refused to touch a penny of the inheritance. The state had taken all of it, but neither he nor Kate cared. Being free of Grand House and its entangling past was enough for both of them.

Her mother's diamonds were another matter, however. Their sale brought in enough money to buy their house in San Francisco and the liens on Elliott's airplanes with a little left over. They weren't rich by California standards, but they had enough. With the income from Carstairs Air, they would never have to worry about money.

"Are you ready?"

Elliott's cheerful call wrenched her out of her thoughts and back to an awareness of where she was. Off to the right, Kate could see the small airstrip that was home to Carstairs Air and a dozen other companies with dreams as big as theirs. She could see the cluster of friends and co-workers who had gathered to watch her first official flight. They'd brought out folding chairs and picnic baskets, ready to celebrate with her once she landed.

Kate twisted around in her seat to look at El. The aviator's goggles hid his eyes, but nothing could hide the joyous smile that split his face.

"You can do it, Kate! Just take the controls. I'll fly it with you until you're ready."

Her heart came into her throat. She'd been preparing for this for weeks, studying books, going up with El so she could get the feel of the yoked controls while he actually flew the plane. She'd worked for this moment. She'd even dreamed of it. But now that the moment was at hand, everything she'd learned, everything he'd taught her, flew out of her head.

"I'm not ready!" she cried, fighting down the panic.

"Yes, you are!"

"No! Not yet!"

"No time like the present," he shouted back.

He was mad. She could *hear* the laughter in his voice. Only a mad man would laugh at a time like this.

She turned back toward him.

"I love you, Elliott Carstairs!" she shouted against the roar of wind and machine.

His grin widened. "I know! But that's not going to get you out of flying this baby on your own. Take the controls, Kate!"

Reluctantly, stomach churning, she did as he said.

For one pass around the airfield, then another, he flew the plane with her. Then he started climbing again, leaving the earth so far behind that the air strip shrank to a ribbon and their gathered friends became specks beneath their wings, then vanished altogether.

The little plane growled in triumph and took them higher. She could feel the controls vibrating beneath her hands, feel the raw power behind them. And she knew, suddenly, that she could really do it.

She laughed, a deep, joyous peal of laughter

361

Anne Avery

that came from the heart, and took a firmer grip on the controls.

"I love you, Kate!" El shouted from behind her. "She's all yours!"

And then he set her free to climb into a welcoming sky that stretched into forever.

A DISTANT STAR

ANNE AVERY

Pride makes her run faster and longer than the others—traveling swiftly to carry her urgent messages. But hard as she tries, Nareen can never subdue her indomitable spirit—the passionate zeal all successful runners learn to suppress. And when she looks into the glittering gaze of the man called Jerrel and feels his searing touch, Nareen fears even more for her ability to maintain self-control. He is searching a distant world for his lost brother when his life is saved by the courageous messenger. Nareen's beauty and daring enchant him, but Jerrel cannot permit anyone to turn him from his mission, not even the proud and passionate woman who offers him a love capable of bridging the stars.

___52335-3 $5.50 US/$6.50 CAN

ALL'S FAIR

ANNE AVERY

For five long years, Rhys Fairdane has roamed the universe, trying to forget Calista York, who seared his soul with white-hot longing, then cast him into space. Yet by a twist of fate, he and Calista are both named trade representatives of the planet Karta. It will take all his strength to resist her voluptuous curves, all his cunning to subdue her feminine wiles. But if in war, as in love, all truly is fair, Calista has concealed weapons that will bring Rhys to his knees before the battle has even begun.

___52257-8 $5.50 US/$6.50 CAN

The Snow Queen
Anne Avery

When Boston-bred Hetty Malone arrives at the Colorado Springs train station, she is full of hope that she will soon marry her childhood sweetheart and live happily ever after. Yet life amid the ice-capped Rockies has changed Michael Ryan. No longer the hot-blooded suitor Hetty remembers, the young doctor has grown as cold and distant as the snowy mountain peaks. Determined to revive Michael's passionate longing, Hetty quickly realizes that no modern medicine can cure what ails him. But in the enchanted splendor of her new home, she dares to administer the only remedy that might melt his frozen heart: a dose of good old-fashioned loving.

_52151-2 $5.99 US/$6.99 CAN

Anne Avery, Phoebe Conn, Sandra Hill, & Dara Joy

LOVESCAPE

WHERE DREAMS COME TRUE...

Do you ever awaken from a dream so delicious you can't bear for it to end? Do you ever gaze into the eyes of a lover and wish he could see your secret desires? Do you ever read the words of a stranger and feel your heart and soul respond? Then come to a place created especially for you by four of the most sensuous romance authors writing today—a place where you can explore your wildest fantasies and fulfill your deepest longings....

_4052-2 $5.99 US/$6.99 CAN